"I'm sorry, Jean-Luc," Q said . . .

"but I can't allow you to be distracted by something as minor as an attack on your ship. Too much is at stake, more than you can possibly imagine."

"Blast it, Q," Picard exploded, provoked beyond all patience. This had gone on long enough, and, as far as he was concerned, Q was the unwanted distraction from more pressing matters. "Explain yourself once and for all—the whole truth and nothing but—or get out of my way!"

"Fine!" Q replied indignantly, sounding almost as if he were the injured party. "Just remember, you asked for it."

What does he mean by that? Picard worried instantly, his worst fears confirmed when a burst of light erupted from Q, sweeping over Picard and carrying him away. Blank whiteness filled his vision. His chair seemed to dissolve beneath him. "Captain!" he heard Troi call out, but it was too late.

Deanna—and the *Enterprise*—were gone.

STAR TREK
THE NEXT GENERATION®

THE Q CONTINUUM

BOOK ONE OF THREE

Q-SPACE

GREG COX

POCKET BOOKS

New York   London   Toronto   Sydney   Tokyo   Singapore

An *Original* Publication of POCKET BOOKS

POCKET BOOKS, a division of Simon & Schuster Inc.
1230 Avenue of the Americas, New York, NY 10020

STAR TREK is a Registered Trademark of Paramount Pictures.

A VIACOM COMPANY

This book is published by Pocket Books, a division of Simon & Schuster Inc., under exclusive license from Paramount Pictures.

ISBN: 0-671-01915-5

First Pocket Books printing August 1998

10 9 8 7 6 5 4

POCKET and colophon are registered trademarks of Simon & Schuster Inc.

Printed in the U.S.A.

Acknowledgments

Thanks to John Ordover for conceiving of this trilogy, to Paula Block and Paramount for sanctioning it, and to my agent, Russ Galen, for handling the contractual details. Thanks also to David and Alexandra Honigsberg for bullfighting tips, and to everyone at Tor Books, for letting me restructure my editorial duties there so that I could give Q all the time and attention he demanded. And to D. C. Fontana, Gene Roddenberry, and John DeLancie for creating Q and bringing him to life (even though Q insists he created them).

Thanks, as ever, to Karen Palinko for providing keen editorial advice at every stage of the saga's creation. And to Alex, our own little Q-kitty, for countless hours of entertainment and distraction.

Q-SPACE

Prologue

LET ME BACK IN!

In back me let!

Beyond the wall, he gibbered. Time meant nothing to him. An instant was the same as an eternity; both were merely subjective measures of his isolation and his madness, which began the moment he was cast out of creation and had been taking its toll ever since. His exile had just begun, and it had lasted forever.

It's not fair, he thought, as he had thought since the wall came into being. *Fair is fair, there is there, and here is nowhere, nowhere, no hope. Isn't that so?*

So it is, he answered himself, since he'd had no one else to talk to for as long as long could possibly be. *So, so, so . . . so how could they lock me up like this? Why could they?*

His feverish mind offered an explanation. *Fear. That was their paltry excuse. Mere fear, sheer fear, that's clear.* He cackled at his own cleverness. *Fear, here. Fair, there. Fear is fair.*

No, it is not, he protested angrily. *I never did*

1

anything, anything that mattered. Matter isn't anything. No, it isn't, is it?

Not at all. All is not. Not is now.

Now. Now. Now.

Now, for the first time since his bleak, barbaric banishment began, something new was happening. There was a weakness in the wall, not enough to allow him to slide his way through, at least not yet, but a certain slackening that perhaps foretold an end to his stubborn struggle to get past the wall. He felt a crack, an infinitesimal fracture in the infinite, that he shouted through with all his might.

Me back in let!

Even if the entirety of his being could not pass through the tantalizingly, tormentingly small lesion, he could still send his ceaseless craving back into the realm from which he had been so unjustly cast out, crying out to anyone who might hear his desperate plea.

Back let me in! he demanded.

And a voice answered back.

Chapter One

Captain's log, stardate 500146.2.

At Starfleet's request, the Enterprise *has arrived at Betazed to take on Lem Faal, a distinguished Betazoid scientist, and his two children. Under Faal's direction, this ship will take part in a highly classified experiment that, if it is successful, may open up a vast new frontier for exploration.*

"ARE YOU QUITE SURE, COUNSELOR, that you do not wish to visit your family while we are here at Betazed?"

"No, thank you, Captain," Commander Deanna Troi replied. "As it happens, my mother and little brother are off on one of her regular excursions to the Parallax Colony on Shiralea VI, so there's not much point in beaming down."

You didn't have to be an empath to detect an unmistakable look of relief on Captain Jean-Luc

3

Picard's face when he learned that Lwaxana Troi was several dozen light-years away. She knew exactly how he felt; even though she genuinely loved her mother, Troi wasn't too disappointed that there would be no parent-daughter reunion on this particular mission. Surviving a visit with Lwaxana always required a lot of energy—and patience. *Maybe it will get easier someday,* she thought. *And maybe Klingons will become vegetarians, too.*

"That's too bad," Captain Picard said unconvincingly. "Although I'm sure our guest must be anxious to get under way." He glanced toward the far end of the conference room, where a middle-aged Betazoid male waited patiently, reviewing the data on a padd that he held at arm's length from himself. *Must be farsighted,* Troi guessed, a not uncommon condition in Betazoids of a certain age. Lem Faal had striking, dark brown eyes, a receding hairline, and the slightly distracted air of a born academic. He reminded Troi of any number of professors she had encountered during her student days at the university, although, on closer inspection, she also picked up an impression of infirmity even though she couldn't spot any obvious handicap. Wearing a tan-colored civilian suit, he looked out of place among all the Starfleet uniforms. Almost instinctively, her empathic senses reached out to get a reading on the new arrival, only to immediately come into contact with a telepathic presence far more powerful than her own. Becoming aware of her tentative probing, Faal looked up from his data padd and made eye contact with Troi from across the room.

Hello, he thought to her.

Er, hello, she thought back. Growing up on Betazed, she had become accustomed to dealing with full telepaths, even though she felt a bit rusty at mind-speaking after spending so many years among humans and other nontelepathic races. *Welcome to the* Enterprise.

Thank you, he answered. She sensed, behind his

4

verbal responses, feelings of keen anticipation, excitement, anxiety, and . . . something else as well, something she couldn't quite make out. Curious, she stretched out further, deeper until she could almost—

Excuse me, Faal thought, blocking her. *I think the captain is ready to begin the briefing.*

Troi blinked, momentarily disoriented by the speed with which she had been shoved out of Faal's mind. She looked around the conference room of the *Enterprise*-E. The other Betazoid's telepathic comment seemed accurate enough; her fellow officers were already taking their places around the curved, illuminated conference table. Captain Picard stood at the head of the table, opposite the blank viewscreen at the other end of the room, where Faal waited to make his presentation. Decorative windows along the outer wall of the conference room offered a eye-catching view of Betazed's upper hemisphere, an image reflected in the glass panes of the display case mounted to the inner wall. Gold-plated models of great starships of the past hung within the case, including a miniature replica of the lost *Enterprise*-D, her home for seven years. Troi always winced inside a little whenever she noticed that model. She'd been at the helm of that *Enterprise* when it made its fatal crash into Veridian III. Even though she knew, intellectually, that it wasn't her fault, she still couldn't forget the sense of horror she had felt as the saucer section dived into the atmosphere of Veridian III, never to rise again. This new ship was a fine vessel, as she'd proven during their historic battle with the Borg a few months ago, but she didn't feel quite like home. Not yet.

Preoccupied with thoughts of the past, Troi sat down at the table between Geordi La Forge and Beverly Crusher. Will Riker and Data were seated across from her, their attention on Captain Picard. Riker's confidence and good humor radiated from him, helping to dispel her gloomy memories. She shook her head to clear her mind and listened attentively as the captain began to speak.

"We are honored to have with us today Lem Faal, a specialist in applied physics from the University of Betazed. Professor Faal has previously won awards from the Daystrom Institute and the Vulcan Science Academy for his groundbreaking work in energy wave dynamics."

"Impressive stuff," Geordi said, obviously familiar with Faal's work. Troi could feel the intensity of his scientific interest seeping off him. No surprise there; she'd expect their chief engineer to be fascinated by "energy wave dynamics" and like matters.

"Indeed," Data commented. "I have been particularly intrigued by the professor's insights into the practical applications of transwarp spatial anomalies." The android's sense of anticipation felt just as acute as Geordi's. *He must have activated his emotion chip,* Troi realized. She could always tell, which certainly demonstrated how genuine Data's on-again, off-again emotions could be.

"Starfleet," the captain continued, "has the greatest of interest in Professor Faal's current line of research, and the *Enterprise* has been selected to participate in an experiment testing certain new theories he has devised." He gestured toward Faal, who nodded his head in acknowledgment. "Professor, no doubt you can explain your intentions better."

"Well, I can try," the scientist answered. He tapped a control on his padd and the viewscreen behind him lit up. The image that appeared on the screen was of a shimmering ribbon of reddish-purple energy that appeared to stretch across a wide expanse of interstellar space. *The Nexus?* Troi thought for a second, but, no, this glowing band did not look quite the same color as the mysterious phenomenon that had obsessed Tolian Soran. It looked familiar, though, like something she might have seen at an astrophysics lecture back at

Starfleet Academy. *Of course,* she realized instantly, *the barrier!*

She felt a temporary surge of puzzlement quickly fade from the room. Obviously, the other officers had recognized the barrier as well. Faal let his audience take in the image for a few seconds before beginning his lecture.

"For centuries," he began, "the great galactic barrier has blocked the Federation's exploration of the universe beyond our own Milky Way galaxy. It completely surrounds the perimeter of our galaxy, posing a serious hazard to any vessel that attempts to venture to the outer limits of inhabited space. Not only do the unnatural energies that comprise the barrier batter a vessel physically, but there is also a psychic component to the barrier that causes insanity, brain damage, and even death to any humanoid that comes into contact with it."

Troi winced at the thought. As an empath, she knew just how fragile a mind could be, and how a heightened sensitivity to psychic phenomena sometimes left one particularly vulnerable to such effects as the professor described. As a full telepath, Faal had to be even more wary of powerful psychokinetic forces. She wondered if his own gifts played any part in his interest in the barrier.

Faal pressed another button on his padd and the picture of the barrier was replaced by a standard map of the known galaxy, divided into the usual four sections. A flashing purple line, indicating the galactic barrier, circled all four quadrants. "The Federation has always accepted this limitation, as have the Klingons and the Romulans and the other major starfaring civilizations, because there has always been so much territory to explore within our own galaxy. After all, even after centuries of warp travel, both the Gamma and the Delta quadrants remain largely uncharted. Furthermore, the distances between galaxies are so incalculably immense that, even if there were a safe way to cross the barrier, a voyage to another galaxy would require a ship to travel for centuries at maximum warp. And finally, to be totally honest, we have accepted the barrier because there has been no viable alternative to doing so.

"That situation may have changed," Faal announced with what was to Troi a palpable sense of pride. *Typical,* she thought. *What scientist is not proud of his accomplishments?* The map of the galaxy flickered, giving way to a photo of a blond-haired woman whose pale skin was delicately speckled with dark red markings that ran from her temples down to the sides of her throat. *A Trill,* Troi thought, recognizing the characteristic spotting of that symbiotic life-form. She felt a fleeting pang of sadness from the woman seated next to her and sympathized with Beverly, who was surely recalling her own doomed love affair with the Trill diplomat Ambassador Odan. Troi wasn't sure, but she thought she sensed a bit of discomfort from Will Riker as well. A reasonable reaction, considering that Will had once "loaned" his own body to a Trill symbiont. She was relieved to note that both Will and Beverly swiftly overcame their flashes of emotion, focusing once more on the present. *They acknowledged their pasts, then moved on,* the counselor diagnosed approvingly. *Very healthy behavior.*

Worf married a Trill, she remembered with only the slightest twinge of jealousy. Then she took her own advice and put that reaction behind her. *I wish him only the best,* she thought.

"Some of you may be familiar with the recent work of Dr. Lenara Kahn, the noted Trill physicist," Faal went on. Heads nodded around the table and Troi experienced a twinge of guilt; she tried to keep up to date on the latest scientific developments, as summarized in Starfleet's never-ending bulletins and position papers, but her own interests leaned more toward psychology and sociology than the hard sciences, which she sometimes gave only a cursory inspection. *Oh well,* she thought, *I never intended to transfer to Engineering.* "A few years ago, Dr. Kahn and her associates conducted a test on *Deep Space Nine,* which resulted in the creation of the Federation's first artificially generated wormhole. The wormhole was unstable, and collapsed only moments after its creation, but Kahn's research team has continued to refine and develop this new technology. They're still years away from being able to produce an artificial wormhole that's stable enough to permit reliable transport to other sectors of the galaxy, but it dawned on me that the same technique, modified somewhat, might allow a starship to open a temporary breach in the galactic barrier, allowing safe passage through to the other side. As you may have guessed, that's where the *Enterprise* comes in."

A low murmur arose in the conference room as the assembled officers reacted to Faal's revelation. Data and Geordi took turns peppering the Betazoid scientist with highly technical questions that quickly left Troi behind. *Just as well,* she thought. She was startled enough by just the basic idea.

Breaking the barrier! It was one of those things, like passing the warp-ten threshold or flying through a sun, that people talked about sometimes, but you never really expected to happen in your lifetime. Searching her memory, she vaguely recalled that the original *Enterprise,* Captain Kirk's ship, had passed through the barrier on a couple of occasions, usually with spectacularly disastrous consequences. Starfleet had declared such expeditions off-limits decades ago, although every few years some crackpot or daredevil would try to break the barrier in a specially modified ship. To date, none of these would-be heroes had survived. She remembered Will Riker once, years ago on Betazed, describing such dubious endeavors as "the warp-era equivalent of going over Niagara in a barrel." Now, apparently, it was time for the

Enterprise-E to take the plunge. She couldn't suppress a chill at the very thought.

"I'm curious, Professor," Riker asked. "Where exactly do you plan to make the test?"

Faal tapped his padd and the map of the galaxy reappeared on the screen. The image zoomed in on the Alpha Quadrant and he pointed at a wedge-shaped area on the map. "Those portions of the barrier that exist within Federation space have been thoroughly surveyed by unmanned probes containing the most advanced sensors available, and they've made a very intriguing discovery. Over the last year or so, energy levels within the barrier have fluctuated significantly, producing what appears to be a distinct weakening in the barrier at several locations."

Shaded red areas appeared throughout the flashing purple curve on the screen. Troi noted that the shaded sections represented only a small portion of the barrier. They looked like mere dots scattered along the length of the line. *Like leaks in a dam,* she thought, finding the comparison somewhat unsettling.

Faal gave her an odd look, as if aware of her momentary discomfort. "These . . . imperfections . . . in the integrity of the barrier are not substantial, representing only a fractional diminution in the barrier's strength, but they are significant enough to recommend themselves as the logical sites at which to attempt to penetrate the barrier. This particular site," he said, pointing to one of the red spots, which began to flash brighter than the rest, "is located in an uninhabited and otherwise uninteresting sector of space. Since Starfleet would prefer to conduct this experiment in secrecy, far from the prying eyes of the Romulans or the Cardassians, this site has been selected for our trial run. Even as I speak, specialized equipment, adapted from the original Trill designs, is being transported aboard the *Enterprise.* I look forward to working with Mr. La Forge and his engineering team on this project."

"Thanks," Geordi replied. The ocular implants that served as his eyes glanced from Data to Faal. "Whatever you need, I'm sure we're up to it. Sounds like quite a breakthrough, in more ways than one."

Troi peered at the spot that Faal had indicated on the map. She didn't recall much about that region, but she estimated that it was about two to three days away at warp five. Neither the captain nor Will Riker radiated any concern about the location Faal had chosen. She could tell that they anticipated an uneventful flight until they arrived at the barrier.

"Professor," she asked, "how similar is the galactic barrier to the Great Barrier? Would your new technique be effective on both?"

Faal nodded knowingly. "That's a good question. What is colloquially known as 'the Great Barrier' is a similar wall of energy that encloses the very center of our galaxy, as opposed to the outer rim of the galaxy. More precisely, the Great Barrier is an *intra*galactic energy field while our destination is an *extra*galactic field." He ran his hand through his thinning gray hair. "Research conducted over the last hundred years suggests that both barriers are composed of equivalent, maybe even identical, forms of energy. In theory, the artificial wormhole process, if it's successful, could be used to penetrate the Great Barrier as well. Many theorists believe both barriers stem from the same root cause."

"Which is?" she inquired.

Faal chuckled. "I'm afraid that's more of a theological question than a scientific one, and thus rather out of my field. As far as we can tell, the existence of the barriers predates the development of sentient life in our galaxy. Or at least any life-forms we're familiar with."

That's odd, Troi mused. She wasn't sure but she thought she detected a flicker of insincerity behind the scientist's ingratiating manner, like he was holding something back. *Perhaps he's not as confident about his theories as he'd like Starfleet to think,* she thought. It was hard to tell; Faal's own telepathic gifts made him difficult to read.

Sitting beside Troi, Beverly Crusher spoke up, a look of concern upon her features. "Has anyone thought about the potential ecological consequences of poking a hole in the barrier? If these walls have been in place for billions of years, maybe they serve some vital purpose, either to us or to whatever life-forms exist on the opposite side of the wall. I hate to throw cold water on a fascinating proposal, but maybe the barrier shouldn't be breached?"

There it is again, Troi thought, watching the Beta-zoid scientist carefully. She sensed some sort of reaction from Faal in response to Beverly's question. It flared up immediately, then was quickly snuffed out before she could clearly identify the emotion. *Fear? Guilt? Annoyance? Maybe he simply doesn't like having his experiment challenged,* she speculated. Certainly he wouldn't be the first dedicated scientist to suffer from tunnel vision where his brainchild was concerned. Researchers, she knew from experience, could be as protective of their pet projects as an enraged *sehlat* defending its young.

If he was feeling defensive, he displayed no sign of it. "Above all else, first do no harm, correct, Doctor?" he replied to Crusher amiably, paraphrasing the Hippocratic Oath. "I appreciate your concerns, Doctor. Let me reassure you a bit regarding the scale of our experiment. The galactic barrier itself is so unfathomably vast that our proposed exercise is not unlike knocking a few bricks out of your own Earth's Great Wall of China. It's hard to imagine that we could do much damage to the ecosystem of the entire galaxy, let alone whatever lies beyond, although the potential danger is another good reason for conducting this preliminary test in an unpopulated sector. As far as we know, there's nothing on the other side except the vast emptiness between our own galaxy and its neighbors." He pressed a finger against his padd and the screen behind him reverted to the compelling image with which he had begun his lecture: the awe-inspiring sight of the galactic barrier stretching across countless light-years of space, its eerie, incandescent energies rippling through the shimmering wall of violet light.

"Starfleet feels—" he started to say, but a harsh choking noise interrupted his explanation. He placed his free hand over his mouth and coughed a few more times. Troi saw his chest heaving beneath his suit and winced in sympathy. She was no physician, but she didn't like the sound of Faal's coughs, which seemed to come from deep within his lungs. She could tell that Beverly was concerned as well.

"Excuse me," Faal gasped, fishing around in the pockets of his tan suit. He withdrew a compact silver hypospray, which he pressed against the crook of his arm. Troi heard a distinctive hiss as the instrument released its medication into his body. Within a few seconds, Faal appeared to regain control of his breathing. "I apologize for the interruption, but I'm afraid my health isn't all it should be."

Troi recalled her earlier impression of infirmity. Was this ailment, she wondered, what the professor was trying so hard to conceal? Even Betazoids, who generally prided themselves on being at ease with their own bodies, could feel uncomfortable about revealing a serious medical condition. She recalled that Faal had brought his family along on this mission, despite the possibility of danger, and she wondered how his obvious health problems might have affected his children. *Perhaps I should prepare for some family counseling, just in case my assistance is needed.*

Faal took a few deep breaths to steady himself, then addressed Beverly. "As ship's medical officer, Dr. Crusher, you should probably be aware that I have Iverson's disease."

The emotional temperature of the room rose to a

heightened level the moment Faal mentioned the dreaded sickness. Iverson's disease remained one of the more conspicuous failures of twenty-fourth-century medicine: a debilitating, degenerative condition for which there was no known cure. Thankfully noncontagious, the disorder attacked muscle fiber and other connective tissues, resulting in the progressive atrophy of limbs and vital organs; from the sound of Faal's labored breathing, Troi suspected that Faal's ailment had targeted his respiratory system. She felt acute sympathy and embarrassment on the part of her fellow officers. No doubt all of them were remembering Admiral Mark Jameson—and the desperate lengths the disease had driven him to during that mission to Mordan IV. "I'm very sorry," she said.

"Please feel free to call on me for whatever care you may require," Beverly stressed. "Perhaps you should come by sickbay later so we can discuss your condition in private."

"Thank you," he said, "but please don't let my condition concern any of you." He held up the hypospray. "My doctor has prescribed polyadrenaline for my current symptoms. All that matters now is that I live long enough to see the completion of my work." The hypospray went back into his pocket and Faal pointed again to the image of the galactic barrier on the screen.

"At any rate," he continued, "Starfleet Science has judged the potential risk of this experiment to be acceptable when weighed against the promise of opening up a new era of expansion beyond the boundaries of this galaxy. Exploring the unknown always contains an element of danger. Isn't that so, Captain?"

"Indeed," the captain agreed. "The fundamental mission of the *Enterprise,* as well as that of Starfleet, has always been to extend the limits of our knowledge of the universe, exploring new and uncharted territory." Picard rose from his seat at the head of the table.

"Your experiment, Professor Faal, falls squarely within the proud tradition of this ship. Let us hope for the best of luck in this exciting new endeavor."

It's too bad, Troi thought, *that the rest of the crew can't sense Captain Picard's passion and commitment the same way I can.* Then she looked around the conference table and saw the glow of the captain's inspiration reflected in the faces of her fellow officers. Even Beverly, despite her earlier doubts, shared their commitment to the mission. *On second thought, maybe they can.*

"Thank you, Captain," Lem Faal said warmly. Troi noticed that he still seemed a bit out of breath. "I am anxious to begin."

This time Troi detected nothing but total sincerity in the man's words.

Chapter Two

"THE MOST DIFFICULT PART," Lem Faal explained, "is going to be keeping the torpedo intact inside the barrier until it can send out a magneton pulse."

"That's more than difficult," Chief Engineer Geordi La Forge commented. He had been reading up on the galactic barrier ever since the briefing, so he had a better idea of what they were up against. "That's close to impossible."

The duty engineer's console, adjacent to the chief engineer's office, had been reassigned to the Betazoid researcher as a workstation where he could complete the preparations for his experiment. To accommodate Faal's shaky health, La Forge had also taken care to provide a sturdy stool Faal could rest upon while he worked. Now he and Geordi scrutinized the diagrams unfolding on a monitor as Faal spelled out the details of his experiment:

"Not if we fine-tune the polarity of the shields to match exactly the amplitude of the barrier at the point where the quantum torpedo containing the magneton pulse generator enters the barrier. That amplitude is constantly shifting, of course, but if we get it right, then the torpedo should hold together long enough to emit a magneton pulse that will react with a subspace tensor matrix generated by the *Enterprise* to create an opening in the space-time continuum. Then, according to my calculations, the artificial wormhole will disrupt the energy lattice of the barrier, creating a pathway of normal space through to the other side!"

"Then it's only two million light-years to the *next* galaxy, right?" Geordi said with a grin. "I guess we'll have to build that bridge when we get to it."

"Precisely," Faal answered. "For myself, I'll leave that challenge for the starship designers and transwarp enthusiasts. Who knows? Maybe a generation ship is the answer, if you can find enough colonists who don't mind leaving the landing to their descendants. Or suspended animation, perhaps. But before we can face the long gulf between the galaxies, first we must break free from the glimmering cage that has hemmed us in since time began. We're like baby birds that finally have to leave the nest and explore the great blue sky beyond."

"I never quite thought of it that way," Geordi said. "After all, the Milky Way is one heck of a big nest."

"The biggest nest still hems you in, as the largest cage is still a cage," Faal insisted with a trace of bitterness in his voice. "Look at me. My mind is free to explore the fundamental principles of the universe, but it's trapped inside a fragile, dying body." He looked up from his schematics to inspect Geordi. "Excuse me for asking, Commander, but I'm intrigued by your eyes. Are those the new ocular implants I've heard about, the ones they just developed on Earth?"

The scientist's curiosity did not bother Geordi; sometimes his new eyes still caught him by surprise, especially when he looked in a mirror. "These are them, all right. I didn't know you were interested in rehabilitative medicine. Or is it the optics?"

"It's all about evolution," Faal explained. "Technology has usurped natural selection as the driving force of evolution, so I'm fascinated by the ways in which sentient organisms can improve upon their own flawed biology. Prosthetics are one way, genetic manipulation is another. So is breaking the barrier, perhaps. It's about overcoming the inherent frailties of our weak humanoid bodies, becoming superior beings, just as you have used the latest in medical technology to improve yourself."

Geordi wasn't sure quite how to respond. He didn't exactly think of himself as "superior," just better equipped to do his job. "If you say so, Professor," he said, feeling a little uncomfortable. Lem Faal was starting to sound a bit too much like a Borg. Maybe it was only a trick of light, reflecting the glow of the monitor, but an odd sort of gleam had crept into the Betazoid's eyes as he spoke. *I wonder if I would have even noticed that a few years ago?* Geordi thought. His VISOR had done a number of things well, from isolating hairline fractures in metal plating to tracking neutrinos through a flowing plasma current, but picking up on subtle nuances of facial expressions hadn't been one of them.

"Chief!" Geordi turned around to see Lieutenant Reginald Barclay approaching the workstation. Barclay was pushing before him an antigrav carrier supporting a device Geordi recognized from Professor Faal's blueprints. "Mr. DeCandido in Transporter Room Five said you wanted this immediately."

The carrier was a black metal platform, hovering above the floor at about waist level, which Barclay steered by holding on to a horizontal handlebar in front of his chest. Faal's invention sat atop the platform, held securely in place by a stasis field. It consisted of a shining steel cylinder, approximately a meter and a half in height, surrounded by a transparent plastic sphere with metal connection plates at both the top and the bottom poles of the globe. It looked like it might be fairly heavy outside the influence of the antigrav generator; Geordi automatically estimated the device's mass with an eye toward figuring out how it would affect the trajectory of a standard quantum torpedo once it was installed within the torpedo casing. *Shouldn't be too hard to insert the globe into a torpedo,* he thought, *assuming everything is in working order inside the sphere.*

"Thanks, Reg," he said. "Professor Faal, this is Lieutenant Reginald Barclay. Reg, this is Professor Faal."

"Pleased to meet you," Barclay stammered. "This is a very daring experiment that I'm proud to be a part—" He lifted a hand from the handlebar to offer it to Faal, but then the platform started to tilt and he hastily put both hands back on the handle. "Oops. Sorry about that," he muttered.

Faal eyed Barclay skeptically, and Geordi had to resist a temptation to roll his ocular implants. Barclay always managed to make a poor first impression on people, which was too bad since, at heart, he was a dedicated and perfectly capable crew member. Unfortunately, his competence fluctuated in direct relationship to his confidence, which often left something to be desired; the more insecure he got, the more he tended to screw up, which just rattled him even more. Geordi had taken Barclay on as a special project some years back, and the nervous crewman was showing definite signs of progress, although some days you wouldn't know it. *Just my luck,* he thought, *this had to be one of Reg's off days.*

"Please be careful, Lieutenant," Faal stressed to Barclay. "You're carrying the very heart of my experiment there. Inside that cylinder is a mononuclear strand of quantum filament suspended in a protomatter matrix. Unless the filament is aligned precisely when the torpedo releases the magneton pulse, there will be no way to control the force and direction of the protomatter reaction. We could end up with merely a transitory subspace fissure that would have no impact on the barrier at all."

"Understood, Professor," Barclay assured him. "You can count on me. I'll guard this component like a mother Horta guards her eggs. Even better, in fact, because you won't have to feed me my weight in silicon bricks." He stared at the Betazoid's increasingly dubious expression. "Er, that was a joke. The last part, I mean, not the part about guarding the component, because that was completely serious even if you didn't like the bit about the Hortas, cause I understand that not everyone's fond of—"

"That will be fine," Geordi interrupted, coming to Barclay's rescue. "Just put the sphere on that table over there. Professor Faal and I need to make some adjustments."

"Got it," Barclay said, avoiding eye contact with Faal. He pushed the carrier over to an elevated shelf strewn with delicate instruments. The antigrav platform floated a few centimeters above the ledge of the shelf. Barclay's forehead wrinkled with anxiety as he looked up and over the carrier to the controls on the other side.

"Let me just scoot over there to even this out," he said, smiling tightly as he began to walk around the carrier to reach the controls.

As soon as Reg took his first step, time seemed to slow down for La Forge. Geordi watched the rise and fall of Reg's footsteps, the gangly engineer's legs grazing the platform, which he didn't give a wide enough berth. La Forge felt his mouth open and heard his own voice utter the first word of a warning. Slowly, excruciatingly slowly, Geordi watched with horror as Lieutenant Reginald Barclay's left elbow plowed into the corner of the platform. The delicate equipment trembled. Reg jumped away. Geordi instinctively covered his eyes. It was one of the few times he wished that medical science had not restored his sight quite so efficiently.

When he finally gathered the courage to look at the equipment and assess the damage, La Forge thought he might faint with relief. The platform had miraculously righted itself. Time sped up to its normal pace again. He dimly heard Barclay's apologies for the near-disaster, but was more concerned for the Betazoid scientist.

He glanced over at Professor Faal. The scientist's face had gone completely white and his mouth hung open in dumbfounded horror. *Has his disease weakened his heart?* he worried. He hoped not, since Lem Faal looked like he was about to drop dead on the spot. He was shaking so hard that Geordi was afraid he'd fall off his stool. *I wonder if I should call Dr. Crusher?*

"Um," Barclay mumbled, staring fixedly at the floor. "Will that be all, sir?"

Geordi offered a silent prayer of thanks to the nameless gods of engineering. He had not been looking forward to telling the captain how his team managed to completely pulverize the central component of the big experiment. He made a mental note to have Barclay schedule a few extra sessions with Counselor Troi. Some more self-confidence exercises were definitely in order . . . as well as a good talking-to.

"Watch it, Lieutenant," he said, his utter embarrassment in front of Faal adding heat to his tone. "This operation is too important for that kind of carelessness." He disliked having to criticize one of his officers in front of a visitor, but Barclay hadn't given him any other choice. He had to put the fear of god into Reg, and let Professor Faal know he had the situation under control.

At least, that was the plan. . . .

"I don't believe it!" Faal exploded, hopping off his stool to confront Barclay. His equipment might have survived its near miss, but the professor's temper clearly had not. Faal's ashen expression gave way to a look of utter fury. His face darkened and his eyes narrowed until his large Betazoid irises could barely be seen. His entire body trembled. "Years of work, of planning and sacrifice, almost ruined because of this . . . this imbecile!"

Barclay looked absolutely stricken. *Yep,* Geordi thought, *Deanna is definitely going to have her work cut out for her.* Barclay tried to produce another apology, but his shattered nerves left him tongue-tied and inaudible.

"I'm sure that looked a lot worse than it actually was," Geordi said, anxious to smooth things over and calm Faal down before he had some kind of seizure. "Good thing we planned on rechecking all the instrumentation anyway."

Faal wasn't listening. "If you only knew what was at stake!" he shouted at Barclay. He drew back his arm and might have struck Barclay across the face with the back of his hand had not La Forge hastily stepped between them.

"Hey!" Geordi protested. "Let's cool our phasers here. It was just an accident." Faal lowered his arm slowly, but still glowered murderously at Barclay. Geordi decided the best thing to do was to get Reg out of sight as fast as possible. "Lieutenant, report back to the transporter room and see if DeCandido needs any more help. You're off of this experiment as of now. We'll speak more later."

With a sheepish nod, the mortified crewman made a quick escape, leaving Geordi behind to deal with the agitated Betazoid physicist. Fortunately, his violent outburst, regrettable as it was, seemed to have dispelled much of his anger. Faal's ruddy face faded a shade or two and he breathed in and out deeply, like a man trying to forcibly calm himself and succeeding to a degree. "My apologies, Mr. La Forge," he said, coughing into his fist. Now that his initial tantrum was over, he seemed to be having trouble catching his breath. He fumbled in his pocket for his hypospray, then applied it to his arm. "I should not have lost control like that." A few seconds later, after another hacking cough, he walked over to the shelf and laid his hand upon the sphere. "When I saw the equipment begin to tip over . . . well, it was rather alarming."

"I understand perfectly," Geordi answered, deciding not to make an issue of the professor's lapse now that he seemed to have cooled off. What with his illness and all, Faal had to be under a lot of stress. "To be honest, I wasn't feeling too great myself for a few seconds there. I can just imagine what you must have been going through."

"No, Commander," Faal answered gravely, "I don't think you can."

Geordi made two more mental notes to himself: 1) to keep Barclay safely out of sight until the experiment was completed, and 2) to remember also that Professor Lem Faal of the University of Betazoid, winner of some of the highest scientific honors that the Federation could bestow, was more tightly wound than he first appeared.

A lot more.

Interlude

LIKE MOST BETAZOIDS, Milo Faal was acutely aware of
his own emotions, and right now he was feeling bored
and frustrated, verging on resentful. Where was his
father anyway? *Probably holed up in some lab,* the
eleven-year-old thought, *same as usual. He's forgotten
all about us. Again.*

Their guest quarters aboard the *Enterprise* were
spacious and comfortable enough. The captain had
assigned the Faal family the best VIP suite available,
with three bedchambers, two bathrooms, a personal
replicator, and a spacious living area complete with a
desk, a couch, and several comfortable chairs. Milo
fidgeted restlessly upon the couch, already tired of the
same soothing blue walls he figured he'd be staring at
for the next several days.

So far, this trip was turning out to be just as boring
as he had anticipated. He had unpacked all their
luggage—with no help from his father, thank you
very much—and put his little sister Kinya down for a
much-needed nap on one of the Jupiter-sized beds in

24

the next room. Monitoring her telepathically, he sensed nothing but fatigue and contentment emanating from his slumbering sibling. With any luck, she would sleep for hours, but what was he supposed to do in the meantime? There probably wasn't another kid his age around for a couple hundred light-years.

In the outer wall of the living room, opposite the couch, a long horizontal window composed of reinforced transparent aluminum provided a panoramic look at the stars zipping by outside the ship. It was a pretty enough view, Milo granted, but right now it only served to remind him how far away he was traveling from his friends and home back on Betazed. All he had to look forward to, it seemed, was a week or two of constant babysitting while his father spent every waking hour at his oh-so-important experiments. These days he often felt more like a parent than a brother to little Kinya.

If only Mom were here, he thought, taking care to block his pitiful plea from his sibling's sleeping mind, lest it disturb her childish dreams. It was a useless hope; his mother had died over a year ago in a freak transporter accident. *Which was when everything started going straight down the gravity well,* he thought bitterly.

Their father, for sure, had never been the same after the accident. *Where in the name of the Second House are you, Dad?* Milo glared at the closed door that led to the corridor outside and from there to the rest of the ship. Sometimes it felt like they had lost both parents when his mother died. Between his illness and his experiments, Dad never seemed to have any time or thought for them anymore. Even when he was with them physically, which wasn't very often, his mind was always somewhere else, somewhere he kept locked up and out of reach from his own children. *What's so important about your experiments anyway? You should be here, Dad.*

Especially now, he thought. Milo knew his father

25

was sick, of course; in a telepathic society, you couldn't hide something like that, particularly from your own son. All the more reason why Lem Faal should be spending as much time as possible with his family . . . before something happened to him. *If* something happened, Milo corrected himself. He could not bring himself to accept his father's death as inevitable, not yet. There was always a chance, he thought. They still had time to turn things around.

But how much time?

Milo flopped sideways onto the couch, his bare feet resting upon the elevated armrest at the far end. His large brown eyes began to water and he felt a familiar soreness at the back of his throat. *No,* he thought, *I'm not going to get all weepy.* Not even when there was no one around to see or hear him. Staring across the living room at the streaks of starlight racing by through the darkness of space, he forced his mind to think more positively.

Flying across the galaxy in Starfleet's flagship had its exciting side, he admitted. Every schoolkid in the Federation had heard about the *Enterprise;* this was the ship, or at least the crew, that had repelled the Borg—twice. *This wouldn't be such a bad trip,* he mused, *if only Dad took the time to share it with us.* He could easily imagine them making a real vacation of it, touring the entire ship together, inspecting the engines, maybe even visiting the bridge. Sure, his father would have to do a little work along the way, supervising the most crucial stages of the project, but surely Starfleet's finest engineers were capable of handling the majority of the details, at least until they reached the test site. They didn't need his father looking over their shoulders all the time.

Of course not.

The entrance to the guest suite chimed and Milo jumped off the couch and ran toward the door, half-convinced that his father would indeed be there, ready to take him on a personal tour of the bridge itself. *About time,* he thought, then pushed any trace of irritation down deep into the back of his mind, where his father couldn't possibly hear it. He wasn't about to let his bruised feelings throw a shadow over the future, not now that Dad had finally come looking for him.

Then the door whished open and his father wasn't there. Instead Milo saw a stranger in a Starfleet uniform. An adult human, judging from the sound of his thought patterns, maybe twenty or thirty years old. It was hard to tell with grown-ups sometimes, especially humans. "Hi," he said, glancing down at the data padd in his hand, "you must be Milo. My name's Ensign Whitman, but you can call me Percy."

Milo must have let his disappointment show on his face, because he felt a pang of sympathy from the crewman. "I'm afraid your father is quite busy right now, but Counselor Troi thought you might enjoy a trip to the holodeck." He stepped inside the guest quarters and checked his padd again, then glanced about the room. "Is your sister around?"

"She's sleeping," Milo explained, trying not to sound as let down as he felt. *Humans aren't very empathic,* he remembered, *so I might as well pretend to be grateful. Just to be polite.* "Hang on, I'll go get her."

I should have known, he thought, as he trudged into Kinya's bedroom, where he found her already awake. She must have heard Percy what's-his-name stumble in, he thought. She started to cry and Milo lifted her from the sheets and cradled her against his chest, patting her gently on the back until she quieted. *Dad would never interrupt his work for us,* he thought bitterly, taking care to shield the toddler from his hurt and anger, *not when he can just dump us with some crummy babysitter.*

The holodeck. Big deal. If he wanted to kill time in

a holodeck, he could have just as easily stayed on Betazed. And it wasn't even his father's idea; it was the ship's counselor's! *Thanks a lot, Dad,* he thought emphatically, hoping that his father could hear him no matter where he was on this stupid starship.

Not that he's likely to care if he does....

Chapter Three

THE DOOR TO THE CAPTAIN'S READY ROOM slid open and Deanna stepped inside. "Thank you for joining us on such short notice, Counselor," Picard said. He waited patiently for her to sit down in one of the chairs in front of his desk, next to Geordi. The door slid shut behind her, granting the three of them a degree of privacy. "Mr. La Forge has informed me of an unpleasant incident involving Lem Faal and I wanted your input on the matter."

Geordi quickly described Faal's confrontation with Lieutenant Barclay to Troi. "It's probably no big deal," he concluded, shrugging his shoulders, "but I thought the captain ought to know about it."

"Quite right," Picard assured him, feeling more than a touch of indignation at the Betazoid scientist's behavior. Granted, Mr. Barclay's awkward manner could be disconcerting, but Picard was not about to let Faal abuse any member of his crew, no matter how prestigious his scientific reputation was. Had Faal actually struck Barclay, he might well be looking at the brig now. "I appreciate your effort to keep me informed," he told La Forge. No doubt Geordi would rather be attending to matters in Engineering, where there was surely much to be done to prepare for the experiment. Picard looked at Deanna. "Counselor, what impression have you formed of Professor Faal?"

Troi hesitated, frowning, and Picard felt a twinge of apprehension. Lem Faal had not struck him as particularly difficult or worrisome. What could Deanna have sensed in the man? Some form of instability? If so, he was concealing it well. "Is there a problem with Professor Faal?" he pressed her.

Her flowing black mane rustled as she shook her head and sighed. "I can't put my finger on anything, but I keep getting a sense that he's hiding something."

"Hiding what precisely?" Picard asked, concerned.

"That's what, I can't tell. Unfortunately, Faal is a full telepath, like most Betazoids, which makes him harder to read. To be honest, sometimes I can half-convince myself that I'm only imagining things, or that I'm merely picking up on the normal anxiety any scientist might feel on the verge of a possible failure." She watched Picard carefully, intent on making herself clear. "Then I get another trace of . . . well, something not quite right, something Faal wants to conceal."

"Are you sure," Picard asked, "that you're not simply sensing some deep-rooted anxieties Faal may have about his medical condition? Iverson's disease is a terrible affliction. It can't be easy living with a terminal diagnosis."

"I've considered that as well," Deanna admitted. "Certainly, he has to be troubled by his illness and impending death, but there may be more to what I'm feeling. When he admitted his condition during the briefing, I didn't get the impression that he was letting go of a deeply held secret. He may be concealing something else, something that has nothing to do with his condition."

"What about his family?" Picard asked. He had been less than pleased to read, in his original mission briefing, that Professor Faal was to be accompanied on this voyage by his two children. The devastating crash of the *Enterprise*-D, along with the heightened tensions of the war with the Dominion, had inspired Starfleet to rethink its policy regarding the presence of children aboard certain high-profile starships engaged in risky exploratory and military missions, much to Picard's satisfaction. His own recommendation had come as no surprise; although he had grudgingly adapted to the family-friendly environment of the previous *Enterprise*, he had never been entirely comfortable with the notion of small children taking up permanent residence aboard his ship. Or even temporary residence, for that matter. "How are his children faring on this voyage?"

"Professor Faal has children?" Geordi asked, caught by surprise. "Aboard the *Enterprise?*"

"Yes," Troi said, both intrigued and concerned. "Hasn't he mentioned them to you?"

"Not a word," Geordi insisted. He scratched his chin as he mulled the matter over. "Granted, we've been working awful hard to get the modified torpedo ready, but he hasn't said a thing about his family."

A scowl crossed Picard's face. "The professor's experiment is not without its dangers. To be quite honest, it hardly strikes me as an ideal time to bring one's children along."

"Any time is better than none at all," Troi explained. "At least that's what the family counselors back on Betazed thought. According to Professor Faal's personal file, which I reviewed after our meeting in the conference room, the children's mother was killed less than six months ago. Some sort of transporter accident."

"The poor kids," La Forge said, wincing. Picard recalled that Geordi's own mother had been missing and presumed dead for only a few years now, ever since the *Hera* disappeared along with everyone aboard; it was none too surprising that the engineer empathized with the children's loss.

"Anyway," Troi continued, "it was felt that now was far too soon to separate them from their father as well, especially since his time after the experiment is completed is likely to be so brief."

"I see," Picard conceded reluctantly. He was no expert on child psychology, but he granted that Faal's terminal condition necessitated special consideration where his children were concerned. "No doubt Faal's illness, as well as the recent tragedy involving his wife, imposes a terrible burden on the entire family. Do you think you might be reacting to whatever difficulties he might be having with his children?"

Troi shook her head. "I'm very familiar with parent-child stresses, including my own," she added with a rueful smile. Picard tried hard not to let his own . . . unflattering . . . feelings toward Lwaxana Troi seep over into Deanna's awareness. "Not to mention helping Worf through all his difficulties with Alexander. . . . No, I know what family problems feel like. This is something different." She frowned again, clearly wishing she could offer Picard advice more specific. "All I can say, Captain, is that Faal is more complicated than he appears, and might behave unpredictably."

"By attempting, for example, to strike Lieutenant Barclay?" Picard suggested. To be fair, he admitted privately, it was Barclay, after all. While he could not condone near-violence against a crew member, Barclay was something of a special case; there were times when Picard himself wondered if Reg Barclay might not be happier in a less stressful environment. The man had his talents, but perhaps not the correct temperament for deep-space exploration.

"For example," Troi agreed. She turned toward La Forge. "Geordi, you've worked more closely with Professor Faal than the rest of us. What are your impressions of him?"

"Gee, I'm not sure," Geordi waffled. "I mean, yeah, he gets pretty intense at times—who wouldn't under the circumstances?—but I don't think he's dangerous or anything, just determined to get the job done while his health is still up to the task. He doesn't talk about it much, but I think his illness weighs on his mind a lot. He's aware that he hasn't got much time left."

"I see," Picard nodded, his irritation at the scientist fading. It was hard not to feel for a man who was facing death just as his life's work neared completion. "Perhaps we should make some allowances for displays of temperament, given the professor's condition." Picard stood up behind his desk and straightened his jacket. Time to conclude this meeting, he decided, and get back to the bridge.

"Faal's reputation is impeccable," he told Troi, thinking aloud. "At the moment, all we can do is keep an extra eye on the professor and try to be ready for any unwelcome surprises." He glanced at the closed door to the bridge. "Counselor, quietly inform both Commander Riker and Lieutenant Leyoro of your misgivings. Mr. La Forge, please keep a careful eye on Professor Faal from now on. We may be worrying unnecessarily, but it's always better to be prepared for any problem that might arise."

"You can count on me, sir," Geordi promised.

"I always do," Picard said, stepping out from behind his desk and gesturing toward the exit. The door slid open and he strode onto the bridge. He nodded a greeting to Commander Riker, who rose from the captain's seat, surrendering it to Picard. "Thank you, Number One," he said. "How goes the voyage?"

"Smooth sailing so far, Captain," Riker reported. He tipped his head at Deanna as she took her accustomed seat beside Picard. Behind them, Geordi disappeared into the nearest turbolift. *Back to Engineering,* Picard assumed.

He settled into his chair, resting his weight against the brown vinyl cushions. All around him, the bridge crew manned their stations; anticipating a straightforward cruise through safe territory, he had chosen to give some of the newer crew members opportunities for valuable bridge experience. On the main viewer at the front of the bridge, stars zipped by at warp five, the maximum speed recommended by Starfleet for non-emergency situations. The familiar hum of ordinary bridge operations soothed his ears. So far, it appeared, their voyage to the edge of the galaxy held few surprises. "No Borg, no Romulans, no space-time anomalies," he commented. "A nice, quiet trip for a change."

"Knock on wood," Riker said with a grin. He glanced around the gleaming metallic bridge. "If you can find any, that is."

"A bit on the dull side, if you ask me," Lieutenant Baeta Leyoro said. The new security officer had joined the ship at Auckland Station. She had previously served aboard the *Jefferson* and the *Olympic* and came highly recommended. Picard had reviewed her file thoroughly before approving her for the post aboard the *Enterprise;* the imposing, dark-haired woman had fought in the brutal Tarsian War in her youth, enduring psychological and biochemical conditioning to increase her fighting skills, before leaving Angosia III and joining Starfleet. In theory, the victorious Angosians had, rather tardily, reconditioned its veterans to peacetime, but how effective that reconditioning was remained open to debate; could any treatment truly undo the hardening effects of years of bloody conflict? Picard found Leyoro's personality slightly abrasive, but that was often the case with the best security officers. Aggressiveness, along with a manageable dose of paranoia, seemed to come with the job. *Just look at Worf,* he thought, *or even the late Tasha Yar.*

"On the *Enterprise,*" he replied to Leyoro, "one learns to appreciate the occasional dull patch . . . as long as they're not *too* long."

"If you say so, sir," she said, sounding unconvinced. Her jet black hair was braided into a long plait that hung halfway down her back. She patted the type-1 phaser affixed to her hip. "I wouldn't want to get too rusty."

"No danger of that, Lieutenant," Riker promised her.

Indeed, Picard thought. On this mission alone, the galactic barrier was nothing to take lightly. The real danger would not begin until they arrived at their destination. "Ensign Clarze," he addressed the pilot at the conn station, a young Deltan officer fresh out of the Academy. "How much longer to the edge of the galaxy?"

Clarze consulted his display panel. Like all Deltans', his skull was completely hairless except for a pair of light blond eyebrows. "Approximately seventy-five hours," he reported promptly.

"Very good," Picard remarked. They were making good time; with any luck, Geordi and Lem Faal should be about ready to commence the experiment by the time they arrived at the barrier. Picard contemplated the viewscreen before him, upon which the Federation's outmost stars raced past the prow of the *Enterprise.* The galactic barrier was still too far away to be visible, of course, but he could readily imagine it waiting for them, marking the outer boundaries of the Milky Way and standing guard over perhaps the most infinite horizon of all. He felt like Columbus or Magellan, prepared to venture beyond the very edge of explored space. *Here there be dragons,* he thought.

A sudden flash of white light, appearing without

warning at the front of the bridge, interrupted his historical ruminations. *Oh no,* he thought, his heart sinking. *Not now!*

He knew exactly what that brilliant radiance foretold, even before it blinked out of existence, leaving behind a familiar personage in front of the main viewer. "Q!" Picard blurted. Beside him, Will Riker jumped to his feet while gasps of surprise and alarm arose from the bridge crew, many of whom had never personally encountered the infamous cosmic entity before.

Standing stiffly at attention before them all, Q was costumed even more colorfully than usual. For some reason that Picard could only hope would become evident, their unexpected visitor had assumed the traditional garb of a Royal Guard at Buckingham Palace, complete with a towering helmet of piled black fur and a crisp red uniform adorned with golden buttons and insignia. A white diagonal sash completed the outfit, along with a sturdy iron pike that he grasped with both hands. He held the pike crosswise before his chest, as though barring them from the stars that streaked by on the screen behind him. "Who goes there?" he intoned ominously.

Picard rose from his chair and confronted his bizarrely attired adversary. "What is it, Q? What are you up to this time?"

Q ignored his queries. He kept his expression fixed and immobile, devoid of his customary smirk, like one of the guards he emulated. "What is your name?" he demanded in the same stentorian tone. "What is your quest?"

Picard took a deep breath, determined not to let Q get under his skin the way he invariably did. Even though he had encountered Q on numerous occasions in the past, he had never devised a truly satisfactory strategy for dealing with the aggravating and unpredictable superbeing. The sad fact of the matter, he admitted silently, was that there was really no way to cope with Q except to wait for him to tire of his latest game and go away. No power the Federation possessed could make Q do anything he didn't want to. Picard liked to think that he had scored a moral victory or two against Q over the years, but here Q was again, ready to try Picard's patience and torment the *Enterprise* one more time. *It's been over two standard years since his last escapade,* he thought, remembering the disorienting trip through time that Q had subjected him to the last time he intruded into their lives. *I should have known our luck was due to run out.*

"What is your quest?" Q repeated. He spun the pike upward and rapped the bottom tip of the iron spear against the duranium flooring, producing an emphatic clang that hurt Picard's ears.

"You know full well who we are and why we're here," he declared. "State your business."

Q's frozen features relaxed into a look of weary annoyance. "Some people have no respect for the classics," he sighed in something closer to his usual voice. He clicked his tongue and the pike disappeared in another blinding burst of light. "Really, Jean-Luc, would it have killed you to play along?"

"No games, Q," Picard insisted. "What do you want?"

Q clutched his hands to his heart, feigning a look of aghast horror. "No games? Why, *mon capitaine,* you might as well ask a sun not to blaze or a tribble not to multiply." He glanced at ship's first officer, poised beside his captain. "Oh, do sit down, Riker, you're not impressing anyone with your manly posing. Except maybe the counselor, that is, and even she can see right through you." He snapped his fingers and Riker was suddenly back in his chair, without having moved a muscle himself. He glared at Q with a ferocity that was nearly Klingon in its intensity, while Troi looked like she would rather be anywhere else.

Why me? Picard thought. Q seemed to take peculiar

delight in afflicting him. "You don't need to show off your powers to us," he said calmly, making what he knew would be a futile attempt to reason with the vainglorious demigod. "We are fully aware of your capabilities." *And then some,* he added mentally. "I am quite busy with other matters. For once, can't you get straight to the point?"

Q looked back and forth before replying, as if disinclined to be overheard. "Permit me to fill you in on a little secret, my impatient friend. When you can do *anything,* nothing is more boring than simply doing it. Getting there isn't half the fun, it's the whole enchilada." He winked at Picard and a drippy Mexican entrée appeared in the captain's hand. "Care for one?"

Picard handed the enchilada back to Q and wiped his greasy fingers on his trousers. He could feel his blood pressure rising at a rate that would surely distress Dr. Crusher. "No, thank you," he said coldly, his temper ascending toward its boiling point. No matter how many times it happened, he could never get used to being made a fool of in front of his crew.

"Your loss," Q said with a shrug, taking a bite from the snack. "Ah, hot and spicy. Reminds me of a supernova I ignited once." Another thought apparently occurred to him and his looming black hat went away. He casually scratched a tuft of unruly brown hair. "Enough of that. It was starting to itch like the devil."

The greatest challenge in dealing with Q, Picard reminded himself, was keeping in mind just how dangerous he could be. Q's antics could be so ludicrous on the surface that it was easy to forget the very real damage he could cause. Whenever Q appeared, Picard made a point of remembering that Q's idea of fun-and-games had already cost the lives of at least eighteen crew members. Q hadn't killed those men and women himself, of course, but he had been perfectly willing to throw the entire ship into the path of the Borg merely to make a point to Picard. *Never again,* Picard vowed. He'd be damned if he'd let Q sacrifice another human life on the altar of his omnipotent ego.

But how did you impose limits on a god?

Lieutenant Leyoro looked ready to try. She had drawn her phaser on Q the moment he appeared, but, to her credit, she had not attempted anything rash. No doubt she was familiar with Q's history from the ship's security logs. "Captain," she inquired, never taking her eyes off Q, "shall I take the intruder into custody?"

Picard shook his head. Why endanger Leyoro with such a pointless exercise? "Thank you, Lieutenant, but I'm afraid that Q is more like an unwanted guest, at least for the time being."

"Your hospitality simply overwhelms me, Jean-Luc," Q remarked sarcastically before turning his gaze on Lieutenant Leyoro. "I see there have been some improvements made." He sniffed the air. "Could it be I no longer detect the barbaric aroma of the ever-feral Mr. Woof?"

"Lieutenant Commander Worf," Picard corrected him, "has accepted a position on *Deep Space Nine.*"

"And good riddance, I say," Q said. A scale model of *Deep Space Nine* appeared in front of him, floating at just below eye level. Q stuck the soggy remains of his enchilada onto one of the miniature docking pylons. Tabasco sauce dripped onto the habitat ring. "I visited that dreary place once. What a dump! I couldn't wait to leave." He waved his hand and both the station and the discarded meal vanished.

"That's not the way I heard it," Picard retorted. Naturally, he had carefully studied all of Q's reported appearances throughout the Federation. "According to Captain Sisko's log, he punched you in the jaw and you never came back." He contemplated his own knuckles speculatively. "Hmmm, perhaps I should have simply decked you years ago."

"I'd be happy to take a crack at it," Riker volunteered.

"Oh, please!" Q said, turning his eyes heavenward but taking a few steps backward. "Really, Picard, with all of creation within my reach, why would I ever return to that woebegone sinkhole of a station? They can't even get rid of the voles."

Despite a strong temptation to argue the point, Picard refrained from defending *Deep Space Nine*. He couldn't expect so flighty a creature as Q to understand all that Benjamin Sisko and his officers had accomplished there over the last several years. He felt a stab of envy, though; Sisko had only the Dominion and the Cardassians to deal with, not a nattering narcissist whose delusions of godhood didn't even have the decency to be delusions. *I wonder if Sisko would be willing to trade the Jem'Hadar for Q?* he thought. Picard would take that deal in a Scalosian second.

"Still, I must congratulate you, Jean-Luc," Q persisted, "in unloading that Klingon missing link. I'm sure he'll fit in perfectly, in a depressingly 'honorable' sort of way, with all the other malcontents and misfits on that station." In the blink of an eye, he teleported from the front of the bridge to the tactical station behind Riker's chair. *"Enchanté, mademoiselle,"* he cooed at Baeta Leyoro, taking her hand and raising it to his lips. "No doubt you have heard nothing but the most extravagant praise of me."

Leyoro yanked her hand back in a hurry. "Listen," she snarled, "I don't care how powerful you're supposed to be. Touch me again and I'll personally send a quantum torpedo up your—"

"Charmed," Q interrupted. He strolled away from the tactical station, taking the long way around the starboard side of the bridge. "Reminds me rather of the late Natasha Yar. Do try to take better care of this one, Jean-Luc."

Picard seethed inwardly. How dare Q make light of

Tasha's tragic death? What did an immortal being even know about the pain and loss associated with mortality? "That's enough, Q," he began, barely reining in his anger.

But Q had already discovered another target. He cocked his head in Data's direction. "What? Can it be true? Did I actually detect a pang of genuine grief from your positronic soul when I mentioned the unfortunate Lieutenant Yar?" Q wandered over to Ops and eyed the android quizzically. Data met his frank curiosity with no visible signs of discomfort.

"Perhaps you are referring to the proper functioning of my emotion chip," he suggested helpfully.

"Indeed I am," Q affirmed, carefully inspecting Data's skull. He crouched down and peered into one of the android's synthetic ears. A beam like a penlight shot from Q's index finger. For a second, Picard feared that Q would simply take Data apart to inspect the chip more closely, but then Q straightened up and stepped away from Data's station. "So the Tin Man finally found a heart . . . of a sort."

"That's enough, Q," Picard said forcefully, "and this 'friendly' reunion has gone on long enough. If you refuse to enlighten us as to the purpose of this visitation, then I see no choice but to get on with our business regardless of your presence." He returned to his chair with every appearance of having dismissed Q from his consciousness, then decided to check on the status of Geordi and Lem Faal's efforts to prepare for the experiment. He tapped his comm badge. "Picard to Engineer—"

Q would not be so easily dismissed. Picard's badge vanished from his chest, reappearing briefly between Q's thumb and index finger before he popped the stolen badge into his mouth and swallowed. "Delicious," he remarked. "Not quite as filling as freshly baked neutronium, but a tasty little morsel nonetheless."

"Q," Picard said ominously as Riker handed Picard his own badge. "You are trying my patience."

"But, Jean-Luc, I haven't even remarked yet on your spanking new *Enterprise.*" He sauntered around the bridge, running a white gloved finger along the surface of the aft duty stations and checking it for dust. "Did you think I wouldn't notice that you've traded up?" He wandered over to the illuminated schematic of the *Enterprise*-E on display at the back of the bridge. "Very snazzy and streamlined, but somehow it lacks the cozy, lived-in quality the old place had. Whatever happened to that bucket of bolts anyway? Don't tell me you actually let Troi take the helm?"

Deanna gave Q a withering look, worthy of her formidable and imperious mother, but otherwise declined to rise to Q's bait. "Very well, Q," Picard said, "it's obvious you've been keeping tabs on us. Now if you don't mind, we have an urgent mission to complete." He started to tap his badge once more, wondering if Q would let him complete his call to Geordi.

Of course not.

"Oh, that's right!" Q said, slapping his forehead. "Your mission. However could I have forgotten? That's why I'm here, to tell you to call the whole thing off."

"What?" Picard hoped he hadn't heard Q correctly.

No such luck. "Your mission," Q repeated. "Your big experiment. It's a bad idea, Jean-Luc, and, out of the goodness of my heart, I've come to warn you." With a flash of light, Q transported himself to directly in front of the captain's chair. He leaned forward until his face was only centimeters away from Picard's. He spoke again, and this time his voice sounded deadly serious. "Read my lips, Captain: Don't even think about breaking the barrier."

Then he disappeared.

Interlude

I SMELL Q, he sniffed. *Q smell I.*

From behind the wall, across the ether, a familiar odor tantalized his senses. Singular emanations, nearly forgotten, impossible to mistake, aroused fragmented flashbacks of aeons past . . . and a personality unlike any other.

Q, Q, that's who, he sang, *Q is back, right on cue!*

Musty memories, broken apart and reassembled in a thousand kaleidoscopic combinations over the ages, exploded again within his mind, sparking an storm of stifled savagery and spite. *It was all Q's fault after all,* he recalled. *False, faithless, forsaking Q.*

He wanted to reach out and wrap his claws around the odor, wring it until it screamed, but he couldn't. Not yet. It was still too far away, but getting closer and closer, too. He flattened himself against the wall,

43

straining impatiently for each new omen of the apostate's approach. A whiff on the cosmic winds. A ripple in space-time. A shadow upon the wall. They all pointed to precisely the same cataclysmic conclusion.

Q is coming. Coming is Q.

And he would be waiting. . . .

Chapter Four

How far could he trust Q? That was the question, wasn't it?

Picard brooded in his ready room, having turned over the bridge to Riker so that he could wrestle with the full implications of Q's warning in private. The music of *Carmen*, the original French Radio recordings, played softly in the background. He sat pensively at his desk as Escamillo sang his Toreador's Song, the infectious melody decidingly at odds with his own somber musings. Picard's weary eyes scanned the dog-eared, leatherbound volumes that filled his bookshelves, everything from Shakespeare to Dickens to the collected poetry of Phineas Tarbolde of Canopus Prime; precious though they were to him, none of the books in his library seemed to offer any definitive solution to the problem of establishing the veracity of an erratic superbeing. At least, he reflected, Dante could be confident that Virgil was telling him the whole truth about the Divine Comedy; the possibility of deceit was not an issue.

So could he believe Q when Q told him that penetrating the barrier was a bad idea? The easy answer was no. Q was nothing if not a trickster. *Mon Dieu,* he had even posed as God Himself once. It was very possible that Q had forbidden the *Enterprise* to breach the barrier for the express reason of tricking them into doing so; such reverse psychology was certainly consistent with Q's convoluted ways. Nor could Picard overlook Q's blatant disregard for the immeasurable value of each human life. *Part of me will never forgive him for that first meeting with the Borg.*

On the other hand, Picard conceded a shade reluctantly, Q's motives were not always malign. When he had briefly lost his powers several years ago, Q had surprised Picard by proving himself capable of both gratitude and self-sacrifice. And every so often Q hinted that he had Picard's best interests at heart. *But,* he thought, *with a friend like Q who needs enemies?* Picard still didn't entirely know what to make of their last encounter; what had truly been the point of that fragmented and disorienting excursion through time? As was too often the case with Q, he had seemed to be both thwarting and assisting Picard simultaneously. The incident frustrated the captain to this day; the more he turned that journey over in his head, the less sense it seemed to make. *It's possible, I suppose, that Q meant well that time around.*

Even Q's most deadly prank, exposing them to the Borg for the first time, had carried a bitter lesson for the future; if not for Q, the Collective might have caught the Federation totally unawares. But who knew what Q's true purpose had been? He could have as easily done so in a fit of pique. Or on a whim.

Whatever his personal feelings toward Q might be, Picard knew he could not dismiss his advice out of hand. He could not deny, as much as he would like to, that Q was a highly advanced being in many respects, privy to scientific knowledge far beyond the Federation's. There might well be some merit to his warning regarding the barrier.

But was Starfleet willing to let the future of humanoid exploration be dictated by a being like Q? That, it seemed to him, was the real crux of the matter. Had not Q himself once declared that the wonders of the universe were not for the timid?

"So I did," Q confirmed, appearing without warning atop the surface of Picard's desk. "How stunningly astute of you to remember, although, typically, you've chosen the worst possible occasion to do so." He shook his head sadly. "Wouldn't you know it? The one time you choose to recall my words of wisdom, it's to justify ignoring my most recent advice."

"I thought such paradoxes were your stock-in-trade?" Picard said, unable to resist such an obvious riposte.

"Touché," Q responded, "or rather I should say, *Olé!"* In fact, he had traded in his guardsman's uniform for the more flamboyant costume of a traditional Spanish matador. A black felt *montera* rested upon his scalp, above his glittering "coat of lights." Golden rhinestones sparkled upon his collar, lapels, and trousers. A thin green tie was knotted at his throat, the chartreuse fabric matching the cummerbund around his waist. A scarlet cape was draped over one arm, although Picard was relieved to see that this would-be bullfighter had left his saber at home.

A strangely appropriate guise for Q, Picard observed, *doubtless inspired by my choice of music.* When he thought about it, Q had much in common with an old-fashioned toreador. Both delighted in teasing and provoking a so-called lesser species for their own sadistic self-glorification. Bullfighting had been banned on Earth since the latter part of the twenty-first century, but Picard doubted that Q cared. "What now?" he demanded. "Why are you here?"

"Votre toast je peux vous le rendre," Q sang in a surprisingly strong baritone, "and one of these days

you might seriously think of offering me a drink, but, anyway, it occurred to me that you might be more likely to see reason in private, when you don't have to strut and preen before your subordinates. Fine, I appreciate your primitive human need to save face in front of your crew. Now that we're alone, though, be a good boy and turn this ship around. I have faith in you, Picard. Who knows why. I'm sure you can think of a suitably plausible excuse if you put your mind to it."

Picard failed to appreciate Q's backhanded flattery. He listened as patiently as he could, then spoke his mind. "First, before you accuse anyone else of strutting and preening, perhaps you should look in the mirror. Second, I have no intention of abandoning my mission unless you can provide me with a compelling reason to do so. Third, get off my desk!"

Q glanced down at his black rhinestone slippers, located only a few centimeters below Picard's chin. "Picky, picky," he clucked, transporting in a flash to the floor facing the sturdy desk. "There, are you happy now?"

"I am rarely happy when accosted by you," Picard answered, holding up his hand to fend off another volley of insults and repartee, "but I am willing to listen to reason. *Why*, Q? I'm giving you a chance. Tell me *why* we should stay within the barrier?"

"Well, why shouldn't you?" Q shot back, but his heart didn't seem to be in it. He chewed on his lower lip and fumbled awkwardly with the satin cape in his hands while he appeared to wrestle with some inner conflict. He opened his mouth, then hesitated, and for a second Picard had an inkling that Q was actually on the verge of saying something genuinely sincere and heartfelt, perhaps ready for the first time to deal with Picard as one equal to another. Pouring out his soul in the background, Don José, the tragic soldier of Bizet's opera, found himself torn between his duty, his heart, and his pride. Picard leaned forward, anxious to hear what Q had to say.

Then the moment passed, and Q retreated to his usual sarcastic demeanor. "Because I say so," he added petulantly. "Really, Jean-Luc, for once in your inconsequential blink of a lifetime, listen to me. Don't let your bruised human ego blind you to my superior wisdom."

"I thought I was about to listen to you," Picard stated, more in sorrow than in anger, "and I don't think it was *my* ego that got in the way." He decided to tempt fate by pushing Q even harder. "If it's that important, Q, why not simply send us home with a wave of your hand? We both know you have the power to do so."

"Forgive me, *mon capitaine*," Q groused, "but perhaps I would prefer not to spend my immortality standing guard over the barrier. I don't want Starfleet sneaking back here every time I'm not looking. I know how blindly stubborn and egomaniacal you mortals are. You're not going to abandon your misbegotten quest unless you think you have some say in the matter."

"Then you must also understand," Picard answered, "humanity's restless urge to explore, to see beyond the next hill." He gestured toward the model starships displayed behind glass on one side of the room, each one a proud reminder of another starship called *Enterprise*. "You're right about one thing. You can turn us back if you want, even destroy this ship if you deem it necessary, but we mortals, as you term us, will not give up that easily. The starships will keep coming, unless you can convince me otherwise."

Q threw up his hands in mock despair. "You're impossible, Picard, thoroughly impossible!" Music soared in the background as the ecstatic citizens of Seville celebrated the coming bullfight. "Well! I'm not about to waste my time here while you're being so pigheaded and primeval, but heed my words, Picard, or you may not live to regret it." He swept his cape off his arm and snapped it with a dramatic flourish. *"Olé!"*

Q vanished, leaving Picard alone with his books and Bizet. *The problem with bullfights,* he reflected soberly, *is that the bull usually ends up dead.*

Chapter Five

DESPITE THE HOUR, the officers' lounge was quite busy. Geordi La Forge spotted Sonya Gomez, Daniel Sutter, Reg Barclay, and several other members of his engineering team seated at various tables around the ship's spacious lounge, trading rumors about Q's most recent appearance, the upcoming assault on the galactic barrier, and other hot topics of discussion. The lights had been dimmed somewhat to give the room more of a murky nightclub ambience, appropriate to the approach of midnight.

Actually, it was a little too dark for his tastes, Geordi decided, so he cybernetically adjusted the light receptors of his optical implants, heightening the visual contrast controls as well. *Ah, that's better,* he thought as Data's gleaming visage emerged from the shadows. Not for the first time, Geordi regretted that the *Enterprise*-D had been destroyed before he got his implants. He would've liked to compare the old Ten-Forward to this new place, yet the switch from his VISOR to the implants made that more or less impossible. The new lounge looked different, all right, but was that because the ship had changed or because his vision had? *Probably a little bit of both,* he guessed.

"It is quite puzzling," Data commented to Geordi. "Spot now refuses to eat her cat food from anything but round plates, even though she has eaten from both round and square plates ever since she was a kitten."

"Cats are just like that," Geordi stated. "Where do you think all those jokes about finicky felines came from? I remember once Alexi, my old Circassian cat, decided that he would only eat if I was eating. Sometimes I'd have to fix myself an extra meal just to get him to finish his dinner. Gained nearly seven kilograms that summer. My parents had to buy me a whole set of clothes for school."

"But it does not make sense, Geordi," Data persisted. Clearly his pet's latest eccentricity was thoroughly baffling his positronic mind. "Why should square plates suddenly become unacceptable for no apparent reason? What if tomorrow she randomly decides that she will only eat from round, *blue* plates?"

Geordi chuckled. "Thank heaven for replicators then." He felt a yawn coming on and didn't bother to suppress it, knowing that the android would not be offended. He and Professor Faal had only finished their prep work less than an hour ago, and he really needed to go to bed soon, but Geordi had learned from experience that, after a day of strenuous mental effort and technical challenges, his mind always needed a little time to unwind before he even tried to fall asleep, which is why he had dropped into the lounge in the first place. Besides, he had been eager to pump Data for details on Q's surprise visit to the bridge.

He'd invited Lem Faal to join them, but the Betazoid scientist had politely declined, pleading exhaustion. *Nothing too suspicious there,* he thought, keeping in mind what Deanna thought she had sensed about

Faal. No doubt the Iverson's had reduced the professor's stamina to some degree. He wished he had more to report to the captain, either to confirm or refute the counselor's suspicions, but, aside from that brief-but-ugly tantrum after Barclay had almost wrecked his equipment, Faal had been on his best behavior. *Too bad all big-name Federation scientists aren't so easy to get along with.* In his capacity as chief engineer aboard the flagship of the fleet, Geordi had worked alongside many of the most celebrated scientific minds in the entire quadrant, and some of them, he knew, could be real prima donnas. Like Paul Manheim, Bruce Maddox, or that jerk Kosinski. By comparison, Lem Faal struck him as normal enough, at least for a genius dying of an incurable disease.

"Another round of drinks, gentlemen?"

Geordi looked up to see a cheerful, round-faced Bolian carrying a tray of refreshments. His bright blue cheeks were the exact color of Romulan ale.

"Thanks," Geordi answered. "Nothing too strong, though. I've got a lot of work in the morning."

Neslo nodded knowingly. "Just as I anticipated. One hot synthehol cider for you," he said, placing a steaming translucent mug on the table, "and for Mr. Data, a fresh glass of silicon lubricant." Complete with a tiny paper umbrella, Geordi noted with amusement. *I wonder whose idea that was, Neslo's or Data's?* He could never tell what his android friend was going to come up with next, especially now that Data was experimenting with genuine emotions.

The blue-skinned bartender was handing the drink to Data when a flare of white light caught them all by surprise. The rest of the drinks tumbled from Neslo's tray, crashing upon the floor, but no one was watching his mishap, not even Neslo. Every eye in the lounge was drawn to the spot by the bar where the flash burst into existence. Blinking against the sudden glare, and wishing that he hadn't turned up his optical receptors after all, Geordi reacted at once, tapping his comm badge and barking, "La Forge to Security. Q is in the officers' lounge!"

Or maybe not. When the light faded, he saw to his surprise that the figure he had expected, Q in all his perverse smugness, was not there. Instead he gazed upon what appeared to be a humanoid woman and a small child. "Fascinating," he heard Data remark.

The woman looked to be about thirtyish in age, slender and tall, with pale skin and a confident air. She was dressed for a safari, with a pith helmet, khaki jacket and trousers, and knee-high brown boots. A veil of mosquito netting hung from the brim of her helmet and she held on to the child's tiny hand while her free hand raised an ivory lorgnette before her eyes. She peered through the mounted lenses and looked about her, seemingly taking stock of her surroundings. She did not appear either impressed or intimidated.

"Well, at least it's a bit more spacious than that other vessel," she commented to the child, quite unconcerned about being overheard, "although what your father sees in these creatures I still can't comprehend."

The toddler, a little boy clad in a spotless white sailor's suit with navy-blue trimming, held an orangish ball against his chest as he searched the room with wide, curious eyes. Geordi, remembering his own little sister at roughly the same age, estimated that the boy was no more than two or three years old. "Daddy?" he inquired. "Daddy?"

Data, as the highest-ranking officer present, approached the strangers. "Greetings," he declared. Geordi rose from his chair to follow behind the android. Bits of glass crunched beneath his feet as he accidentally stepped into a puddle of spilled synthehol and lubricant gel. *Yuck,* he thought as the syrupy mess clung to the soles of his boots.

The crackle of the shattered glasses attracted the woman's attention. "Disgraceful," she said, staring through the lorgnette at the remains of Neslo's meticulously prepared drinks, "leaving sharp edges like that lying around where any child might find them." She lowered the lorgnette and there was another flash of light at Geordi's feet. When he looked down again, the entire mess, both the spilled liquids and the fragments of glass, had completely disappeared. The floor shone as if it had been freshly polished. *Uh-oh,* he thought, *I think I see where this is heading.*

"Children are not customarily permitted in the officer's lounge," Data explained evenly. "I am Lieutenant Commander Data of the Federation starship *Enterprise.* Whom do I have the privilege of addressing?"

Bet I can answer that one, Geordi thought. If the lady was not in fact Q in disguise, then she had to be a relation of some sort. That little trick with broken glass cinched it as far as he was concerned.

The woman looked skeptically at Data, as though noticing him for the first time. "A clockwork humanoid," she observed. "How quaint."

"Robot!" the child chirped happily. "Robot!"

"I am an android," Data volunteered. "And you are?"

"Q," she replied haughtily.

The double doors at the entrance to the lounge snapped open, faster than was usual, and Baeta Leyoro charged into the lounge, brandishing a type-3 phaser rifle. Two more security officers followed hot on her heels, each armed with an equally impressive firearm. "Where is he?" she demanded, searching the room with her eyes.

The security team's dramatic arrival startled the little boy. His ball slipped from his hand, landing with a surprisingly solid thunk and rolling across the floor. Tears poured from his eyes and he let out an ear-piercing wail that Geordi guessed could be heard all over the ship. Lieutenant Leyoro, confronted by a crying toddler rather than Q as she had expected, looked a bit surprised as well. The muzzle of her rifle dipped toward the floor.

"Now see what you've done," clucked the woman who called herself Q. She waved her lorgnette like a magic wand and all three phaser rifles disappeared. Turning her back on Leyoro and the others, she knelt to console the child. "There, there, baby. Those naughty lower life-forms can't hurt you. Mommy's here."

The boy's frightened cries diminished, much to the relief of Geordi's eardrums, replaced by a few quiet sniffles and sobs. The woman's lorgnette transformed instantly into a silk handkerchief and she wiped the child's runny nose. Leyoro stared in amazement at her suddenly empty hands, then eyed the woman with a new wariness. Only Data appeared unfazed by the most recent turn of events.

"Lieutenant Commander?" Leyoro asked the android, keeping her gaze on the woman.

"Permit me to introduce Q," Data replied, but Leyoro did not look satisfied with his answer. The skeptical expression on her face was that of a person who thought someone else was trying to pull a fast one—and was going to regret it if she had anything to do about it.

"I've met Q," she said. "This doesn't look like him."

"I believe," Data elaborated, "that we are encountering another representative of the Q Continuum."

"Well, of course," the woman stated. She lifted the snuffling child and rested his head against her shoulder. "Even a bunch of unevolved primates such as yourselves should be able to figure that out without the help of a mechanical man." She patted the child gently on his back while she glared at the crowd of men and women surrounding her. "I am Q," she insisted.

Another Q, Geordi thought in wonder, *and a baby Q as well!* He hoped that this woman was less irresponsible and more congenial than the Q they were accustomed to. *So far we don't seem to have gotten off to a very good start.*

Hoping to salvage this first-contact scenario, he scurried under a table to retrieve the child's ball. The orange globe was about the size of a croquet ball and heavier than he expected, like a ball of a concrete. It also felt distinctly warm to the touch. Shifting to infrared mode, he was surprised to discover that the globe had a core of red-hot, molten ore. *Wait a second,* he thought, increasing the magnification on his optical sensors. A cracked, rocky surface came into view, with odd-looking craters and outcroppings: hills and valleys, mesas and canals, riverbeds, plateaus, and mountain ranges.

"Er, Data," he said, carrying the ball ever more gingerly toward the woman and her child. "I'm not sure, but I think this is a *planet.*"

Even Data appeared a trifle nonplussed by Geordi's announcement. He paused only a second before tapping his comm badge. "Captain, I believe we need you in the officers' lounge immediately."

"I'm on my way," Picard answered.

57

Interlude

SWIFT AS IT WAS, the turbolift ride to the guest quarters felt interminable to Lem Faal. His body was too anxious to rest in the privacy of his own suite, while his mind resented the loss of any of his precious time. He had too much to do, and too little time to do it, to waste precious seconds simply getting from one place to another. The restrictions of mere physicality chafed at him, filling him with bitter anger at the sheer injustice of the universe. *By the Fourth House,* he thought, *I can't even depend on my own pathetic body anymore.*

In fact, his legs ached to shed the burden of supporting his weight. Every day he felt the effects of Iverson's more and more. It wasn't only in his lungs anymore; now the creeping weakness and shortness of his breath had undermined both his strength and his stamina, leaving him ever slower to recover after each new exertion. Working with Chief Engineer La Forge all day had left him exhausted and badly in need of rest. His breath wheezed in and out of his heaving chest, bringing him little in the way of sustaining oxygen. *The experiment has to succeed,* he mused as the turbolift came to a stop. *I can't endure this much longer.*

He staggered out of the lift into the corridor, grateful that none of the *Enterprise* crew were present to witness his debilitated state. The entrance to his quarters was only a short walk away; Faal felt as though he'd trudged across the scorched plains of Vulcan's Forge, through as thin an atmosphere, by the time he got to his door, which slid open at his approach, concealed sensors confirming his identity. Overhead lights came on automatically, illuminating the chambers beyond.

Captain Picard had generously provided Faal and his children with the best accommodations upon the *Enterprise.* The generously appointed suite was a contrast to the cramped Betazoid transports he had traveled on in his youth, in which open space had been at quite a premium. There were some advantages, he reflected, to living in the latter part of the twenty-fourth century. He could only hope that he would somehow live to see the dawn of the twenty-fifth, no matter how unlikely that seemed at this moment.

Despising his own mortal frailty, he sank onto the couch, a sigh of relief escaping his lips despite his determination to defy the ravages of his disease. His breathing remained labored, and his fingers toyed with the hypospray in his pocket. He considered giving himself another dose of medicine, but decided against it; the polyadrenaline helped his breathing, true, but it sometimes kept him awake as well. *I might as well sleep,* he thought. *There's nothing more I can do until the ship nears the barrier.*

He had faith in his technology, but the unexpected arrival of this "Q" character troubled him. Although he had not actually witnessed the mysterious entity's manifestation upon the bridge, La Forge had informed him of some of the ways Q had previously harassed the crew of the *Enterprise.* The engineering chief had taken care to emphasize that Q was more mischievous than dangerous, although Faal suspected La Forge of holding back many of the more alarming details, but his appearance now, on the very brink of the most important experiment of Faal's lifetime, could not bode well. What if Q seriously tried to obstruct the experiment? How could anyone stop him? Faal had heard about creatures like Q before; such supremely powerful energy beings had been known to Federation science since at least the Organian Peace Treaty of 2267. And there were other strange forces at work in the universe, he knew, forces glimpsed only in prophecies and dreams. . . .

Faal felt the hand of destiny upon him. In a way, Q's intervention only confirmed the ailing scientist's conviction that he was on the verge of a breakthrough of apocalyptic proportions. The inexorable tide of evolution carried him forward and he would let no one stop him, not even a godlike being like Q. He shook his fist at the unseen entity, his entire frame trembling with fervor. *Do your worst,* he defied Q. *Greater powers than you propel me and they will not be denied.*

Exhausted by this spontaneous outpouring of emotion, Faal sagged forward, his chin dipping against his chest. Milo and Kinya were away at the *Enterprise*'s child-care center, he recalled. He needed to collect them eventually, of course, but not right away; he didn't have the strength to cope with two demanding youngsters, not the way he was currently feeling. The children were in capable hands. He'd try to sleep a few hours first.

It was a mistake bringing the children on this mission in the first place. He had neither the strength nor the time to look after youngsters and conduct his experiment at the same time. He would have left them behind on Betazed, but the counselors had been too insistent, in their relentlessly compassionate way, to resist. *Perhaps I should have put up more of a fight,* he thought. There was no room for the children in what remained of his life. They would have to learn to get by without him, one way or another. He had to keep his mind and priorities focused on the larger picture; ultimately, mere biological offspring were no substitute for the sort of immortality he sought. Anyone who thought otherwise had not stared into oblivion as hard as he had been forced to.

Shozana would not agree, he suspected, a pang of guilt going almost unnoticed amid his other constant aches and pains, but, in a very real sense, it was his late wife who had brought him to this critical juncture. Her death in that transporter mishap was the defining moment that taught him the true impermanence of physical existence. . . .

There had been no warning at all. Shozana had stepped lightly onto the transporter pad, then turned to wave back at him, her russet hair gleaming in the warm afternoon sunlight that poured through the clear crystal skylights of the public transport station. *See you soon,* she thought to him as a young transoperator, who looked like he ought to be in school, not behind a control panel, prepared to beam her to a xenobiology conference in the southern hemisphere.

Enjoy yourself, he thought back. *We'll be fine.* There had really been no reason why he had accompanied her to the station that day—it wasn't as if she was leaving on a starship or something—but he had done so anyway. It was a ritual of theirs, one that had always brought them luck before. *Love you,* they thought to each other simultaneously.

Her body evaporated in the golden shimmer of the transporter effect, and he started to leave—until he saw the ashen look on the face of the operator. "What is it? What's happening?" he called out, knowing at once something was wrong, but the panicky youth ignored his cries. His face pale and bloodless, the operator frantically worked the controls while babbling urgently to his counterpart at the other end of the transmission about a "pulsar surge" and "losing the pattern." Faal couldn't follow what the young fool was saying, but the truth hit home with heartbreaking clarity. Shozana was gone. . . .

In the end, there hadn't even been a body to bury. Her signal lost, her flesh and spirit reduced to an entropic stream of disordered particles, Shozana Faal had ceased to exist in the space of a moment. Right then and there, Lem Faal saw the shape of the future. Physical existence was not enough; it was too brief and insubstantial. His own body was disintegrating much more slowly than Shozana's had, but just as inevitably. Soon his pattern, too, would be lost.

An evolutionary breakthrough was required, a transcendent leap to a higher level of being. The old, onerous limitations of the past had to be overcome once and for all. Breaking the galactic barrier was only the first step. . . .

Fatigue overwhelmed his fervent ambitions. Unable to traverse the terrible gulf between the couch and his bedroom, he closed his eyes and collapsed into sleep beneath the bright overhead lights. He twitched restlessly upon the couch, visions of apotheosis filling his dreams.

Chapter Six

ASIDE FROM THE TWO COMMAND OFFICERS, La Forge and Data, and Lieutenant Leyoro's security team, the lounge had been largely evacuated by the time Picard arrived. *A wise precaution,* he decided. If this new Q chose to start turning people into frogs right and left, the fewer warm bodies around the better. He took comfort in knowing that, should anything happen to him, Will Riker was safely in charge of the bridge.

Data had brought him up to speed while he took the turbolift from his ready room to the lounge, so he was not surprised to see the woman and the child waiting for him. The woman had a distinctly imperious air about her that reminded Picard far too much of her infuriating male counterpart; he flattered himself that he could have identified her as a Q even if he hadn't been warned in advance. He took note of her unusual costume as well. *No doubt,* he realized, *she thinks she's on an expedition among savages.* The child, whose scream he had indeed heard nine decks away, he spotted sitting crosslegged on a tabletop nearby, playing with his . . . planet?

Picard repressed a shudder at the thought of what this small boy might be capable of. Dealing with children of any sort was never one of his favorite things to do, but an omnipotent child? Wesley was difficult enough on occasion, and he had merely been a prodigy.

Leyoro met him at the door and escorted him to the woman, who scanned him from head to toe with an appraising look. "You must be the one he talks about all the time," she said, mostly to herself. "Luke John, isn't it?"

"I am Captain Jean-Luc Picard of the *Starship Enterprise*," he informed her. He had no doubt whom the "he" she had mentioned referred to, and couldn't help wondering what Q might have told her about him. *Nothing very complimentary, I'm sure.* "May I ask what brings you here?"

She removed her pith helmet and laid it down on an empty chair. Auburn curls tumbled down to her shoulders, framing her face. If nothing else, she was a good deal more attractive than the usual Q. Her face looked vaguely familiar, but he couldn't place where he might have seen her before.

"I'm looking for my husband," she declared. "Besides, I've always meant to find out why Q finds this primitive vessel so interesting." She glanced around, then shrugged her shoulders. "I must admit, I don't see it yet, but now that we have a family I intend to share more of his interests, however bizarre and unappealing."

"Your husband," Picard repeated, momentarily flummoxed. The only thing more disturbing than the idea of Q married was the realization that he had actually reproduced. *Just what the universe needs,* he thought, *a chip off the old block.* He looked over at the empty bar, wishing Guinan were there. She knew a lot more about the Q Continuum than she usually let on. He generally preferred to respect her privacy regarding her sometimes mysterious past, but he could certainly have used her advice now. *I wonder if I should contact Earth and have her put on a shuttle right away?*

Probably a bit drastic, he decided. *God knows I've coped with the other Q on my own more times than I care to remember.*

"You are correct," he told the woman. "Q was here, a few hours ago, but he has departed."

"Nonsense," she said, looking past him. "He's here, all right. Q," she said firmly, placing her hands on her hips. "Show yourself."

"You called, dearest?" an unmistakable voice rang out, accompanied by a flash of light. Picard spun around to see Q materialize atop the bar counter, stretched out on his side like a model posing for a portrait. He had traded in his anachronistic matador's garb for an up-to-date Starfleet uniform. "Honey, I'm home!"

"This is *not* your home," Picard barked automatically. Q disappeared in a flash, then reappeared next to his alleged spouse. It briefly registered on Picard that this was the first time he had seen Q in the new plum-colored uniforms instituted shortly before the Borg Queen's assault on the Earth. As usual, the sight of Q in uniform seemed grossly inappropriate and offensive.

"Oh, don't be such a sourpuss, Jean-Luc," Q replied. "Allow me to introduce you to my better half, Q." He teleported over to the adjacent table and patted the child on the head. "And this, of course, is little q."

"Daddy!" the boy said gleefully. In his excitement, he forgot to hold on to his "ball," which rolled inexorably toward the edge of the table. With a muted cry of alarm, Geordi La Forge ran over and caught the sphere right as it went over the brink. He let out a sigh of relief and turned toward Picard.

"It doesn't look like an M-class planet," the engineer informed his captain, "but who can be sure?"

"I can," Q stated flatly, taking back the globe from Geordi, who hesitated for a heartbeat before surrendering it. Q grinned and gently shook his finger at the child. "How many times have I told you to be more careful with your toys? Let's put this back into its solar system where it belongs." The orange sphere vanished from sight. "That's a good boy."

This picture of Q as a doting and responsible parent was almost more than Picard could stomach. He didn't know whether to laugh or grimace, so he spoke to the mother instead. "I am happy to meet you," he said diplomatically. "I was unaware that Q had a family."

"Oh, it's a new development," Q explained cheerfully. He snapped his fingers and a rain of white rice descended on the lounge. "We're newlyweds. Isn't it delightful?" The deluge of grain ceased and Q rejoined his bride at her side. "Sorry we couldn't invite you to the ceremony, Jean-Luc, but it was something of a shotgun wedding." He winked at the female Q, as if sharing a private joke with her. A generous assortment of fragrant red roses appeared in the woman's arms. "I'd offer to rethrow the bouquet, but I see that neither the counselor nor Dr. Crusher is present." He raised his hand in front of Picard's face and rubbed his thumb and his index finger together. "Of course, I can always remedy that situation."

"Leave Counselor Troi and the doctor where they are," Picard said more quickly than his pride would have preferred. He didn't know for sure that either Beverly or Deanna was sleeping, but he knew that neither woman would appreciate being yanked from whatever she was doing merely to serve as the butt of one of Q's puerile jokes. He angrily brushed the fallen rice off his uniform while his fellow crew members did the same. Curiously, not a grain appeared to have stuck to either Q.

"Spoilsport," Q said with a scowl. He exchanged a look with his wife. "See what I mean about him?"

The woman gave Picard another frank appraisal. "I still don't understand," she admitted. "He doesn't seem very amusing."

He gave her an affectionate peck on the cheek. "That's because, darling, you've forgotten the ancient, primeval concept of the straight man."

Her eyes lit up. "Oh, now I see it." She blushed and peered at Q through her lashes as if mildly scandalized. "But, Q, that's so . . . carbon-based of you!"

"Isn't it just?" he said, preening. They both tittered slyly at his apparent outrageousness. The child, seeing his parents laughing, started giggling as well, although Picard rather suspected the boy didn't get the joke. He wasn't sure he wanted to either, although he derived a degree of satisfaction and relief from this confirmation that Q was considered something of a reprobate and rascal even among his own kind. The idea of an entire race of godlike beings just as mischievous and troublesome as Q was enough to fill him with utter dread. *I suppose it's too much to hope,* he thought, *that Q will settle down now that he's a husband and a father.*

As often happened with toddlers, the child's attack of the giggles escalated to a full-scale bout of hysterical silliness. He began bouncing up and down on the tabletop, shrieking at the top of his lungs—which sounded like it was in the upper decibel range. Everyone except Data and the elder Q's covered their ears to keep out the deafening peals of laughter. The android hurried toward the table, evidently concerned that the boy might fall and hurt himself, but the pint-sized entity Q had christened q slipped from between Data's arms and hurled himself upward, ricocheting off the ceiling and bouncing around the lounge like a rubber ball flung with the force of a particle accelerator. The child struck the floor only centimeters from Picard's feet, then took off at an angle toward Leyoro and the security team. They yelped in unison and dropped to the floor only an instant before q zipped by overhead. Chairs and tables went flying in all directions as q collided with them, and Geordi and Data took cover behind the bar. A bottle shattered and the smell of Saurian brandy filled the lounge, soon joined by the clashing aromas of Gamzain wine and Trixian bubble juice. Q and Q beamed at each other as their hyperactive offspring wreaked havoc throughout the lounge. Picard saw their lips move and, even though he couldn't hear a thing over the child's wild laughter, felt sure they were saying something like, "Isn't he adorable?"

Picard knew he had lost control of the situation, nothing new where any Q was concerned. "Q!" he shouted, not caring which one heard him. "Stop this at once!"

Q conferred with his spouse, who shrugged and nodded her head. He surveyed the chaos, smiled proudly, then clapped his hands. The silence was immediate. Picard noticed the absence of the din a second before he realized that he was no longer in the lounge.

None of them were. Picard looked around in amazement and discovered that he, Data and Geordi, the security team, and all three Q's had been instantaneously transported to the bridge of the *Enterprise*. It was a close call who was the most surprised, the bridge crew or the new arrivals. Riker leaped from the captain's chair, his eyes wide and his mouth open. "Captain!" he exclaimed.

"At ease, Number One," Picard assured him. He cocked his head toward the Q family, knowing that was all the explanation that was required. The baby q now rested securely within his father's arms, while Picard found himself standing between the command area and Ops. Baeta Leyoro rushed over to the tactical console and stood guard over the weapons controls.

Riker got it, untensing his aggressive stance only a little. A newly replicated comm badge adorned his chest. "I see," he said, glaring suspiciously at Q. "And the woman and child?"

"Q's wife and heir." Riker's jaw dropped again, and Picard shook his head to discourage any further inquiries. "Don't ask. I'll explain later, if I can." He turned and confronted the omnipotent trio. "Q?" he demanded.

Q, the usual Q, lowered his child to the floor and strolled toward Picard with a look of unapologetic assurance on his face. "I felt it was time for a change in venue," he said, loudly enough for all to hear. Q glanced furtively at his mate, who was inspecting the aft engineering station, and whispered in Picard's ear. "To be honest, that other place reeked too much of *her*."

"Guinan?" Picard asked aloud. He found it hard to imagine that Q could truly be honest about anything.

"Don't say that name!" Q hissed, but it was too late. The woman glowered at Q the second Picard mentioned the former hostess of Ten-Forward, then huffily turned her back on him. She took her son by the hand and took him on a tour of the bridge.

"I'm going to pay for that," Q predicted mournfully, "and so will you—someday."

Picard refused to waste a single brain cell worrying about Q's domestic tranquillity. Perhaps Q had inadvertently done him a favor in returning them all to the bridge. The best thing he could do now was ignore Q's attempts to distract him and get on with the business of running the *Enterprise*. He took his place in the captain's chair and swiftly assessed the crew assignments. "Mr. Data, please relieve Ensign Stefano at Ops. Mr. La Forge, if you could arrange to send a repair crew to the lounge."

"You needn't bother, Captain," the female Q commented. "Any and all damage has been undone. Your tribal watering hole has been restored to its pristine, if woefully primitive, condition." As an afterthought, she lifted a hand and retrieved her pith helmet from the ether.

"Thank you," Picard said grudgingly. Despite her condescending attitude, which seemed to go along with being a Q, he entertained the hope that this new entity might prove less immature than her mate. *Heaven help us if she's worse,* he thought. "Never mind, Mr. La Forge." He glanced at the chronometer, which read 0105. "You're relieved from duty if you wish."

"If it's all the same to you," Geordi said, crossing the bridge to the engineering station, "I think I'd rather stay here and keep an eye on things."

Picard didn't blame him. How often did they have three omnipotent beings dropping by for a visit? He considered summoning Counselor Troi to the bridge, then rejected the notion; Deanna's empathic powers had never worked on Q and his ilk.

"Besides," Geordi added, "there's still plenty I can do here to get ready for the experiment." He manipulated the controls at his station. "Data, let's double-check to see if the parameters for the subspace matrix have been fully downloaded into the main computer."

"Yes, Com—" Data began to answer, but Q interrupted, literally freezing the android in midsentence. He laid his hand on the flight controls and shook his head sadly.

"Jean-Luc, I'm very disappointed with you. I can't help noticing that your little ship is still on course for what you ignorantly call the galactic barrier." He sighed loudly and instantly traded places with Ensign Clarze at the conn. The displaced crewman stood in front of the main viewer, blinking and befuddled. "How about a little detour? I hear the Gamma Quadrant is lovely this time of year." His fingers danced over the conn and the distant stars veered away on the screen. "We could take the scenic route."

Picard didn't know what indignity to protest first. Did Q really think he could cancel their mission just by silencing Data? Riker appeared more worried about the flight controls. He strode over to the conn and dropped a heavy hand on Q's shoulder. "Get out of that seat, Q!"

"Overdosing on testosterone again, Number One," he asked, not budging a centimeter, "or are you merely picking up the slack now that everyone's favorite atavism, the redoubtable Worf, is gone?"

"I'm warning you, Q," Riker said with emphasis. Picard admired his first officer's nerve. Q had them hopelessly outmatched in raw power, but maybe Riker could prevail through sheer force of personality. Stranger things had happened.

"Oh, very well," Q grumbled, rising from the chair. Riker nodded at Ensign Clarze, who gulped once, then resumed his place at the conn. "I hardly wanted to steer this pokey hulk for the rest of eternity." He gave Riker a disgusted look. "I can't believe I ever saw fit to offer you the powers of a Q."

That piqued the other Q's interest. "This is the one?" she asked, her mysterious grudge against Q and Guinan forgotten for the moment. She walked over and circled Riker, then placed her hand over her mouth and tried, not very successfully, to keep from laughing. The baby q mimicked his mother's merriment. "Well, that would have certainly shaken up the Continuum. Small wonder they stripped you of your powers after that."

"Don't remind me," he said sullenly. Caught up in their quarrel, neither Q seemed to notice as the *Enterprise* returned to its previous heading. Picard thanked providence for small favors, but his frown deepened as his gaze fell upon the frozen form of Data. The android officer remained immobile, his mouth open in silent reply to his captain's inquiry.

"Q!" he barked, unwilling to let his first officer take on all the risks of defying Q.

"Yes?" the two elder Q's replied simultaneously.

Picard felt a headache coming on. "You," he specified, pointing at his longtime nemesis. "Restore Mr. Data immediately."

That Q glanced impatiently at the inert android, as though Data were a minor annoyance already dismissed from his mind. "Priorities please, Jean-Luc. We still haven't settled this matter of the barrier."

"Might I remind you, Q," Picard observed, "that Mr. Data once saved your life, at considerable risk to his own existence."

For once, Q looked vaguely taken aback. He gazed back at the android with a chastened expression. "But surely," he blustered, "I have repaid that debt many times over with my invaluable services to this vessel."

"Reasonable people might dispute that point," Picard said dryly. He lifted his eyes to espy the female Q and her child. "Your family is here, Q. Is this really the example you wish to set for them?"

Q peeked back over his shoulder at the woman and the boy. His wife raised a curious eyebrow. The child sucked on his thumb, watching Q with awe and adoration.

"Fine!" he said indignantly. He pantomimed a pistol with his thumb and index finger and pointed it at Data's head. "Bang."

"—tenant," Data finished, coming back to life. He paused and assumed a contemplative expression. "How unusual. There appears to be a discrepancy between my internal chronometer and the ship's computer." He surveyed the bridge until his gaze fell upon the party of Q's. "May I assume that one of our visitors is responsible?"

"Precisely so," Picard confirmed, relieved that Data appeared to be back to normal. "Now then, Mr. Data, you were about to inform Mr. La Forge of the status of a particular computer program."

"Really, Jean-Luc!" Q complained, storming up to the command area. "If I didn't know better, I'd swear you were beginning to take me for granted." He shook a warning finger at Picard. "You really shouldn't do that, you know. You're not the only Starfleet captain I can bestow my attentions on, in this or any other quadrant."

What does he mean by that? Picard wondered, although he was far more concerned with the report from Data that Q seemed so determined to postpone. "I'm sure Captain Sisko would welcome a second round of fisticuffs," he told Q, then turned his attention back to Data. "Please proceed with your report."

Data eyed Q curiously, waiting for a second to see if the impertinent entity would interrupt him a third time, but Q seemed to have given up for the present. Q leaned sideways against a nonexistent pillar, looking rather like a gravity-defying mime, and pouted silently.

"It appears that the program is showing a degree of calibration drift," Data stated. "It is possible that an unknown fraction of the data may have been lost during the start-up routine."

Picard paid little attention to the specifics of the problem, which Data and Geordi were surely capable of resolving, but found it eminently reassuring to hear the business of the ship proceeding despite the presence of their unwanted visitors. Displaying a similar hope that order had been restored, Riker took his place at the starboard auxiliary command station.

"Well," Geordi replied to Data, "that explains the eight percent falloff in AFR ratios I keep seeing." His artificial eyes zeroed in on the engineering monitor as he scratched his head. "There must be a problem in the diagnostic subroutines. Maybe we need to completely recalibrate."

"Captain," Leyoro spoke up, her face grim, "I have to protest any discussion of a top-secret mission in front of these unauthorized civilians." She eyed the Q trio dubiously. "All details of a technological nature are strictly classified."

"As if we would have any interest in your pathetic little scientific secrets," Q said scornfully. "You might as well try to hide from us the secret of fire. Or maybe the wheel."

"Wheel!" the baby q chirped, and began rotating slowly above the floor until his mother set him upright again. Thankfully, he was not inspired to summon fire.

"Your point is well taken, Lieutenant," Picard said, sympathizing with Leyoro's concerns; on one level, it felt more than a little strange to be conducting this discussion in front of a party of intruders. "But I'm afraid that Q is correct in this instance. Realistically, it is doubtful that the Federation possesses any technological secrets that the Q Continuum could possibly covet." Besides, he admitted silently, there was little point in concealing their efforts; Q had proved time and time again that he was supremely capable of spying on them regardless of the time or place. "You may proceed with your work, gentlemen."

"Must they?" Q asked peevishly. "It's all academic anyway. There isn't going to be an experiment."

Geordi did his best to ignore Q. "Now I'm getting a drop-off in the triple-R output," he informed Data. "We might have a bigger problem than the diagnostic subroutines."

"Possibly," Data conceded, "but it could simply be a transtator failure. That would also be consistent with calibration errors of this nature."

"And so on and so on," Q broke in, his voice dripping with boredom. He righted himself until he was perpendicular to the floor once more. "Are you done yet? We have infinitely more important matters to get back to."

Q's offspring, Picard noted, no matter how young he might actually be, seemed to possess a greater reserve of patience than his egomaniacal father. "Mr. Data," he said, "I do not pretend to be intimately acquainted with the finer points of Professor Faal's computer programs. Do you anticipate any difficulties working out these problems prior to our arrival at the barrier?"

"No, sir," Data said. Fortunately, the android did not require sleep like the rest of them, although Data often chose to simulate a dormant state in order to further his exploration of humanity, so Picard had no doubt that Data would work through the night if necessary.

Q yawned, and not from fatigue. "Are we quite through with this dreary business?" he inquired. A nervous-looking Ensign Clarze, who was surely less than eager to be teleported away from his post again, kept his eyes determinedly focused on the screen ahead of him even as Q ambled back to the conn. "Then can I finally prevail upon you to abandon this monumentally misguided exercise? Leave the barrier alone. It is not for the likes of you to tamper with."

Maybe it was exhaustion, maybe it was simply that he had reached his limit, but Picard had suddenly had enough of Q's perpetual snideness and high-handed pronouncements. "Get this straight, Q. I take my orders from Starfleet and the United Federation of Planets, not from the Q Continuum and most especially not from you!"

Q recoiled from Picard's vehemence. "Somebody woke up on the wrong side of the Borg this morning," he sniffed. He raised his eyes unto heaven and struck a martyred pose. "Forgive him, Q, for he knows not what he says. I try to enlighten these poor mortals but their eyes are blind and their ears are deaf to my abundant wisdom." He shrugged his shoulders, dropped his arms to his sides, and turned to his mate. "Honeybunch, you talk to him. Tell him I know what I'm talking about."

The female Q was busy wiping her son's nose, but

she looked up long enough to fix her brown eyes on Picard and say, "He knows what he's talking about, Captain." She returned to her son and muttered under her breath, "If only he didn't."

"Big wall!" the toddler interjected, adding his own two cents' worth. "Bad! Bad!" He stamped his tiny foot on the floor and the entire bridge lurched to starboard. Picard grabbed on to his armrests to keep from being thrown from the chair. Data padds and other loose instruments clattered to the floor. Riker stumbled forward, but managed to keep his footing. Baeta Leyoro swore under her breath and shot a murderous glare at Q and his family. Yellow alert lights flashed on automatically all around the bridge. An alarm sounded.

"Now, now," the female Q cooed to her son. "Be gentle with the little spaceship. You don't want to break it." She patted the child on the head and he looked down at his feet sheepishly. Picard felt the *Enterprise*'s flight path stabilize.

He silenced the alarm and ended the yellow alert by pressing a control on his armrest. Although the crisis seemed to have passed, he was unnerved by this demonstration of the baby's abilities. Suppose the child threw a real tantrum? Not even the entire fleet might be able to save them. "Q," he began, addressing the male of the species, "perhaps there is a more suitable location for your son? Children do not belong on the bridge," he said quite sincerely.

"Really?" Q asked. "You gave that insufferable Wesley the run of the place as I recall." He stood on his tiptoes and peered over everyone's heads, as if expecting to find young Wesley Crusher hidden behind a console. Then he lowered his soles to the floor and considered his son. Little q held on to his mother's leg while watching the viewscreen through droopy eyelids. "Still, you may have a point," Q told Picard. "He is looking a trifle bored."

"————?" he said to his wife in a language that

bore no resemblance to any tongue Picard had ever heard before, one so inhuman that even the Universal Translator was stumped.

"———," she replied.

An instant later, the baby disappeared. Picard felt an incalculable sense of danger averted until a new suspicion entered his mind. "Q," he asked warily, "where exactly did the child go?"

Q acted surprised by the question. "Why, Jean-Luc, I understand the *Enterprise* has excellent child-care facilities."

He and the other Q vanished from sight.

Chapter Seven

ALTHOUGH ENTIRE FAMILIES no longer lived permanently on the *Starship Enterprise,* Holodeck B could be converted into a children's center to accommodate the offspring of the various diplomats, delegations, and refugees who often traveled aboard the ship. During such times, the holographic center was kept open twenty-four hours a day, to handle the varying circadian rhythms of each alien race as well as to allow for emergency situations. Since alien encounters and other crises could hardly be expected to occur only during school hours, there had to be some place where any mothers and fathers aboard the ship could safely stow their children during, say, a surprise Romulan attack. The last thing anyone wanted was visiting scientists or ambassadors who were unable to assist in an emergency because they couldn't find a babysitter.

Ensign Percy Whitman, age twenty-five, didn't mind working the graveyard shift at the children's center. The Faal children were still living on Betazed time, according to which it was roughly the middle of the afternoon, but they seemed well behaved and remarkably quiet. *That's the nice thing about telepathic kids,* he thought. *They can talk among themselves without disturbing anyone else.* All of which gave him more time to compose his work-in-progress, a holo-novel about a sensitive young artist who works nights at a kindergarten for nocturnal Heptarians until he is recruited by Starfleet Intelligence to infiltrate the Klingon High Command.

Tonight the writing was going unusually well. He was already up to Chapter Seven, where the hero, Whip Parsi, fights a duel to the death with the treacherous heir to a hopelessly corrupt Klingon household. "His mighty *bat'leth* sliced through the sultry night air, keening a song of vengeance, as Whip struck back with all the skill and fury of one born to battle," he keyed into the padd on his desk. *Yeah,* he thought, transfixed by his own output, *that's great stuff.* He'd work out the holographic animation later.

A squeal of high-pitched laughter yanked him away from his gripping saga. He looked up from the padd to check on his charges. Everything seemed in order: the two smaller children, roughly two years old in human terms, played happily on the carpeted floor, stacking sturdy durafoam blocks into lopsided piles that inevitably toppled over, while their eleven-year-old brother played a computer game in one of the cubicles at the back of the room. Childish watercolor paintings of stars and planets decorated the walls.

Another meter-high tower of multicolored blocks collapsed into rubble and the toddlers squealed once more. *Nothing to be alarmed about here,* Whitman thought. He started to go back to his masterpiece-in-the-making, then paused and scratched his head. Say, hadn't there been only *one* little tyke before?

He put aside his personal padd and checked the attendance display on the center's terminal. *Let's see . . .* Kinya and Milo Faal. That was one all right, a little Betazoid girl and her older brother. He stood up behind the desk and checked out the smaller children again.

The girl was easy to identify. Her blond curls and striking Betazoid eyes distinguished her from the other gleeful youngster. But where had that child, a brown-haired boy in a white sailor's costume, come from? Had someone dropped off another kid without him noticing? He wasn't aware of any other children visiting the ship, but he was only an ensign; no one told him anything.

Could this be some sort of test or surprise inspection? Maybe the new kid wasn't really here at all but was just a holographic image that had appeared from nowhere while he wasn't looking. He checked out the holographic control display embedded into his desk, but found nothing out of the ordinary.

"Milo?" he called out. Perhaps the eleven-year-old had noticed something. "Did you see anybody come by in the last half hour or so?"

"Uh-uh," Milo grunted rather sullenly, never looking away from his computer game. Whitman suspected that Milo thought he was much too old for the children's center and was taking it out on the baby-sitter.

"Are you sure?" Whitman asked. It just didn't make any sense. How could there be an extra kid?

"Uh-huh," Milo said, extremely uninterested in anything any grown-up had to say. On the terminal before him, several invading Tholian warships bit the dust in a computer-generated blaze of glory.

Whitman closed his eyes and massaged his temples, growing increasingly agitated by this uncrackable dilemma. The way he saw it, there was no way he could ask anyone for an explanation without looking like a careless and incompetent idiot. His stomach began to churn unhappily. *Maybe if I just keep my eyes shut,* he thought desperately, *and count to ten, everything will go back to normal and I'll have the right number of kids again.*

It was a ridiculous, pathetic fantasy, but it made as much sense as what had already happened so far. He squeezed his eyes shut and counted slowly under his breath. He swallowed hard, then opened his eyes.

Only one toddler sat on the carpet, staring up at the ceiling with unrestrained wonder. Whitman couldn't believe his luck, until he noticed the wobbly stack of blocks rising up in front of him. He craned his neck back and followed the tower of blocks to its top—where he saw the other child, the one in the sailor suit, teetering at the top of an impossibly tall block pile that reached above Whitman's head. The boy's unruly brown hair brushed the ceiling and he giggled happily, completely unfrightened by his precarious perch. The other child clapped her tiny hands together, cheering him on.

"Oh . . . my . . . god," Whitman gasped, unable to believe his eyes. Then he clapped his hands over his mouth, afraid to exhale for fear of bringing down the tower of brightly colored blocks. Across the room, Milo, intent on his one-man war against the Tholian marauders, was oblivious of the miracle.

The baby reached out his hand and two more blocks lifted off the floor and drifted upward into his waiting fingers. Whitman rubbed his eyes and struggled to figure out what was happening. Could something have gone wrong with the artificial gravity? Could this be some bizarre holographic malfunction? Stranger things had been known to happen; he'd heard a few horror stories about near-fatal accidents within the old *Enterprise*'s holodecks, like that time a holographic Moriarty had almost taken over the ship. Or when Counselor Troi was nearly gunned down during a Western scenario.

Whitman picked up his padd and dropped it over the desk. The padd fell straight down, just like it was supposed to, so the gravity was working fine. But how then had the little boy managed to erect such a ridiculous structure?

He cautiously snuck out from behind the desk, arms outstretched to catch the teetering toddler if and when he plummeted to the floor. He had to fall soon, Whitman told himself. The ramshackle pile of blocks looked like an avalanche waiting to happen. It could collapse at any second. When it did, would he be able to grab the kid before he crashed to the ground? What would Whip Parsi do at a time like this? He hit the medical emergency alert button, summoning help in advance of the ghastly plunge that was sure to come.

The child continued to stack his blocks. Having run out of room between himself and the roof, the boy blithely turned himself upside down and crawled out onto the ceiling. He began lining up his new blocks in a row across the length of the ceiling while he hung there effortlessly like a fly upon a wall. "Choo-choo!" he burbled.

Whitman suddenly felt very silly holding his arms out. *A gravity screwup,* he thought. *It has to be.* Never mind that he still didn't know how this kid got here in the first place. He was about to contact Engineering when the door whished open and Counselor Troi rushed in. Her hair was disheveled and she looked like she'd come straight from bed, pausing only to throw on a fresh uniform.

"Gee, you're fast," Whitman said, remembering his medical alert from mere moments ago.

"The captain sent me," she explained.

"No security team?" Baeta Leyoro asked, sounding both incredulous and offended.

"That is correct, Lieutenant," Picard confirmed. "I believe that Counselor Troi is better suited to handle this situation." If the infant q had indeed been deposited in the holographic children's center, then Deanna's empathic skills and training were more likely to keep the child under control than a squadron of phaser-wielding security officers, assuming that any of them had even a prayer of stopping q from wreaking havoc aboard the ship. *This is all Q's fault,* he thought angrily. *He simply can't resist making my life difficult.*

Leyoro fumed visibly. The dark-haired security chief abandoned her station at tactical and marched into the command area to face Picard. "Permission to speak frankly, sir?" she requested. Her eyes blazed like a warp-core explosion.

"Go ahead, Lieutenant," he said. With Q and his mate absent for the time being, there might be no better time to hear what Leyoro had to say. Will Riker paid close attention to the irate officer as well, while the rest of the crew carried on with their work, no doubt listening attentively.

She stood stiffly in front of him, her hands clasped behind her back. "With all due respect, sir, I cannot do my job effectively if you keep countermanding my recommendations. If you have no faith in me as your head of security, then perhaps you should find someone else."

Just for a second, Picard wished that Worf had never accepted that post at *Deep Space Nine.* "Your service record is exemplary," he told her, "and I have a great deal of confidence in you. However, dealing with Q, any Q, is a unique situation that calls for unorthodox approaches, like sending a counselor in place of a security team."

"I believe I am accustomed to coping with unexpected circumstances," she maintained. "In the past, I have smuggled defectors across the Neutral Zone in an uncloaked ship, rescued political prisoners from a maximum-security Tarsian slave labor camp, and even repelled a Maquis raid with nothing more than a single shuttlecraft and a malfunctioning photon torpedo."

Having thoroughly examined Leyoro's file before

granting her the post of security chief, Picard knew that she was not exaggerating in the slightest. If anything, she was understating her somewhat colorful (and faintly notorious) history. *Not to mention rebelling against her own government when the Angosian soldiers escaped from that lunar prison colony,* he thought.

Still.

"Despite your varied accomplishments," he insisted, "a Q is unlike any threat that you could have encountered before. Force and shows of force can accomplish nothing where a Q is concerned." He hoped Leyoro would understand what he was saying and not take the matter personally. "This is not about you or your capabilities, but about what a Q can do. Namely, anything."

Leyoro appeared mollified. She relaxed her stance and stopped radiating anger. The furnace in her eyes cooled to a smolder. "So," she asked, "how do you deal with an entity like Q?"

"Lieutenant," he answered, "I've been trying to figure that out for a good ten years now."

Beverly Crusher arrived at Holodeck B only minutes after Troi. Not that any of them really needed to have hurried. The baby q looked quite content to play with his blocks up on the ceiling. Watching him was a disorienting, vaguely vertiginous experience. Troi kept glancing down at the floor to make sure that she wasn't simply looking at a reflection in a mirrored ceiling.

She wasn't.

"Now what do we do?" she asked aloud. "Send a shuttle up there to fetch him?"

"I may have a better idea," Beverly answered, "but first let's get the rest of these kids out of here." At the doctor's suggestion, Percy Whitman began corralling the little Faal girl and herding her toward the door. Troi felt sorry for the poor ensign; she could sense his anxiety and confusion. She had attempted to explain to him quickly about Q and Q and q, but he remained as rattled as before.

"Percy," she whispered as he passed by. "Feel free to drop by my office later if you want to talk about this."

He nodded weakly and gave the tiny Betazoid girl a pat on the back to keep her moving. Enthralled by the astounding spectacle of her peer's visit to the ceiling, the other toddler was not very eager to leave. She started crying, but Percy ssshed her effectively and led her out the door. Sitting upside down above everyone's heads, merrily stringing his blocks across the ceiling, q did not notice his playmate being escorted away. Troi breathed a little easier when the youngest of Professor Faal's children disappeared into the corridor. She had summoned Faal himself to the holodeck, but the scientist could just as easily claim the children outside the chamber, safely away from the baby q's unpredictable activities.

That left only the eleven-year-old at the computer terminal. *Milo,* she recalled from Lem Faal's personal files. She began to inch her way along the edge of the chamber, hoping to sneak the older boy out without attracting q's attention. "Milo," she called in a hushed tone. "Milo?"

Caught up in his game, he had not yet observed any of the oddities taking place nearby, nor did he hear her call his name. Troi admired the intensity of his focus even as she wished that he would lift up his head from the screen for just one moment. She had no idea what the baby q might do to another child if provoked, but she didn't want to find out.

The door to the holodeck was sliding shut behind Ensign Whitman when Lem Faal stormed into the simulated child-care center. His thinning hair was disordered and a heavy Betazoid robe, made of thick, quilted beige fabric, was belted at his waist. "What's this all about?" he said irritably, sounding as if he had been unpleasantly roused from sleep. "What's going on with my children? First, I got an urgent call, then that strange young man out there"—he gestured toward the corridor—"said something about an upside-down baby?" Beverly tried to shush Faal, fearing he'd startle q, but the scientist spotted the child upon the ceiling first. "By the Sacred Chalice," he whispered, taken aback. His red-rimmed eyes widened. His mouth fell open and he gasped for breath.

The situation was getting more complicated by the moment, Troi realized. She had to get both Faal and the remaining child out of here. *"Milo?"* she thought urgently, hoping to reach the Betazoid child on a telepathic level.

"Ha!" the boy shouted in triumph, leaning back in his chair and pumping his fist in the air. "Eat hot plasma, Tholian scum!"

His cry of victory startled q, who evidently forgot about canceling gravity. Durafoam blocks rained upon the floor while the surprised baby dropped like a rock. "Oh no!" Beverly shouted.

Without thinking about it, Troi ran to the center of the room and threw out her arms. Will had always teased her about her total inability to play the ancient Terran game of baseball, but now she relied on every hour she had ever spent practicing in the holodeck to wipe the grin from his face. Her heart pounded. Her breath caught in her throat. Nothing else mattered. There was only the falling baby and the hard metal floor beneath the orange carpeting.

Ten kilograms of quite corporeal child landed in her arms and she breathed once more. She hugged the boy against her chest, taking care not to press her comm badge by mistake. For the spawn of two transcendental, highly evolved beings, little q felt surprisingly substantial. Tears sprung from his eyes as Troi shifted her load to make him more comfortable.

Memories of her own infant, Ian Andrew, and of holding him much like this, came back to her with unexpected force.

Beverly Crusher rushed to her side, a medical tricorder in her hand.

"Is he all right?" Troi asked her urgently. It felt very strange—and scary—not to be able to sense the baby's emotions. "Was he hurt by the fall?"

"I don't even know if it's possible for him to be hurt," Beverly answered. She began to scan the child with the peripheral unit of her tricorder, then remembered impatiently that conventional sensors were useless where a Q was concerned. She put the tricorder away and examined the boy with her hands. "No swelling or broken bones," she announced after a moment. "I think he's more scared than injured."

The baby's descent, and Troi's spectacular catch, had seized the attention of both Professor Faal and his son.

"Dad?" Milo said, spotting his father from across the room. "What's happening? Where did that baby come from?" Another thought occurred to him and he looked around the simulated child-care facility. "Hey, where's Kinya?"

But Faal was too intent upon the miraculous, gravity-defying infant to answer his son's queries, or even look away from the bawling child in Troi's arms. "I don't understand," he protested, his gaze shifting from q to the ceiling and back again. "Was that some sort of trick?"

"It's a baby Q," Troi volunteered, trying to put a little distance between Faal and Beverly so that the doctor would have more room to work in.

"Q," he whispered, awestruck. Troi didn't like the sound of his breathing, which was wet and labored. She felt glad that Beverly was close by, and not only for the baby's sake. "But it looks so . . . ordinary?"

Milo left his computer game behind and hurried to join his father. He looked completely baffled, but Troi sensed his happiness at his father's arrival. "Q?" he asked. "What's a Q?"

"An advanced life-form," Faal intoned, more to himself than to the boy. He remained intent on the baby Q. "A higher stage of evolution, transcending mere corporeal existence."

"That?" Milo said, incredulous. Troi detected a spark of jealousy within him, no doubt ignited by his father's absorption with the superhuman infant. "It's just a stupid baby."

Did little q understand him? For whatever reason, the baby started crying louder, approaching the ear-splitting wail that had earlier resounded throughout the entire ship. "Hush," Troi murmured, rocking him gently, but the child kept crying.

"Hang on," Beverly said, "I bet I have a prescription for that." She reached into the pocket of her blue lab coat and pulled out a cherry-red lollipop. "Here, try this."

The child's cries fell silent the moment he saw the bright red sweet. His pudgy fingers wrapped around the stick and he began sucking enthusiastically on the candy. Troi didn't require any special gifts to sense q's improved spirits.

"The oldest trick in pediatric medicine," Beverly explained with a smile. "I never come to a children's center, holographic or otherwise, without one. Once I got here, I had planned to use it to lure him down off the ceiling." She approached Troi to inspect the baby. "You know, he actually looks a little like Q."

"Try not to hold that against him," Troi said. The sucker had calmed q for a time, but she wondered how long that could last. She didn't mind holding the child for a while, even though she realized that wasn't much of a long-term solution. *He looks so angelic now, it's easy to forget how dangerous he might be.*

Troi hoped the doctor had brought some extra

lollipops for later. "You say his mother is much like Q?" Crusher asked.

"So I'm told," Troi answered. She had to admit that she was curious to meet Q's mate. *I guess there really is someone for everyone,* she thought. "At least her ego is supposed to be just as immense."

Professor Faal's interest in the child remained more scientific. He scrutinized the baby like it was a specimen on a petri dish, squinting at the child the closer he got to Troi and the baby Q. Troi was struck by the intensity of his fascination with the child. *Then again,* she recalled, *maybe I've simply become too accustomed to Q and his kind.* She imagined that any scientist would find a Q an irresistible puzzle. "Doctor," Faal said to Crusher, noticing the equipment she was carrying, "might I borrow your tricorder at once."

"It won't do you any good," she warned him, but handed him the instrument. He began scanning q with the tricorder, then scowled in frustration at the (non) readings it displayed. "Dammit, it's not working." At his side, Milo tried to see what his father was reacting to, standing on his tiptoes to peer past his father's arm. Frankly, Troi wished she could somehow persuade Faal to return with Milo to his own quarters, leaving them alone to deal with q, but she suspected it would take wild horses to drag the scientist away from such a unique specimen of advanced alien life.

Beverly considered the child thoughtfully. "It's funny," she said eventually. "I'm kind of surprised that his mother would be willing to leave him alone in the care of a primitive species like us."

"Unless maybe she thought we couldn't possibly do him any harm?" Deanna suggested. "Even if we tried, that is."

"If's he like any other toddler," Beverly said, "then he's perfectly capable of hurting himself by accident." She frowned, disturbed by her own chain of reasoning. Troi could sense her concern growing. "It just doesn't make sense. Why leave a precious child like this with people who completely lack the ability to look after him properly?"

A unexpected burst of light caught them all off guard. "If you must know," said the woman who suddenly appeared in their midst, "I had my eye on him the whole time."

This had to be the female Q, Troi realized. She looked much as the captain had described her, except that now she had assumed the attire of a twentieth-century American tourist on a summer vacation: sandals, pink plastic sunglasses, a large-brimmed hat, and a light cotton sundress with a Hawaiian print design. She held a paper fan in one hand and a flyswatter in the other, both rather gratuitous in the controlled environment of the *Enterprise. Where does she think she is,* Troi wondered, *the Amazon rain forest?* She recognized a bit of baby q in his mother's features, finding this evidence of a family resemblance vaguely reassuring in its similarity to a common, everyday aspect of humanoid parentage.

The woman noticed Troi inspecting her. "Well," she asked acidly, "is my ego as large as you anticipated?"

Troi blushed, recalling her remarks of a few moments ago. She hoped that the woman was equipped with a sense of humor to go with her extraordinary abilities; otherwise Troi might be in serious trouble. "My apologies. I had no idea you were listening."

"Oh, never mind," the Q stated wearily, as if the matter were far too trivial to waste her time upon. "I suppose divinity must resemble egotism to evolutionarily disadvantaged creatures such as yourself." She swept the children's center with a withering stare. To Troi's surprise, Professor Faal stepped backward apprehensively. The Betazoid scientist remained hard to read, but he almost seemed frightened of the female Q. *I guess a harmless baby is one thing,* Troi thought, *but a full-grown Q in her prime is a good deal more intimidating, even for one of the Federation's finest minds.* She reminded herself that Faal, not to mention Milo, were nowhere near as used to encountering the unknown as the crew of a starship. *Especially when she just appears out of nowhere.*

Having surveyed her surroundings, the female Q focused once more on Deanna. "Which one are you?" she asked. "The headshrinker or the witch doctor?"

Any lingering embarrassment Troi might have felt for inadvertently insulting this Q evaporated abruptly. "I am the ship's counselor, Lieutenant Commander Deanna Troi," she declared, "and this is Dr. Beverly Crusher."

"Whatever," Q replied, sounding faintly bored, but her patrician manner softened a bit when her gaze fell upon the child in Troi's arms. The fan and the flyswatter popped out of existence, and she patted his tiny nose with her finger. "Hello, little fellow, have you been having fun among the silly primitives?"

The boy, who was obviously accustomed to his mother appearing from out of nowhere, smiled and showed her his lollipop. "Mama!" he gurgled, and waved the half-eaten sucker in her face. "Yum-yum!"

Troi hoped that his mother approved of giving candy to babies. "That's very yummy, I'm sure," Q said to her child and lifted him from Troi's grasp. The Betazoid counselor willingly surrendered q, her tired arms grateful for the break. She had forgotten how heavy babies could get after a while. Q gave q a tender hug, then looked at the other two women with a marginally more charitable expression on her face. "I suppose I should thank you for tending to my baby as diligently as you were able, not that you can be expected to fully understand the unique needs of such a special and profoundly gifted child, who is, after all, the literal embodiment of the ultimate potential of the Q."

"I wouldn't be so sure of that," Beverly challenged her, understandably annoyed by the woman's attitude. Troi both sensed and shared Beverly's irritation, although Lem Faal, despite his anxiety, seemed to hang on her every word. He couldn't take his eyes off the female Q and her child. "My own son, Wesley, is quite gifted."

"Well, by humanoid standards, perhaps," Q said, distinctly less than impressed.

"Not necessarily," Beverly pointed out. "An entity much like yourself, who called himself the Traveler, judged Wesley worthy of his attention and tutelage."

"The Traveler?" Q asked, sounding intrigued despite herself. She clearly recognized the name. "The Traveler chose *your* son?"

"Exactly," Beverly informed her. Troi could feel her friend's pride in her son, as well as the pain of Wesley's long absence from the *Enterprise*. "I have every reason to believe that he may be on the threshold of entering a higher level of existence."

"For that matter," Troi added, unable to resist joining this game of maternal one-upmanship, "my own son, Ian Andrew, grew up to be a noncorporeal life-form exploring the cosmos."

In fact, the full story was more complicated than that; her son had been an alien entity who had impregnated her with himself in order to learn more about humanoid existence, but she saw no reason to explain all that to this particular Q, who could obviously use being taken down a peg or two. *For her own good, of course,* Troi thought.

The female Q could not believe her ears. Professor Faal looked equally surprised. "Your son," she echoed, "transcending the inherent limitations of matter-based biology? You must be joking."

"Not a bit," Troi stated. "If you doubt either me or Dr. Crusher, you can always consult the ship's logs."

Her son's head resting contentedly on her shoulder, Q subjected Troi and Crusher to more intensive scrutiny than before. "Hmmm," she murmured, mostly to herself, "I think I may be starting to see what Q finds so compelling about you funny little creatures. You may not be as primitive as you appear."

Mother and child both disappeared, leaving the two women, along with Faal and his son, alone in the holographic children's center at roughly three in the morning. Both the holodeck and the ship had survived the visitation intact, although Faal looked as though he had just undergone a religious experience. "I can't believe it. How amazing," he murmured, oblivious of Milo, who tugged on his father's arm but failed to distract the older man from his preoccupation. "Pure energy and power in humanoid form," Faal rhapsodized. "The manifestation—and reproduction—of noncorporeal existence. Animate, anthropomorphized thought!" His breath was ragged, but he didn't seem to notice. He stared inward, poring over his memories for the secrets of the Q's existence. "What did she mean," he asked, "that the child was the embodiment of the Q's potential? Do you think she was implying an even further development in their evolution? Why, the implications are astounding . . . !"

"I think it's getting very late," Troi said simply, uncertain how to respond. Despite all the wondrous events of the last hour, she found she could not ignore the wounded look on Milo's face as his father theorized about the scientific importance of the infant Q. When the other parents, human and otherwise, boasted of their children, she recalled, Faal had not even mentioned his own. Troi could feel the boy's pain. Why couldn't Faal? *Is he unable to sense it somehow,* she wondered, *or does he simply not care?*

Chapter Eight

Captain's log, supplemental:

> As we approach the outer boundaries of the galaxy, neither Q nor any member of his family has been heard from for several hours. If nothing else, this welcome respite has given both myself and my officers a chance to get some much-needed rest. I anticipate the commencement of Professor Faal's ambitious experiment with renewed optimism and vigor, even as I remain convinced that we have not heard the last of Q.

THE GALACTIC BARRIER shimmered on the viewscreen. Red and purple energies coursed along its length, charging the barrier with enough power to threaten even a Sovereign-class starship. On this side of that incandescent ribbon of light, the Milky Way galaxy as they knew it, home to the Federation and the Dominion and the Borg and millions of worlds and races as yet unknown. On the other side, a vast and inconceivable emptiness holding countless more galaxies as large or larger than their own. *This is truly the final frontier,* Picard mused, contemplating the galactic barrier from his chair on the bridge, *one boundless enough to be explored forever.*

"An awesome sight," he commented to Lem Faal. The Betazoid physicist and Geordi La Forge had joined them on the bridge to witness the barrier as it came within visual range of their sensors. Faal stood behind Data's station at Ops, regarding the radiant barrier with open wonder. "I imagine you must be eager to be under way with your experiment," Picard said.

"More than you could ever comprehend," Faal answered. His pale face held a mixture of reverence and ill-disguised rapacity, like King Midas beholding his hoard of gold. "Did you know that the energy that composes the barrier is unlike anything we've ever encountered, aside from the Great Barrier at the galactic core? Why, at first it didn't even register on any of the primitive sensors of the previous century."

"So I gathered," Picard said. He had taken the time to review Starfleet's past encounters with the barrier, particularly the daring voyages of Captain James T. Kirk of the original *Enterprise,* who had braved the barrier in his flimsy ship not once but *three* times. Kirk had mentioned in his log that the barrier had originally been invisible to every sensor except visual, emitting no conventional forms of radiation nor producing any measurable gravimetric effects. Picard smiled sadly at the thought of Jim Kirk; meeting Kirk himself in the Nexus remained one of the high points of his career. *Too bad he didn't live to see this day. This was exactly the kind of pioneering expedition he loved most.*

"How soon until we're within firing range?" Faal asked. A modified quantum torpedo, holding his crucial apparatus, waited within one of the forward torpedo launchers. Faced with the barrier in all its immensity and enigmatic splendor, Picard found it hard to visualize how any man-made object, no matter how specialized, could hope to make a dent in that heavenly wall. Then again, why would Q warn them to leave the barrier alone unless he actually thought Faal might succeed?

"Approximately three hours, forty-seven minutes, and twelve seconds," Data answered helpfully. He increased the magnification on the main viewer and the image of the barrier expanded to fill the screen.

"Wow," Geordi said, from his seat at the engineering station. "That is impressive." Picard wondered how the barrier appeared to Geordi's optical implants.

"You can say that again," added Riker, who was seated at the starboard auxiliary command station. The first officer was as wide-eyed as the rest of them. "I have to admit, Professor, I don't see any sign of those weak spots you mentioned before."

Faal chuckled at Riker's remark. "Everything's relative, Commander. The fractures are there, you can be certain of it, but even the weakest point in the barrier appears impregnable to the naked eye." He never looked away from the screen, enraptured by the magnified vision of the barrier in all its glory. "Three hours, you say. Captain, could we possibly go a little faster?"

"Only in an emergency," Picard stated. He sympathized with the scientist's impatience, but he failed to see a need to exceed Starfleet's recommended cruising speed of warp five, imposed when it was discovered that higher warp speeds caused ecological damage to the very structure of space. "I'm sorry, Professor, but we should be within range soon enough."

"I understand, Captain," Faal said, accepting the verdict. His fingers toyed with his ever-present hypospray. "I've waited years for this opportunity. I suppose I can wait a few hours more."

Picard was grateful that the scientist did not press the issue. Overall, Lem Faal had been fairly easy to work with so far; could Deanna have been mistaken when she detected some hidden dark side to the man's temperament? He glanced to the left and was reassured to see that the counselor was watching the barrier and not Faal; he assumed this meant that the professor was not radiating any particularly disturbing emotions at present. *Let us hope that she misread Faal initially,* the captain thought. Q and his family were enough of a headache for any voyage. He hardly needed further problems.

"Captain," Data reported, "our external sensors are detecting unusual tachyon emissions."

Picard leaned forward in his chair, responding to Data's unexpected announcement. "From the barrier?"

The golden-skinned android turned to face Picard. "Negative, Captain. I was monitoring radiation levels outside the ship when I noted an intriguing phenomenon. In theory, the ambient radiation should decrease steadily the farther we travel away from the galactic center. However, peripheral sensors on the ship's hull are recording a steadily rising number of subatomic tachyon collisions, and not exclusively from the direction of the barrier."

"I see," Picard answered. He exchanged a quizzical look with Riker. The captain had learned to rely on Data's scientific expertise when dealing with unexpected interstellar phenomena; if the android thought these microscopic collisions with faster-than-light particles were worth mentioning, then they deserved his full attention. "Do the tachyon emissions pose a threat to the ship or the crew?"

"No, sir," Data stated. "The tachyon particles are passing through our deflector shields, but the number of particles would need to increase by approximately 1000.45 orders of magnitude before they constituted a hazard to either organic or cybernetic systems. I was merely calling to your attention an unexpected statistical pattern."

Data didn't sound particularly concerned, Picard noted, but the on-again, off-again nature of the android's emotions often made it hard to gauge his reaction to any given development. When he wanted to be, Data could be as unflappable as a Vulcan high priest, no matter how dire the circumstances. Picard didn't think this was one of those times, though; Data was also capable of conveying a sense of urgency as well, and Picard was not getting that impression from the android officer.

"Is there anything that could account for all this heightened tachyon activity?" Riker asked Data.

"There are only two possible explanations," the android stated. His golden eyes carefully monitored the readouts at the Ops console. "An unusual natural phenomenon, such as a wormhole or quantum singularity, or an artificial tachyon bombardment engineered by parties unknown."

"Artificial?" Leyoro asked.

Data elaborated calmly. "I cannot rule out the possibility that the emissions are being deliberately directed at the *Enterprise*."

"To what purpose?" Picard asked. He didn't like the sound of this. In theory, only Starfleet Command was aware of the *Enterprise*'s present location.

"That I cannot yet determine," Data responded. "Shall I devote more of the sensor array's resources toward identifying the source of the emissions?"

Picard nodded gravely. "Make it so, and continue to monitor the impact of the tachyons upon the ship." He turned to address Geordi. "Mr. La Forge, is this tachyon surge likely to interfere with your plans for the experiment?"

"We may need to recalibrate our instruments," Geordi answered. "Some of the equipment is pretty delicate." Professor Faal nodded in agreement, and

Geordi considered the barrier upon the screen. "Before we release the torpedo containing the magneton generator, I want to launch a class-2 sensor probe into the barrier first, just to see what kind of readings we can get before the probe is destroyed. Then we can fine-tune the settings in the torpedo before we send it into the barrier."

"Professor Faal, is this acceptable to you?" Picard asked.

The scientist sighed impatiently, but nodded his head. "Yes, Captain," he said. "Naturally, I would prefer to go straight to creating the wormhole, but, under the circumstances, sending in a probe first would be a wise precaution. The more accurate our data on the barrier is, the better chance for success."

"Very well," Picard said. "Prepare to launch the probe as soon as we're within range of the barrier."

Confident that Geordi could cope with this new development, he considered Data's suggestion that the tachyons were being purposely directed at the ship. Could they constitute a signal of some sort? "Mr. Data, is there any pattern to the emissions that might suggest an attempt to communicate with us?"

"Negative, sir," the android replied. "I have, in fact, run a statistical record of the tachyon emissions through the Universal Translator without success. The only discernible pattern is one of steady growth, suggesting that the source of the emissions is either growing in intensity and/or drawing nearer to the ship."

"In other words," Riker said, "it could be growing stronger *and* getting closer." He scowled through his beard. "That could be trouble."

Lieutenant Leyoro seemed to feel likewise. "Perhaps we should modify the deflector shields to keep the tachyons out," she suggested. "Maybe by adding more power to the subspace field distortion amplifiers."

"That seems a bit premature," Picard decided after

a moment's consideration. Increasing the power of the shields tended to reduce the effectiveness of their scanners. "This doesn't feel like an attack and if it is, it's a singularly ineffective one." He mulled over the possibilities, his arms crossed atop his chest. "Counselor," he asked Troi. "Do you sense anything unusual?"

"No, Captain," she answered. "Nothing from outside the ship. Of course, there are plenty of life-forms out there who don't register on my radar, so to speak. Like the Ferengi, for instance."

"This can't be the Ferengi," Riker quipped. "There hasn't been a price tag attached."

Picard smiled at Riker's joke. "Thank you, Counselor," he said to Deanna. "I appreciate your efforts." He leaned back into his chair and contemplated the viewscreen. *Could this have something to do with our mission?* he wondered. *Is someone trying to sabotage the experiment even before we come within range of the galactic barrier? But why such a subtle approach, employing carefully minute emissions, unless the supposed saboteurs are truly determined to avoid detection?* It seemed unlikely that the Cardassians or their Jem'Hadar allies could get this far into Federation space without someone raising the alarm, but either the Klingons or the Romulans could have slipped a cloaked ship past the borders. Granted, the Klingons were supposedly the Federation's allies once more, but Picard knew better than to trust Gowron too far, especially when there was revolutionary new technology at stake.

And then there were always the more unpredictable factors, like the Tholians or the Gorns. They had been keeping a fairly low profile for the last few decades, but who knew what might draw them out of their isolationist policies?

And, of course, there was Q. . . .

"Captain," Leyoro persisted, "with all due respect, we have to assume hostile intention until we can prove otherwise. Request permission to modulate the shield harmonics to repel the tachyons."

Picard weighed the matter carefully before reaching his decision. "No, Lieutenant, if we start to assume a hostile intent behind every unusual phenomenon we encounter, then our charter to explore the unknown will be severely compromised. For all we know, these harmless emissions may be the first overtures of an entirely new species of being, or evidence of a previously unknown natural phenomenon, and we would do ourselves and our mission a grave disservice if we prematurely cut ourselves off from that evidence out of fear and distrust."

Besides, he thought, sometimes a statistical blip was just that. The universe was all about probabilities, according to standard quantum theory, and if there was one thing he had learned during his long career in Starfleet, it was that the galaxy was big enough and old enough that even the most unlikely probabilities came to pass occasionally.

As if to prove the point, Q appeared upon the bridge. "Scans. Probes. Deflectors," he mimicked. "Don't you ever get fed up with those tired old tricks?" He posed between the captain and Troi, resting his left elbow on the back of the counselor's chair. His standard-issue Starfleet uniform made him *almost* inconspicuous upon the bridge. "I have an idea. Why don't you simply turn around and go home? That would sure catch those pesky tachyons by surprise."

"Go home?" Lem Faal asked anxiously. "Captain, you can't listen to this . . . being!" Picard assumed that Q required no introduction, but noted that Faal appeared more disturbed by Q's opposition to the experiment than by Q's startling entrance. The Betazoid was flushed and trembling at the prospect of watching his plans unravel. Picard heard his weakened lungs laboring strenuously. "You can't cancel the experiment now!"

"I don't intend to," Picard informed the scientist while looking Q firmly in the eye, "not unless our visitor can provide me with a compelling and indisputable reason to do so."

"A reason . . . from this creature?" Faal exclaimed, clearly aghast at the very notion of giving Q a say in the matter. "You can't be serious, Picard. Are you out of your mind?"

"I've often wondered the same thing," Q commented. "You really should consider an insanity defense, Jean-Luc, the next time humanity's on trial."

"This is ridiculous," Faal protested, scurrying toward Picard, but Troi rose and placed a gentle but restraining hand upon the scientist's arm, leaving the captain to deal with the insouciant intruder.

A thought came to Picard and he stared at Q through narrowed eyes. "Do either you or your family, Q, have anything to do with the surge in tachyon collisions we're experiencing?"

"Moi?" The interloper in the Starfleet uniform was the very picture of astonished innocence.

"Vous," Picard insisted, making himself perfectly clear. "Are you responsible for the excess tachyons?"

"Please," Q said, dismissing the notion with a wave of his hand, "I haven't played with tachyons since I was smaller than dear little q. They're far too slow-moving to occupy a mature Q's attention."

"I think you protest a bit too much," Picard said. He remained unconvinced by Q's denials. He knew from experience just how devious Q could be. Why, this very creature had once tried to convince him that Guinan was a deadly threat to the *Enterprise.* What was that name again that Vash had told him that Q had acquired in the Gamma Quadrant? Oh yes, "The God of Lies." *A more than suitable description,* he thought.

Q pursed his lips in mock amazement. "Ooh, a graceful allusion to the mawkish scribblings of a preindustrial mammal. Was that supposed to impress me?" He stared balefully at the captain with a trace of genuine menace in his tone. "Cross my heart, Picard, neither me nor mine have sicced these zippy little particles on you and your ship. You'll have to look elsewhere for the answer to that particular conundrum."

Q vacated the bridge as abruptly as he had arrived, leaving Picard with the unsettling realization that, for once, he actually believed Q was telling the truth.

About the tachyons, at least.

Interlude

"PLEASE STATE THE NATURE of the medical emergency."

Beverly Crusher was working in her office, checking the crew manifest against the annual vaccination schedule for Rigelian fever while half-listening to the musical score of the new Centauran production of *West Side Story,* when she heard the holographic doctor's voice. *Who the devil turned that thing on?* she wondered. Although she liked to think of herself as open to new ideas and equipment, she still had her doubts about this particular innovation. While the program's medical expertise seemed competent enough, its bedside manner left a lot to be desired.

She found the hologram standing in Ward One, beside a row of empty biobeds. She had given Nurse Ogawa the day off, barring further emergencies. Thankfully, there were currently no casualties recuperating in sickbay. "I'm sorry," he said, more snippishly than Beverly liked, "please rephrase your request."

At first, she couldn't see who he was speaking to.

Then she stepped to one side and lowered her gaze. "Yum-yum?" asked the baby q, to the utter bafflement of the emergency medical program. Beverly couldn't help wondering how the child had managed to activate the program in the first place.

"I'm sorry," he replied, "but I am afraid I am not programmed to dispense . . . yum-yums."

"End program," Beverly said with a smirk, feeling more than a little reassured regarding her job security. The hologram vanished as quickly as a Q, and she knelt down to look the child in the face. He wore a miniature version of the Starfleet uniform his father often adopted. "Hello there," she said warmly. "Come for another treat, have we?"

"Yum-yum," he repeated, his current vocabulary less infinite than his potential. He held out a small, pudgy hand.

"Come on," she said, standing up and taking him by the hand. "I think I can take care of this." She led him around the corner to the ship's pediatric unit, which featured a row of smaller biobeds as well as a state-of-the-art intensive care incubator in the center of the facility, beneath an overhead sensor cluster. The room was as deserted as the adult ward. Although no children resided permanently on the *Enterprise*-E, as they had on the previous ship, the pediatric unit was kept ready for any injured youngsters brought aboard during rescue and evacuation efforts; only a few weeks ago, the facility had been filled with the pint-sized survivors of a deadly radiation storm on Arcadia VI. Thankfully, Beverly recalled, all those children had been safely delivered to relatives on *Deep Space Seven*. The small q did not appear particularly dangerous, but she was glad she didn't have to worry about any underage bystanders during this encounter.

She kept a supply of replicated lollipops in a container in one of the equipment cupboards. Fishing a bright blue sucker from her depleted stock, she offered it to q. "How's this?" she asked. "Do you like uttaberry?"

"Yum!" he said gleefully, popping the candy into his mouth. It occurred to Beverly that q could probably wish his own lollipops into existence, in whatever flavor and quantity he desired, but who knew how the mind of a baby superbeing worked? *Probably just as well that he associates me with sweets,* she thought, *and not castor oil.*

She looked q over; had he been truly as human as he appeared, she would have guessed that he was eighteen to twenty-four months old, but how did one estimate the age of a Q? For all she knew, this harmless-looking toddler could be as old as the pyramids. "So how old are you?" she asked aloud. "One century? Two?"

"Actually, he's only been alive for a couple of your standard years," a voice volunteered from behind her.

Beverly jumped forward and clutched her chest, then spun around to face the female Q, who had just appeared in the nursery.

Something to remember, she told herself. *When the child is present, the mother is never very far away.* The Q's outfit was identical to the doctor's, right down to an exact duplicate of Beverly's favorite blue lab coat. *When in Rome, I guess,* Beverly thought. She waited for a second to steady her breathing, then addressed the woman. "You have to give people a little more warning before popping in like that," she advised. "It's not good for our hearts."

"Really?" the woman said. "I seem to have improved your circulation."

In the best interests of diplomacy, Beverly refrained from comment. "Can I help you?" Beverly asked the female Q. She found it hard to think of her as just Q, although it was probably technically correct to do so; that "name" was all too vividly linked in her mind to another face. Why couldn't this female entity just make life easier for them all and pick another letter in the alphabet?

The Q did not answer her immediately, preferring to stroll around the nursery, running a languid hand over the contours of the small beds and occasionally peeking into the cupboards. The child trailed after her, sucking away at his uttaberry lollipop. "You appear to have a distinct talent for handling small children," she commented to Beverly. The incubator caught her attention and she contemplated it for several seconds, looking quite lost in thought. "Are there many children aboard this vessel?" she asked finally.

"Not at present," Beverly answered. She rather missed the children who had helped populate the old *Enterprise;* it had been a point of pride that she'd known all of them by name.

The female Q drew the little boy nearer and patted him lovingly on his tousled head. "My own son is quite unique: the first child born to the Continuum since we transcended physicality untold aeons ago."

Beverly thought that over for a moment. "What about Amanda Rogers?" she asked, recalling the young Starfleet officer who had discovered that she was actually a Q. "She was born on Earth only a few decades back."

The woman sniffed disdainfully. "That creature was conceived in a primitive, strictly humanoid fashion." She shuddered at the very thought.

Don't knock it if you haven't tried it, Beverly thought, but kept her remark to herself. Still, the Q gave her a peculiar look, as if well aware of Beverly's unspoken sentiments.

If she was, however, she chose to ignore them. "I've observed the individual you mentioned," the Q conceded. "It's a wonder she has any gifts at all, given her atrocious origins. I suppose, however, that the poor creature should not be blamed for the sordid activities of her notorious progenitors. She's more to be pitied, really. It was quite magnanimous of Q to take her under his wing the way he did."

He threatened to kill her, Beverly recalled, wondering if the Q could read that in her mind as well. *Maybe it would be best to change the subject.* "Your son is quite charming," Beverly said. "You must be very proud of him." That certainly seemed like safe ground, she judged. Q or not, few mothers could object to praise of their child.

"He is the future of the Continuum," the female Q stated matter-of-factly. "The first of an entirely new generation of immortals. A true mingling of two divine essences, a future messiah, quite unlike that ignorant urchin you called Amanda Rogers."

Better not let Professor Faal hear you talking like that, Beverly thought. The Betazoid scientist had seemed all too fascinated by the Q child to begin with. She could readily imagine his interest in a genuine "future messiah." He'd probably want to ship the baby straight to his lab on Betazed. *Somehow I don't think his mother would approve of that kind of attention.*

The female Q gazed down at the child, who was content to suck quietly on his treat by his mother's side. Her eyes narrowed and she chewed upon her lower lip as if troubled. "I confess I find the responsibility of motherhood rather . . . daunting."

A-ha, Beverly thought. *Now I get it. Faced with the ancient concept of parenting, which no Q has reckoned with for millions of years, why not come to us humble primitives for our crude but simple wisdom?* She wondered whose idea it really was to drop in on sickbay, the child's or the mother's?

"Don't we all," she confided sympathetically. She couldn't blame the Q for her worries. Every new mother had doubts about her ability to cope with raising a child; how much harder it must be when you're the first of your kind to face that prospect since the dawn of time. Beverly had trouble imagining the devious Q as an innocent Adam—he struck her as more the serpent type—but her heart went out to this nervous new Eve.

She circled around the incubator and took the Q by the hand. The woman flinched at the intimacy, but did not draw away. "You seem to be doing fine," Beverly said. "I know it's scary, but millions of mothers have faced the same challenges and survived. The trick is learning when to say no and when to let them learn from their own mistakes."

"Exactly!" the Q responded, acting amazed and grateful that another living creature understood what she was going through. "Little q has all the power of a Q, but he doesn't know how to use it responsibly."

Like father, like son, Beverly thought. "I know he needs to explore his potential, but I'm afraid to let him out of my sight for a fraction of a nanosecond."

"You'll get by somehow," she promised. "Just remember to enjoy this time while you have it. I'll tell you the honest truth: the hardest part of having children is letting them go when they're grown. Of course, for all I know, you might not have to worry about that for millions of years."

"Only millions?" the Q said, apparently sincerely. She tugged q nearer to her, sounding both sad and surprisingly human.

"You'll be amazed how fast the time will fly," Beverly cautioned. Part of her still thought of Wesley as the fragile, acutely vulnerable infant she and Jack had brought home so many years ago. "Don't let this time slip by you without taking a moment every now and then to savor the experience. You might tell his father the same thing," she added, feeling generous toward Q for possibly the first time in her life. *Imagine having Q for a dad,* she thought. *The poor kid.*

She hoped he'd take after his mother instead.

"Thank you for your time," the woman said. Beverly tried to remember whether the other Q had ever thanked anyone for anything. The Q squeezed her hand once, then released it. "You know, my darling q's godmother is one of your kind."

A Q with a human godmother? Beverly was intrigued. "And who would that be?"

"Let me see," the woman began, her gaze turning inward as she combed her memory for this apparently insignificant piece of trivia, "I think her name was—"

Chapter Nine

TWO HOURS, FORTY MINUTES, and only Data knew how many seconds after the *Enterprise* came within sight of the galaxy's edge, Professor Faal and Geordi prepared to launch the sensor probe into the barrier. Although Data had reduced the magnification on the main viewer by several orders of magnitude, the energy barrier filled the screen, bathing everyone on the bridge in its ineffable radiance. *There's something almost mystical about it,* thought Picard, who usually resisted superstitious impulses. He felt much as Moses must have felt when he first beheld the burning bush, or when Kahless drew the original *bat'leth* from the lake of fire.

"Are we far enough away for safety's sake?" he asked. The barrier looked as if it could sweep over them in a matter of minutes, like the largest tsunami in the galaxy.

"I believe so, Captain," Data reported. "As predicted, the barrier yields no harmful radiation or gravitational disturbances. The surrounding space is not affected by the barrier at this distance."

"No evidence of hostile action," Leyoro conceded, looking only a trifle disappointed. "Deflectors at minimum strength."

"No unusual stresses on the hull," Geordi concluded. He looked up in amazement from the engineering monitors to confirm that there actually was a glowing barrier looming before them. "It's like the crazy thing isn't really there."

"Oh, it's most definitely there," Faal whispered avidly, "and more real than any of us has ever been." Turning away from Geordi's monitors, he looked over at Picard, his eyes aglow with anticipation. Picard noticed that he was breathing heavily. "Don't worry, Captain, my artificial wormhole will carve us a safe passage through the barrier, have no fear."

His voice had a fervid tinge that worried Picard. The captain regarded Deanna Troi, who was watching Faal carefully with an apprehensive eye. Faal's outburst during Q's recent visit had given new life to her earlier concerns about the dying scientist's emotional state. Picard frowned, uneasy even though everything seemed to be under control. "How are we doing, Mr. La Forge?" he asked.

"As well as can be expected," Geordi said, his fingers tapping upon the remote controls. Faal, standing behind Geordi, inspected his every move. "The probe should give us the most up-to-date information possible on wave amplitudes within the barrier so we can adjust the shields on the torpedo appropriately. If everything checks out, we should be able to launch the torpedo itself within a few hours." He paused to wipe the sweat from his forehead. "Those tachyon emissions aren't making anything easier, but I think we can work around them."

"There is no question," Faal emphasized, his voice hoarse and strained. Picard was not surprised to see Faal resort to his hypospray once more. Was it only his imagination or was Faal requiring his medication ever more often? "We will make it work," Faal wheezed, "no matter what."

Geordi wandered over to the primary aft science stations, consulting the displays there. "La Forge to Engineering," he said, tapping his comm badge. "Begin rerouting the pre-ignition plasma from the impulse deck to the auxiliary intake. We're going to need that extra power to generate the subspace matrix later on." He placed his hands on the control panel. "Permission to launch the probe, Captain?"

Picard held up his hand to delay Geordi. "Just a minute, Mr. La Forge," he said. A nagging concern preyed on his mind. "Mr. Data, has the tachyon barrage continued to accelerate?"

"Slowly but surely," the android affirmed.

"Have you formed any theory concerning the source of the emissions?" Picard asked. The inexplicable nature of the tachyon surge troubled him to a degree. Launching a simple probe was hardly a risky matter, but he disliked doing so while any scientific irregularities remained unaccounted for.

"Some intriguing possibilities have presented themselves," Data stated, "but I am reluctant to venture a hypothesis on such minimal evidence."

"Do so anyway, Mr. Data," Picard instructed, hoping that the resourceful android could cast some light on the mystery. A tenuous explanation was better than none at all. "Which of your working theories present a cause for concern?"

"An interesting question, sir." Data cocked his head as he considered the issue. "You may find one hypothesis particularly intriguing, although I must emphasize that the evidence supports approximately 75.823 other interpretations."

"Your caveats are duly noted," Picard said. "Go on, Mr. Data."

"Very well, Captain." He manipulated the controls beneath his fingers at superhuman speed, summoning up the relevant information. "Although profoundly weaker in intensity, these persistent emissions are gradually coming to resemble the tachyon probe used by the Calamarain to scan the *Enterprise* on stardate 43539.1."

"The Calamarain?" Riker said, echoing Picard's own reaction as he recalled a cloud of energetic plasma, as large as the *Enterprise*-D or bigger, that had seemed to house a community of gaseous beings possessed of remarkable power. The *Enterprise* had barely survived its first meeting with the Calamarain; if these mounting tachyon emissions had anything to do with those enigmatic beings, then the situation might be more serious than they had first thought.

"Excuse me, Captain," Lem Faal asked, understandably concerned about the effect of Data's theory on his experiment, "but who or what are the Calamarain?"

"An unusual life-form," Picard told him, "that we encountered many years ago. They exist as swirls of ionized gas within a huge cloud of plasma traveling through open space. The Calamarain took hostile action against the *Enterprise,* but their real target was Q himself, who, at that point in time, had lost his powers and taken refuge aboard the ship. Apparently, Q made an enemy of the Calamarain sometime in the past, and they intended to take advantage of his temporary weakness to get their revenge once and for all."

"Can hardly blame them for that," Riker commented. Like most anyone who spent any length of time with Q, the first officer had no great love for the vexatious entity. Picard wondered if the female Q ever felt the same way.

"Agreed, Number One," he said. "Ultimately, Q regained his powers and repelled the Calamarain, and that's the last we had heard of them until now." Picard leaned forward in his chair as he considered all the possibilities. "Data, how likely is it that this is the work of the Calamarain?"

Data analyzed the readings on his console. "That is difficult to say, Captain. Their initial scans in our previous encounter consisted of very broad-based emissions, registering seventy-five rems on the Berthold scale." Picard nodded, remembering vividly the intensity of the alien scan they had experienced years ago: a brilliant deluge of light that had seemed to blot out everything in sight. The Calamarain's first few scans had actually blinded everyone on board momentarily. "These new emissions are far less intense, by several orders of magnitude, but it is a difference of degree, not kind. They may simply be observing us in a more subtle and surreptitious manner." Data swiveled in his chair to address Picard directly. "On the other hand, the tachyon surge could also be caused by any number of unusual natural conditions. It may be that the barrier itself has effects on the surrounding space that we are unable to detect at present."

"Last time the Calamarain attacked us because Q was aboard," Riker pointed out. "If the Calamarain are spying on us, and I realize that's a fairly big 'if,' I think we can safely assume that Q is involved somehow."

"That is a plausible assumption," Data agreed.

"What I don't understand," Geordi said, "is why would the Calamarain be interested in us now? This is hardly the first time we've hosted Q since that time he lost his powers."

Would that it were so, Picard thought privately. He could've done without that vision of his future self suffering from the effects of Irumodic syndrome.

"They've never come after us the last several times Q showed up," Geordi continued, "and it sure doesn't look like he's been turned into a mortal again."

"Far from it," Baeta Leyoro added with obvious regret. Picard suspected that she would love to get her hands on a powerless and vulnerable Q. *She could probably sell tickets,* he thought.

"We should not jump to assumptions," he stated firmly. "The Calamarain have not been observed in Federation space for over a decade, and our previous encounter with them was several hundred light-years from this vicinity." Picard rose from his chair and looked over Data's shoulder at the readings on the Ops console; a rising line charted the growth of the tachyon effect as it approached a level established by the Calamarain so many years ago. "Still, we should be prepared for any possibility." He turned toward the science station. "Mr. La Forge, when the Calamarain attacked us before, you managed to adjust the harmonics of our deflector shields to provide us with a measure of protection against their tachyon blasts. Please program the ship's computer to do so again should the need arise."

"Yes, sir," Geordi said. "I'll get on that right away."

Picard exchanged a look with Lieutenant Leyoro at tactical. Her eyes gleamed and the corners of her lips tipped upward in a look of much-delayed gratification, but she resisted, with admirable restraint, whatever temptation she might have felt to say, "I told you so."

"Captain Picard," Faal said, "this is all very interesting, but perhaps we should proceed with launching the probe?" He fingered his hypospray anxiously. "I cannot stress how eager I am to attempt the experiment."

"Mr. La Forge?" Picard asked. "Do you require any more time to reprogram the deflectors?"

"No, sir," Geordi reported with admirable efficiency. "The adjusted settings are on call." *Excellent,* Picard thought, glad that they were ready for even the most unlikely of scenarios. Now it was simply a matter of continuing with their mission before Q—or the Calamarain, if they were truly close at hand—

could intervene. "You may launch the probe as planned, Mr. La Forge," he stated.

Geordi reached for the launch controls, only to be caught off guard by a blinding flash directly in front of him. For a second, Picard feared that the science station had exploded; then he realized what the flash really entailed. *Blast,* he thought. *Not again!*

Q was back, sitting upon the launch controls, clad in the unearned honors of a Starfleet uniform. Geordi stepped backward involuntarily, and Q peered at him with interest. He took a closer look at Geordi. "Are those new eyes, Mr. Engineer? I can't say they're very flattering, although I suppose it beats wearing a chrome fender in front of your face."

He looked past Geordi and cast a dour eye on the shimmering barrier upon the main viewer. "You disappoint me so, Jean-Luc. I never thought suicide missions were exactly your style." He hopped nimbly off the science console and strolled toward Picard. "Leave the galaxy? Why, you foolhardy humans couldn't put one foot into the Gamma Quadrant without starting a war with the Dominion. What makes you think the rest of the universe is going to be any better?"

"That's enough," Riker said. "The captain has better things to do with his time than listen to you."

Q paid the first officer no heed. "Tell me, Jean-Luc, I know you have a childish fondness for hard-boiled detective yarns." He held out a palm on which a single white egg now balanced upon its end. A caricature of Picard's scowling face was painted on the shell of the presumably hard-boiled egg. "Bit of a resemblance, isn't there?" Q commented. He blew on his hand and the egg wafted away like a mirage. "But haven't you ever paid attention to some of your species' old monster movies?" His voice dropped several octaves, taking on a sepulchral tone. "There are some things that insignificant, short-lived mortals are meant to leave alone." He gave Picard what seemed, for Q, a remarkably sober look, and when he spoke again his voice sounded notably free of irony or sarcasm. "The barrier is one of them, Picard. Trust me on this."

Trust? Q? Of the many surprising and exceptional developments in this highly eventful mission, this suggestion struck Picard as the most unlikely of all. He wasn't sure Q could be direct and honest if his own immortal existence depended on it. "That's not enough," Picard told him. "You need to tell me more than that."

"It's none of your business!" he said petulantly, apparently unable to maintain a sincere appearance for more than a moment or two. "You try to offer a few helpful tips to an inferior organism, but do they appreciate it? Of course not!" He paced back and forth in front of the viewscreen, looking exasperated beyond all measure. "Why can't you simply admit that we Q are older and wiser than you are?"

"Older, certainly," Picard said, "but not necessarily wiser. If you are at all typical of your kind, then the fabled Q Continuum is not above mere pettiness and spite." He rose from his chair and confronted Q. *Let's have this out here and now,* he determined. "As you might imagine, I've given the matter a great deal of thought, and I've come to the conclusion that the Continuum is more fallible and prone to error than you care to admit. Let's look at what we mere mortals have learned about their behavior," he said, ticking his points off on his fingers.

"They put lesser life-forms on trial for the mere crime of not rising to their exalted level, all the while ignoring most of the conventions of due process recognized by supposedly inferior societies. They strip you of all your powers, placing you in mortal jeopardy, after having failed to keep your mischievous excesses under control. Then they reverse their decision and let you run amok through the galaxy again." Q harrumphed indignantly, but Picard showed him no mercy. "According to your own admission, the Continuum summarily executed Amanda Rogers's parents for choosing to live as human beings, left the orphaned child—one of their own—to be raised among we so-called primitive humans, then had the audacity to return years later and threaten Amanda herself with death unless she relinquished her own humanity." He shook his head slowly. "Banishment. Executions. Threats of genocide against less gifted races. These don't strike me as the actions of an advanced and enlightened society. Indeed, I could argue that the Klingons or the Cardassians have a higher claim to social progress."

Q snorted in derision. "Now you're just being ridiculous as well as insulting."

"Am I?" Picard asked, refusing to give any ground. "At least the harsher aspects of their cultures arose from, respectively, a demanding environment and severe economic hardships." He recalled Gul Madred's self-justifying evocations of the famine and poverty that first brought the Cardassian military regime to power generations ago. "Nor are those the only comparisons I could make," he continued, warming to his theme. "The tyranny of the Founders is said to be a response to centuries of Changeling persecution in the Gamma Quadrant, while the militaristic Romulan Empire of the present evolved from an arduous diaspora from ancient Vulcan millennia ago. And who knows what terrible, inexorable forces drove the Borg to first form their Collective?

"But even with the powers of the gods at your disposal, having conquered all the material challenges that trouble humanoid civilizations, the Q Continuum consistently behave in an arbitrary and draconian manner, one better suited to Dark Age despots than the evolved life-forms you claim to be." Picard returned to his chair and faced the viewscreen, his expression stony and resolute. The more he thought about it, the more certain he became that he could not permit Q to deter them from their mission.

"When you say to stay away from the barrier, you are saying that the rest of the universe is not for us. I'm sorry, but with all due respect to your self-proclaimed omniscience, that's not your decision to make." He nodded at Geordi, and when he spoke again his voice was steely in its conviction. "Mr. La Forge, launch the probe at once."

"Yes, sir!" Geordi responded. Keeping one eye on Q, he reached out and pressed the launch controls. Picard looked on as the class-2 probe, looking something like a duranium ice-cream cone, arced away from the *Enterprise,* its trajectory carrying it toward the nearest segment of the galactic barrier. He anticipated that the probe would pass into the barrier in less than ten minutes, beaming back a full spectrum of EM and subspace readings right up to the instant of its destruction, which would probably occur within nanoseconds of its initial contact with the barrier. He heard Lem Faal inhale sharply in anticipation.

"Captain!" Data said emphatically. "Tachyon levels are multiplying at a vastly accelerated rate." He turned to face Picard. "It *is* the Calamarain, sir, and they are approaching rapidly."

"Oh, them again," Q said without much enthusiasm. He had not been nearly so blasé, Picard recalled, when he faced the wrath of the Calamarain without his godlike powers. "Hail, hail, the gang's all here."

Lem Faal eyed Q with alarm, but Picard did his best to ignore Q's inappropriate attempt at humor. Q or no Q, he would not allow the *Enterprise* to be taken by surprise by the Calamarain. "Red alert!" he barked. "Shields up." Crimson warning lights flared to life around the bridge. Lieutenant Leyoro kept her hands poised above the weapons controls, while Riker looked ready to tackle Q if he so much as tried to interfere with Picard's ability to command the ship during this moment of crisis.

Q couldn't have cared less. "Oh dear," he said sourly, "I fear we're going to have to do this the hard way." He stepped between Picard and the viewscreen. "I'm sorry, Jean-Luc, but I can't allow you to be distracted by this minor complication. Too much is at stake, more than you can possibly imagine."

"Blast it, Q," Picard exploded, provoked beyond all patience. This had gone on long enough, and, as far as he was concerned, Q was the unwanted distraction from more pressing matters. "Explain yourself once and for all—the whole truth and nothing but—or get out of my way!"

"Fine!" Q replied indignantly, sounding almost as if he were the injured party. "Just remember, you asked for it."

What does he mean by that? Picard worried instantly, his worst fears confirmed when a burst of light erupted from Q, sweeping over Picard and carrying him away. Blank whiteness filled his vision. His chair seemed to dissolve beneath him. "Captain!" he heard Troi call out, but it was too late.

Deanna—and the *Enterprise*—were gone.

Interlude

"I THINK HER NAME WAS——"

The red alert siren sounded, interrupting the female Q just as she was about to divulge the name of baby q's human godmother. Beverly Crusher instantly went into crisis mode. "Excuse me," she said to her visitor as Beverly tapped her comm badge. "Crusher to the bridge. What's happening?"

I was afraid of this, she thought instantly. After their initial briefing on Professor Faal's project, Beverly had reviewed the reports on the original experiments at *Deep Space Nine,* and discovered that in one of the early trials, the artificial wormhole had collapsed prematurely and produced a massive graviton wave. A plasma fire had broken out aboard the *Defiant* and three people had nearly been killed. In theory, the cause of the collapse—some sort of unexpected reaction between the tetrion field and the shielding on a probe—had been isolated and remedied since that near-disaster, but what if something similar had happened again?

122

Dire possibilities raced through her mind in the split second it took for the bridge to respond to her page. "The captain has been abducted by Q," Lieutenant Leyoro informed her succinctly; Beverly guessed that Commander Riker was otherwise occupied. "And the ship is about to engage the Calamarain."

"What!" Beverly was shocked by the news. The Calamarain? But they hadn't been heard from in years! Where had they come from all of a sudden? This was the last thing she had expected to hear. And Jean-Luc missing?

"I would prepare for casualties," Leyoro advised. "Do you require any further information or assistance, Doctor?"

Beverly contemplated the female Q and her child. Unlike the doctor, Q's mate evinced no reaction to the startling news. She occupied herself while Beverly was busy by wiping a smear of blue uttaberry flavoring off q's face with the sleeve of her imitation lab coat. "No, I don't think so," Beverly told Leyoro. It sounded like Will and the others had a lot on their hands at the moment; she decided she could handle the Q on her own. "Crusher out."

Her hand fell away from the badge and she confronted the other woman. "Well?" she demanded.

"Well?" the Q echoed, blithe disregard upon her features. She sopped up the last dab of blue from around the child's lips, then lifted him into her arms. *So much for female bonding,* Beverly thought. Whatever warm feelings she might have harbored for the Q were washed away by concern for Jean-Luc. "You know what I mean. What has Q, the other Q, done with the captain? Where has he taken him?"

"Am I my Q's keeper?" She gave Beverly what the doctor supposed was intended to be a reassuring smile. "Really, there's no need to be concerned, I'm certain that wherever Q has taken your captain, he has done so for a very good reason."

123

Beverly didn't find that terribly comforting. "But we need the captain here now. We're on an important mission, and we've just encountered an alien, possibly hostile life-form." She tried a personal appeal. "As one mother to another, can't you do something?"

"Why should I have to do anything?" the woman answered. She took a moment to inspect her reflection in the shining, silver surface of a sealed cupboard, then tucked a few stray curls back into place. "My child is perfectly safe."

"I'm glad to hear it," Beverly shot back, shouting to be heard over the blaring alarm, "but how about the rest of us?"

The female Q shrugged. "The way Q talks, you people live this way every day. If it's not the Dominion or the Borg, it's a temporal anomaly. If it's not an anomaly, it's a warp-core breach or a separated saucer." She smiled indulgently. "I wouldn't want to interfere with your quaint and colorful way of life. It's far more educational for q to see you in your natural environment."

"This is not a field trip!" Beverly protested, despite a growing sense of futility. The original Q had never taken human lives seriously, so why should his mate be any different?

"I beg to differ," the Q said, then she and her beaming baby boy disappeared without so much as a goodbye.

Beverly feared she knew where the omnipotent pair were heading. Where else would they find a better view of the developing crisis? Before she silenced the alarm and summoned Ogawa and the rest of her emergency personnel, she paused long enough to tap her comm badge. "Crusher to the bridge. Expect company."

Chapter Ten

WILLIAM RIKER SUDDENLY FOUND himself in command. Before he could react, before he could even rise from his seat, Q vanished from the bridge, taking Captain Picard with him. "Captain!" Deanna called out, but the captain's chair was empty.

For a fleeting second, Riker worried about what might be happening to Captain Picard, but there was nothing he could do for the captain now. The safety of the crew and the ship had to be his number-one priority. *This isn't the first time Q has snatched the captain,* he recalled, *and Q's always brought him back before.* He could only pray that this time would be no exception.

"Scan for any nearby concentrations of ionized plasma," Riker ordered Data. "I want to know the instant the Calamarain come within sensor range." He stood and walked to the center of the command area, quickly considering the problem posed by the Calamarain. They didn't know for sure that the alien cloud-creatures posed a threat to the ship, but he didn't intend to be caught napping.

"Commander," Data stated. "The Calamarain are coming into visual range now."

A great cloud of incandescent plasma drifted between the *Enterprise* and the barrier, obscuring Riker's view of the shimmering wall of energy. The lambent cloud had a prismatic effect, emitting a rainbow's range of colors as it swirled slowly through the vacuum of space. Although the gaseous phenomenon, several times larger than the Sovereign-class starship, bore little resemblance to sentient life as Riker was accustomed to it, looking more like a lifeless accumulation of chemical vapors, he knew that this was the Calamarain all right, an entity or collection of entities capable of inflicting serious harm upon humanoid life if they chose to do so. Riker had no way of knowing if these were precisely the same beings who had menaced them before, but they were clearly of the same breed. "Mr. La Forge," he asked, "how are our shields?"

"They should stand up to them, Commander," Geordi reported. "I've set the shield harmonics to the same settings that worked last time." He double-checked the readouts at the engineering station and nodded at Lieutenant Leyoro, who monitored the shields from her own station at tactical. "Let's just hope the Calamarain haven't changed their own parameters over the last few years."

"I don't understand," Lem Faal wheezed, slowly coming to grips with a radically altered situation upon the bridge. "Where is Captain Picard?" His bloodshot gaze swung from the captain's empty chair to the bizarre alien apparition upon the main viewer. "Commander Riker!" he exclaimed, seizing upon the first officer as his only hope. "You have to stop that entity, drive it away. The probe . . . they could ruin everything!"

"Mr. Mack," Riker barked to a young ensign stationed near the starboard aft turbolift. "Escort Professor Faal to his quarters." He sympathized with the unfortunate scientist, but the bridge was no place for a civilian during a potential combat situation, and Riker didn't need the distraction.

"Commander, you can't do this!" Faal objected, hacking painfully between every word. He looked back at the screen as the young ensign took him by the arm and led him toward the nearest turbolift entrance. "I have to know what's happening. My experiment!"

Ensign Mack, an imposing Samoan officer, stood a head above the stricken Betazoid researcher, and had the advantages of youth and superior health besides, so Riker had every confidence that the ensign would be able to carry out his orders. Soon enough Faal's gasping protests were carried away by the turbolift, and Riker turned his attention to more critical matters: namely, the Calamarain.

He stared at the breathtaking spectacle of the immense, luminescent cloud; under other circumstances he would have been thrilled to encounter such an astounding life-form. *If only there was a way to communicate with them,* he mused, knowing that Captain Picard always preferred to exhaust every diplomatic effort before resorting to force. Unfortunately, the Universal Translator had proven useless the last time they confronted the Calamarain, whose unique nature was apparently too alien for even the advanced and versatile language algorithms programmed into the Translator. "Counselor," he asked Troi, "can you sense anything at all?"

"Aside from Professor Faal's distress?" She closed her eyes to concentrate on the impressions she was receiving. "The Calamarain are more difficult to read. All I'm picking up from them is a sense of rigid determination, a fixity of purpose and conviction. Whatever they are about, they are committed to it without doubt or hesitation."

He didn't like the sound of that. In his experience, an utterly fixed viewpoint could be the hardest to achieve a mutual understanding with. Fanatics were seldom easy to accommodate. He could only hope that the goal the Calamarain were so set upon did not involve the *Enterprise*.

We should be so lucky, he thought doubtfully.

"Commander," Leyoro called out, "the Calamarain are pursuing the probe."

It was true. The scintillating cloud receded into the distance as it abandoned the *Enterprise* in favor of chasing the much smaller projectile. The speed and accuracy of its flight belied any lingering doubts about the cloud's sentience. Through the prismatic ripples of the cloud, he saw the glitter of discharged energy outlining the probe as its protective forcefield struggled to shield it from the attack of the Calamarain. *Why are they doing this?* Riker wondered. *The probe poses no threat to them.*

"The readings from the probe are going berserk," Geordi said. "A massive overload of tachyon emissions." He studied the output at the science station. "Commander, if we could retrieve the probe at this point, examine its hull, we might be able to learn a lot more about the offensive capabilities of the Calamarain."

That may be for the best, Riker thought, taking his place in the captain's chair. It was obvious that the probe was not going to fulfill its original mission within the barrier. "Bring us within transporter range," he ordered. "Mr. La Forge, prepare to lock on to the probe."

"Commander!" Lieutenant Leyoro exclaimed. "That will mean lowering our shields. In my opinion, sir, the probe's not worth risking the ship for."

"If we don't learn more about the Calamarain, we may pay for it later on," he pointed out. "They don't seem interested in us at the moment, only the probe."

Why is that, he wondered. *The probe came nowhere near them. Why did they go after it?*

The starship soared toward the amorphous, living fog that now held the probe in its grasp. Puzzled, Riker witnessed the coruscating shield around the probe growing weaker and less effective before his eyes. The flaring bursts of power came ever more sporadically while the targeted projectile rocked back and forth beneath the force of the cloud's assault. How much longer could the probe withstand the fury of the Calamarain?

"Shields down," Leyoro reported unhappily.

"I'm trying to lock on to the probe," Geordi said, having transferred the transporter controls to his science station, "but the Calamarain are interfering."

"Deliberately?" Riker asked.

"Hard to say," Geordi answered. "All I know is those tachyon emissions are making it hard to get a solid lock on the probe."

"Do what you can," Riker instructed, "but be prepared to abort the procedure at my command." Leyoro was right to a degree; if the Calamarain showed any interest in coming after the ship itself, they would have to sacrifice the probe and its data.

His comm badge beeped, and he heard Dr. Crusher's voice, but before he could respond a white light flared at the corner of his eye. For a second Riker hoped that maybe Q and the captain had returned, then he spotted the female Q and her child sitting behind him on a set of wooden bleachers that had materialized at the aft section of the bridge, blocking the entrances to both of the rear turbolifts. The child now wore an antiquated Little League uniform and baseball cap instead of the sailor suit that had clothed him earlier. His mother wore a matching orange cap and jersey, with a large capital Q printed in block type upon the front of her uniform, as opposed to the lower-case q upon the little boy's jersey. "See," she told q, pointing toward the main viewer, "this is what they call an emergency situation. Isn't it funny?"

The boy laughed merrily and pointed like his mother. "'Mergencee!" he squealed, bouncing up and down upon the bleachers so forcefully that the timbers creaked.

Riker seldom resorted to profanity on the bridge, but he bit down a pungent Anglo-Saxon expression as he tore his gaze away from the grossly inappropriate tableau that now occupied the bridge. He'd have to deal with the two sightseeing Q's later; right now his attention belonged on the sight of the endangered probe, its shields flashing within the vaporous depths of the Calamarain. Still, he felt less like the commander of a mighty starship than like the ringmaster of a three-ring circus.

"Now, pay attention," the female Q instructed her child. "This is supposed to be educational as well as entertaining." She plucked a pair of red and black pennants from out of the air and handed one flag to little q, keeping the other one for herself as she sat upon the bleachers. The pennants were made of stiff red fabric with the word "Humanoids" embossed on one side. "While your father is occupied elsewhere, let's make an outing of it, assuming the funny humanoids can keep their ship in one piece for that long."

"Pieces!" little q chirped. "Pieces!"

On the screen, a flash of crimson flame erupted from the side of the probe as its hull crumpled beneath the stresses exerted by the Calamarain. "Mr. La Forge?" Riker asked, guessing that soon there would be nothing left of the probe to salvage.

"I think I've got it," Geordi called out. "Energizing now."

The golden flicker of the transporter effect raced over the surface of the probe, supplanting the futile sparking of its failing forcefield. The probe faded away completely, leaving behind only the spectacular sight of the Calamarain floating 'twixt the *Enterprise* and the galactic barrier.

"One point to the lowly humans," the female Q announced, writing a neon-yellow Arabic number one in the air with her index finger. The fiery numeral hung suspended above the floor for a breath before evaporating. A silver whistle appeared on a cord around her neck. She blew on it enthusiastically, hurting Riker's ears with the shrill sound, before declaring, "Game on!"

The great cloud that was the Calamarain drifted in place for a moment, perhaps unaware at first that its prey had escaped, but then it raced toward the screen, growing larger by the instant. Smoky tendrils reached out for the *Enterprise*. "It's coming after us," Leyoro said.

"Estimate interception in one minute, thirty-two seconds," Data stated.

Riker heard Troi gasp beside him. He wondered if she was feeling the Calamarains' hostile emotions, but there was no time to find out. "Mr. La Forge," he called out. "Is the transport complete?"

"We have it, Commander," Geordi assured him. "It was close, but we beamed it into Transporter Room Five."

"Raise shields," he ordered Leyoro. The incandescent cloud filled the screen before him. Unknown vapors churned angrily, stirring up ripples of ionized gas. He tried to distinguish individuals within the mass of radiant fog, but it was impossible to single out one strand of plasma among the whole. *It's possible,* he thought, *that each Calamarain does not exist as a single entity the way we do. They may be closer to a hive-mind mentality, like the Borg.*

That comparison did nothing to reassure him.

"Already on it," Leyoro said promptly, with a fierce gleam in her cold gray eyes. Riker suspected she was never truly happy except when fighting for survival. A dangerous attitude in the more civilized and peaceable regions of the Federation, but possibly a valuable trait on a starship probing the boundaries of known space. *You can take an Angosian out of the war,* he thought, *but you can't always take the war of out an Angosian.* Not unlike a certain Lieutenant Commander Worf. . . .

The plasma cloud surged over and around the *Enterprise.* Riker felt the floor vibrate beneath his boots as their deflectors absorbed and dispersed some variety of powerful force. A low, steady hum joined the background noise of the bridge, buzzing at the back of his mind like a laser drill digging into solid tritanium. He could practically feel the grating sound chafing away at his nerve endings. *That's going to get real old real fast,* he thought.

"Permission to open fire?" Leyoro asked, eager to return fire. Her survival instincts could not be faulted, Riker knew. They had kept her alive during both the war and the veterans' revolt that came afterward.

He shook his head. "Not yet. Let's not rush into battle before we even know what we're fighting about." Their shields had fended off the Calamarain before. He was confident that they would buy them a little breathing space now.

A jolt shook the bridge, which rocked the floor from starboard to port and back again before stabilizing a moment later. Everyone on the bridge caught their breath, except for the female Q, who cheerily turned to her child and said, "Come to think of it, I believe we may be rooting for the wrong team." The stiff cloth pennants the pair clutched in their hands switched from red fabric to something slick and, in its shifting spectrum of colors, reminiscent of the Calamarain. Riker noted that the lettering on the miniature flags now read "Nonhuman life-forms."

"One point to the Calamarain," she said, blowing sharply on her referee's whistle, "and the score is tied."

Riker refused to be baited, not while his ship was under attack. "Report," he instructed his crew. "What caused that shock?"

"Really, Commander Riker," the female Q chided, "who do you think caused it? The Calamarain, of course. Do you see any other threatening aliens in the vicinity?"

"Just you," Riker said curtly. "Mr. Data, please define the nature of the attack."

"Yes, Commander," Data said, scanning the readouts at Ops. From the captain's chair, Riker could see a string of numerals rushing across Data's console faster than a human eye could follow. "The tachyon barrage emitted by the Calamarain has increased by several hundred orders of magnitude. The intensity of the tachyon collisions is now more than sufficient to fatally damage both the ship and its inhabitants if not for the protection afforded by our deflectors."

"I see," Riker said, none too surprised. The Calamarain had demonstrated the potency of their offensive capabilities the last time they ran afoul of the *Enterprise.* "Mr. La Forge, are our shields holding?"

"For now," Geordi affirmed, "but we can't maintain the deflectors at this level forever."

"How long can we keep them up?" Riker asked. He watched the luminous plasma coursing across the screen, the iridescent hues swirling like a kaleidoscope. *It's strangely beautiful,* Riker reflected, regretting once more that humanity and the Calamarain had to meet as adversaries.

"Exactly?" Geordi said. "That depends on what they throw at us." The circuit patterns upon his implants rotated as he focused on his engineering display. "If they keep up the pressure at this intensity, the shields should be able to withstand it for about five hours. Four, if you want to play it safe."

Good, Riker thought. At least they had time to get their bearings and decide on a strategy. He didn't intend to stay a sitting duck much longer, but it might be in this instance that a judicious retreat was the better part of valor. There was too much unknown about both the Calamarains' motives and their abilities for him to feel comfortable committing the *Enterprise* to an all-out armed conflict. And as for their mission, and Professor Faal's experiment . . . well, that was looking more unlikely by the moment.

"I can do more from Engineering," Geordi offered. "Permission to leave the bridge?"

"Go to it, Mr. La Forge," Riker said crisply as Geordi headed for the turbolift. He looked at Troi and saw that the counselor still had her eyes closed, a look of intense, almost trancelike concentration upon her face. "Deanna?" he asked quietly, not wanting to jar her from her heightened state of sensitivity.

"They're all around us," Troi answered, slowly opening her eyes. "Surrounding us, containing us, confining us. I'm sensing great anger and frustration from every direction, but that's not all. Beneath everything, behind the rage, is a terrible fear. They're desperately afraid of something I can't even begin to guess at."

"How typically vague and ominous," the female Q said from the bleachers, rolling her eyes, to the amusement of her offspring. "Perhaps, young lady, you'd get better results with tea leaves."

"Never mind her," Riker said to Troi. "Thank you, Deanna." He tried to interpret her impressions, but too much remained unknown. How could such powerful entities, capable of thriving in the deadly vacuum of space, possibly be afraid of the *Enterprise?* The very idea seemed laughable, especially when a much more probable suspect sat only a few meters away.

He spun his chair around to confront the anachronistic wooden bleachers and the incongruous duo resting upon them. Riker inspected the female Q. She was an attractive woman, he noted, more so than Q deserved, in his opinion. Remarkably tall, too; it wasn't often Riker met women who were the same height as he, but the individual standing in front of him met his gaze at near eye-level. *She looks almost as imposing as a Klingon woman,* he thought. *Although I guess an omnipotent being can be as tall as she wants.*

"You," he accused. "Are you at the heart of this business? Are the Calamarain afraid of you?"

"Me?" the woman asked. She added ketchup to a hot dog that had not existed a heartbeat before. Neither had the ketchup, for that matter.

"Yes," Riker answered. "The Calamarain tried to kill your husband before. Is it you they fear?"

"They should," she said darkly, then assumed a more chipper expression, "but I'm in a forgiving mood today. No, First Officer, that's not it; the Calamarain have far more to worry about than me and little q these days."

"What do you mean?" Riker demanded. He didn't get the impression the woman was dissembling, unlike the original Q, who always came off as about as sincere as a Ferengi used-shuttle salesman, but who could tell with a Q? As he understood it, this wasn't even her true appearance. "Explain yourself."

The little q reached for his mother's hat, so the female Q amused him by trading their headwear with a snap of her fingers. The oversized hat looked ridiculous on the child's small head, but q giggled happily, his face all but concealed by the drooping brim of the hat.

"About the Calamarain," Riker prompted firmly. Even with their shields defending them from the Calamarain's lethal tachyons, he had no desire to linger in their grasp any longer than necessary. This Q could play the doting mother on her own time. "I'm still waiting for an explanation."

"Such a one-track mind," the Q sighed. "Q is right. You creatures really do need to learn how to stop and smell the nebulas now and again." She tapped the child-sized baseball cap upon her head and it expanded to fit more comfortably. "I'm sure if my

135

husband wanted you to understand about the Calamarain and their selfish grievances, he would have
explained it all to you. Mind you, I don't blame him
for keeping mum where this whole business is concerned. Kind of an embarrassing anecdote, especially
since it was all his fault in the first place."

What in blazes does she mean by that? Riker briefly
wished that he had hung on to the supernatural
powers Q had granted him years ago, just so he could
threaten to kick this other Q off the ship if she didn't
start giving him straight answers. "Embarrassing?" he
said with deeply felt indignation. "Your husband
kidnapped our captain. For all I know, he sicced the
Calamarain on us, too. I call that more than 'embarrassing' and I want to know what you intend to do
about it, starting with telling us just where Q has
taken Captain Picard."

The female Q peered down her nose at Riker. "I'm
not sure I approve of your tone," she said icily,
placing her hands over baby q's ears. The child,
curious, grew a new pair of velvety silver bunny ears
out of the top of his scalp, foiling his mother's well-
intentioned efforts.

"I don't want your approval," Riker said. The hum
of the Calamarain buzzed in his ears, reminding him
that he had more important things to do than waste
his breath trying to reason with a Q. "I want you to
lend a hand, answer my questions, or get off the
bridge."

His harsh tone got through to little q, whose childish grin crumpled into tears and sobs. The mother
fixed a chilly stare on Riker, who felt his life expectan-
cy shrinking at a geometrical rate. "Well, if that's how
you're going to be," she huffed. Without another
word, she disappeared from the bridge, taking little q
and the bleachers with her.

Well, that's something, he thought, thankful that
members of the Q Continuum tended to leave as
unexpectedly as they arrived. *For indestructible, im-*

mortal beings, they sure seem pretty thin-skinned. He swiveled his chair around to face the prow of the bridge. On the main viewer, he saw a portion of the Calamarain, its iridescent substance drifting past the window like some lifeless chemical vapor. The roiling gases outside the ship looked more agitated than before. The rainbow colors darkened, the separate fumes clumping together in heavy, swollen accumulations that promised an approaching storm. Flickers of bright electricity leaped from billow to billow, sparking like bursts of lightning through the all-encompassing cloud. Riker felt like they were trapped inside the galaxy's biggest thunderhead. "Deflectors?" he asked, wanting a status report.

"Shields holding," Leyoro informed him, "although I'm detecting an increase in harmful tachyon radiation."

"That is correct," Data confirmed from Ops. "The Calamarain have rapidly raised the intensity of the emissions directed against the ship, possibly in an attempt to penetrate our defenses." He peered intently at the display at his console. "By placing further pressure upon our shields, the amplified nature of the Calamarain's attack reduces our safety factor by 1.531 hours."

"Understood," Riker said, "but we're not going to stick around that long." The captain was missing. The ship was under attack. A prudent departure was definitely in order, he judged. He knew he did not need to worry about leaving the captain behind; Q could find the *Enterprise* anywhere in the universe if he felt so inclined. It seemed a shame to turn tail and run when all they had managed to do so far was misplace Jean-Luc Picard, but there was no compelling reason to continue the experiment in the face of an enemy; it was a pure research assignment after all. The barrier had been around for billions of years. It could wait a little longer. "Mr. Clarze, prepare to go to warp."

"Commander," Lieutenant Leyoro pointed out, "we haven't even tried to strike back at the Calamarain yet. Perhaps we can drive them away with our phasers?"

Riker shook his head. "There's no reason to get into a shooting war, not if we can simply turn around. For all we know, the Calamarain may have legitimate interests in this region of space." He saw Deanna nod in agreement. "Take us out of here, Mr. Clarze."

"Yes, sir," the young Deltan said from the conn, entering the appropriate coordinates into the helm controls. Riker noted a light sheen of perspiration upon the pilot's domed skull; he'd probably never been caught inside a sentient cloud before. *Could be worse,* Riker thought. According to the history tapes, Kirk's *Enterprise* had once been swallowed by a giant space amoeba. "Heading?" Clarze asked.

"The nearest starbase," Riker said, "to report our findings." *Too bad we never got the chance to take on the galactic barrier,* he thought. Still, no experiment was worth risking the *Enterprise,* especially with civilians and children aboard. Starfleet would have to challenge the barrier another day, with or without Professor Faal. It was tragic that the dying scientist had to be thwarted this close to the completion of his final experiment, but the Calamarain had given them no other choice. Who knows? Maybe someday they might even get another chance to establish genuine contact with the Calamarain.

At the moment, though, he found himself more worried about the fact that the viewscreen still held the image of the Calamarain despite his order to go to warp. "Mr. Clarze?"

"I'm trying, Commander!" Clarze blurted, jabbing at the control panel with his fingers. "But something's wrong with the warp engines. I can't get them to engage."

"What?" Riker reacted. If the warp engines were down, the *Enterprise* was in serious trouble. He knew from experience that they could not outrun the Calamarain on impulse alone. He glanced over his shoulder at the crew member manning the aft science station. "Mr. Schultz, what's our engine status?"

"I'm not sure, sir," Ensign Robert Schultz said, peering anxiously at the monitors and display panels at the aft engineering station. "The warp core is still on-line and the plasma injectors seem to be functioning properly, but somehow the warp field coils are not generating the necessary propulsive effect. I can't figure out why."

"That's not good enough," Riker said. Hoping that Geordi had already made it back to Engineering, he tapped his comm badge. "Geordi, this is Riker. What the devil is going on down there?"

"I wish I could tell you," the chief engineer's voice answered, confirming the speed and efficacy of the ship's turbolifts. "We can initiate the pulse frequency in the plasma, no problem, but something's damping the warp field layers, keeping our energy levels below eight hundred millicochranes, tops. We need at least a thousand to surpass lightspeed."

"Understood," Riker acknowledged, remembering basic warp theory. He glanced at Data, wondering if he should pull the android off Ops and send him to assist Geordi in Engineering. *Not unless I absolutely have to,* he decided. "What about the impulse drive?"

"That's still up and running," Geordi stated, "at least for now."

That's something, I suppose, Riker thought, although what he really needed was warp capacity. "Anything you can do to fix the field coils in a hurry?"

"I can run a systems-wide diagnostic," Geordi suggested, "but that's going to take a while. Plus, I've already got half my teams working overtime to maintain the deflectors."

In the meantime, we're stuck here, Riker thought, *with our shields failing and the Calamarain at the door.* "Do what you can, Mr. La Forge." He clenched his fists angrily, frustrated by this latest turn of affairs. It seemed retreat was no longer an option, at least not at present. They might have to fight their way out after all. A strategic notion occurred to him, and he reopened the line to La Forge. "Geordi, have an engineering officer look at the remains of the probe the Calamarain attacked. I want to find out as much as we can about their modes of attack."

"You got it," Geordi promised. "I'll put Barclay on it right away."

Riker experienced a momentary qualm when Reg Barclay's name was mentioned. Deanna insisted that Barclay was making substantial progress, and certainly the man had come in useful when they had to repair Zefram Cochrane's primitive warp vessel back in 2063, but even still . . . Then again, it dawned on him, analyzing the probe was probably less stressful under the circumstances than working on the shields or engines, so the probe and Barclay made a good fit. *I should never have doubted Geordi's work assignments,* he thought. *He knows exactly what his people are capable of.*

Just as Riker knew what a certain android officer could do when the chips were down. "Mr. Data, since we can't get away from the Calamarain, we need to find out what they want. I want you to give top priority to establishing communication with the Calamarain. Perhaps our sensor readings can give you what you need to bring the Universal Translator up to speed. Work with Counselor Troi, if you think she can help. Maybe her nonverbal impressions can provide you with the clue you need to crack their language."

"Yes, Commander," the android replied. He sounded like he was looking forward to tackling the problem. "A most intriguing challenge." He studied the displays at Ops, swiftly switching from one sensor mode to another until he found something. "Counselor Troi," he said after a few moments, "I am detecting a directed transmission from the entity on a narrower wavelength than their tachyon barrage. It may be an attempt at communication. Can you sense its meaning?"

Riker could not see Deanna's face from his chair, but he could well imagine the look of concentration on her face. Even after all these years, her empathic abilities still impressed him, although he could recall more than a few instances when he'd wished that she had not been able to see through him quite so easily. *Like that time on Risa,* he thought.

Deanna Troi shut her eyes, doing her best to filter out the emotions of the crew members present in the conference room as well as, more faintly, throughout the ship. *Speak to me,* she thought to the gaseous mass outside the ship. *Let me know what you're feeling.*

Suddenly, an unexpected "voice" intruded into her thoughts. *You have to talk to the commander,* it urged her silently. *Make him understand. I have to go on with my work. It's vitally important.*

She recognized the telepathic voice immediately. Lem Faal. How desperate was he, she worried, that he would take advantage of her sensitivity like this? *Please,* she told him. *Not now. Please leave me alone.* She needed to have all her faculties focused on the task of reading the Calamarain.

But my work! he persisted. His telepathic voice, she noted, lacked the hoarseness and shortness of breath that weakened his physical voice. It was firm and emphatic, unravaged by disease.

Fortunately, years of dealing with her mother had given her plenty of experience at dispelling an unwanted telepathic presence from her mind. *No!* Faal protested as he felt her squeeze him out of her consciousness. *Wait! I need your help!*

"Leave me alone," she repeated, before banishing him entirely.

"Deanna?" Will Riker asked. Her eyes snapped open and she saw him watching her with a confused, anxious expression. So were Data and Lieutenant Leyoro and the others on the bridge. She hadn't realized she had spoken aloud.

"I'm sorry," she said. "I was . . . distracted."

"By the Calamarain?" the commander asked. She could feel his concern for her well-being.

"No," she answered, shaking her head. She would have to speak to the commander about Faal later; there was something frightening about the scientist's obsession with his experiment, beyond simple determination to see his work completed before death claimed him. First, though, there were still the Calamarain. "Let me try again," she said, closing her eyes once more.

This time Faal did not interfere. Perhaps he had finally gotten the message to keep out of her head. Screening out all other distractions, she opened herself up to the alien emotions seeping into the ship from outside.

They tasted strange to her mental receptors, like some exotic spice or flavor she couldn't quite place. Was that anger/fear or fear/anger or something else altogether? She felt queer impressions suffusing the air around her, like the steady drone of the humming she had heard in the background ever since the cloud had surrounded the ship. They were relentlessly consistent, never quavering or varying in tone or intensity. She couldn't name the feeling, but it was a constant, unchanging, a firm and unshakable conviction/resolution/determination to do what must be done, whatever that might be. She probed as hard as she was able, but the feeling never changed. That was all she could sense, the same inflexible purpose surrounding the *Enterprise* on all sides.

Convinced that she'd heard enough, she opened her eyes slowly, took a few deep breaths, and let the alien emotions recede into the background. "I'm picking up an increased sense of urgency, of alarm mixed with fury," she stated. "There's a feeling of danger, whether to us or from us I can't say." She hesitated for a second, reaching out across the gulf of space with her empathic senses. "I think it's a warning . . . or a threat."

That's a big difference, Riker thought, listening carefully to Deanna's report. *Do the Calamarain want to help us or hurt us?* Judging from the way they'd knocked the probe about earlier, he'd bet on the latter.

"Thank you, Counselor," Data said, comparing Deanna's impressions against his readings and entering the results into his console. "That was quite helpful. I now have several promising avenues to explore."

Could Data really use Deanna's empathic skills as a Rosetta Stone to crack the Calamarain's language? Riker could only wonder how the android was managing to translate Deanna's subjective emotional readings into the mathematical algorithms used by the Universal Translator. Then again, he remembered, Data had knowledge of hundreds, if not thousands, of languages stored in his positronic brain, making him something of an artificial translator himself. *If anybody can do it,* he thought.

"Excuse me, Commander," Leyoro said, "but what's that old human expression again? The one about the best offense . . . ?"

Riker permitted himself a wry smile. "Point taken, Lieutenant. Don't worry, I haven't forgotten our phasers."

Given a choice, he'd rather talk than shoot, but the time for talking was swiftly running out.

Interlude

BUG.

It was buzzing over there, just out of reach. *A shiny, silver bug.* He could see it now, the image refracted through the lens of the wall, deformed and distorted, true, but definitely there. *Itty-bitty little bug, buzzing about on the other side, doing teeny-weeny, buggy little things.*

Busy bug, he crooned. *How fast can you fly? How quick can you die?*

He couldn't wait to swat it with his hungry hand. No, not swat it, he corrected himself. He'd play with it first, teach it tricks, then pull off its wings. *Soon,* he promised, *soon to its ruin.*

Then the bug wasn't alone anymore. A wisp of smoke drifted over to where the bugs flitted. *Bug and smoke,* he cursed, his mood darkening. He remembered that smoke, oh yes he did, and remembering, hated. *A joke on the smoke, ever so long ago. Choke on the smoke. Smoking, choking . . . choking the bug!* Through the fractured glass of the wall, he watched as the thin, insubstantial wisp of vapor surrounded the bug. *No! You can't have it!* he raved. *It's mine, mine to find, mine to grind!*

Impatiently, he reached out for the bug and the smoke, unable to wait any longer, forgetting for the moment all that lay between him and his prizes. But his will collided against the perpetual presence of the wall and rebounded back in pain and fury. He drew inward on himself, nursing his injured pride, while the bug and the smoke circled each other just beyond his grasp. *Not now,* he recalled, *not how. But when, when, WHEN . . . ?*

He howled in frustration—and a voice answered. The same voice that had greeted his cries not very long ago. It was a small, barely audible voice, but it sounded faintly louder than it had before, like it was coming from some place not nearly so far away.

(I'm here,) the voice said, *(I'm almost with you).*

WHEN? he pleaded, his own voice sounding like an explosion compared to the other. *WHEN?*

(Soon. There are a few obstacles to overcome, but soon. I give you my word.)

What did it mean by that? The message was too vague, too indefinite, to curb his constant craving to defeat the wall. The bug and the smoke tormented him, teasing him with their pretended proximity. He needed an answer now.

Let me in, he said. *Let you out. Away, away, no more decay. Let me in, again and again.*

(Yes!) the voice affirmed. *(I will make it happen, no matter what.)*

The voice droned on, but he grew bored and stopped listening. The bug captured his attention once more, so small and fragile, but not yet undone by the suffocating smoke. *Buzz, buzz, little bug,* he whispered. *Flitter free while you can.* He assumed the shape of an immense arachnid, stretching out his will in all directions like eight clutching limbs.

A spider is coming to gobble you up. . . .

Chapter Eleven

HE WAS NO LONGER on the bridge. A cool white mist surrounded Picard on all sides, obscuring his vision, but the familiar sounds and smells of the bridge were gone, informing him unequivocally that he had left the *Enterprise*. He looked around him quickly and saw only the same featureless fog everywhere he glanced. *The Calamarain?* he wondered briefly, but, no, this empty mist was utterly unlike the luminescent swirls of the living plasma cloud. This place, odorless, soundless, textureless, was more like . . . limbo. He stamped his feet upon whatever surface was supporting him, but the mist absorbed both the force and the sound of his boots striking the ground so that not an echo escaped to confirm the physicality of his own existence. He was lost in a void, a sensation that he remembered all too well.

I've been here before, he thought. *That time I almost died in sickbay and Q offered me a chance to relive my past.* The memory did nothing to ease his concerns. That incident had been a profoundly disturbing, if ultimately illuminating, experience, one that he was in no great hurry to endure again. More important, what about the *Enterprise?* Only seconds before, or so it seemed to him, he had placed the ship on red alert in response to the approach of the Calamarain. "Dammit," he cursed, punching a fist into his palm in frustration. This was no time to be away from his ship!

"Q!" he shouted into the mist, unafraid of who or what might hear him. "Show yourself!"

"You needn't bellow, Jean-Luc," Q answered, stepping out of the fog less than two meters away from Picard. His Starfleet uniform, proper in every respect, hardly suited his sardonic tone. "Although I wish you could have simply listened to me in the first place. You have no idea how strenuously I regret that you forced me to go to such lamentable lengths to convince you."

"I forced you?" Picard responded indignantly. "This is intolerable, Q. I demand that you return me to the *Enterprise* at once."

Q tapped his foot impatiently. "Spare me, Picard. Time is scarce. Just this once, can't we skip the obligatory angry protestations and get on with business?"

"Your business, you mean," Picard said. "My business is on my ship!"

"That's what you think," Q replied. He crossed his arms upon his chest, looking quite sure of himself. "Take my word for this, Jean-Luc. You're not going back to the *Enterprise*—E, F, or G—until we are finished, one way or another. Or don't you trust Riker to keep the ship in one piece that long?"

That's not the point, he thought, but part of him was forced to concede the futility of talking Q out of anything. If there was one thing he had learned since their first meeting in Q's "courtroom" over a decade ago, it was that attempting to reason with or intimidate Q was a waste of time. Perhaps the best and only option was to let the charade play out as quickly as possible, and hope that he could get back to his life and duties soon enough. *Not a very appealing strategy,* he thought, *but there it is.*

He took stock of their surroundings, ready to take on Q's latest game. The empty mist offered no clue as to what was yet to come. "What is this place, Q," he asked, "and don't tell me it's the afterlife."

"Like you'd know it if you saw it," Q said. "You wouldn't recognize the Pearly Gates if you had your pathetic phasers locked on them." He paused and scratched his chin reflectively. "Actually, they aren't so much pearly as opalescent . . . but I digress. This shapeless locale," he said, sweeping out his arms to embrace the entire foggy landscape, "is merely a starting point, a place between time, where time has no sway."

"Between time?" Picard repeated, concentrating on every word Q said. This duplicitous gamester played by his own arcane rules, he knew, and sometimes doled out a genuine hint or clue in his self-aggrandizing blather. The trick was to extract that nugget of truth from the rest of Q's folderol. "I thought you said earlier that time was scarce."

"By the Continuum, you can be dim, Jean-Luc," Q groaned, wiping some imaginary sweat from his brow. "Sometimes I feel like I'm teaching remedial metaphysics to developmentally stunted primates. Here, let me demonstrate."

Q grabbed hold of the drifting fog with both hands and pulled it aside as though it were a heavy velvet curtain. Picard glimpsed two figures through the gap in the mist, standing several meters away. One was a tall, balding man in a red-and-black Starfleet uniform that was a few years out of style. A lethal-looking scorch mark marred the front of his uniform, above his heart. The other figure was clad in angelic white robes that seemed composed of the very mist that framed the scene. A heavenly light illuminated the second figure from behind, casting a sublime radiance that outlined the robed figure with a shimmering halo. Looking on this tableau, one could be forgiven for assuming that this auroral figure was a veritable emissary from Heaven, if not the Almighty Himself.

Picard knew better. He recognized the figures, and the occasion, instantly. They were himself and Q, posed as they had been when he first confronted Q in this very same mist, shortly after he "died" from a malfunction in his artificial heart. Caught up in their own fateful encounter, the other Picard and Q paid no heed to the onlookers now witnessing themselves at an earlier time. Picard could not hear what his younger self was saying to the younger Q, but he remembered the exchange well enough. There had been a time, after he woke up in sickbay under Beverly Crusher's ministrations, when he had half-convinced himself that he had merely experienced an unusually vivid and perceptive dream, but, in his heart of hearts, which bore no relation to the steel and plastic mechanism lodged in his chest, he had always known that the entire episode had really happened. Even still, it gave him a chill to watch the bizarre occurrence unfold once more.

He was tempted to shout out a warning to his earlier self, but what could he say? "Whatever you do, don't let Q tempt you into changing your past"? No, that would only defeat the entire purpose of that unique, autobiographical odyssey and deprive his other self of the hard-earned insights he had so painfully achieved over the course of that unforgettable journey. He couldn't bring himself to say a word.

"Seen enough?" Q asked. He withdrew his hands and the fog fell back into place, sealing away the vision from the past. "I must say, I seemed particularly celestial there. Divinity looks good on me."

"So you think," Picard retorted, but his heart was not in the war of words. That flashback to his old, near-death experience shook him more than he wanted to admit. "Why show me that?" he asked. "I have not forgotten what happened then."

"You still don't understand," Q said. "That didn't happen before. It's happening now. Here, everything happens now. But when we return to the boring, linear reality you know, the clock hands will resume their dogged, dreary rounds." He held his hands up in front of his face. "Excuse me while I watch my fingernails grow. Let me know when you're through with your futile efforts to comprehend the ineffable."

Picard ignored Q's taunts. Figuring out the rules of this game was the only way he was going to find his way back to the *Enterprise*. "Is that what this is all about? The same routine as before, you're going to make me face up to another chapter of my past?" He couldn't help trying to guess what heartrending tragedy he might be forced to relive. The death of Jack Crusher? That nasty business back at the Academy? His torture at the hands of Gul Madred? *Dear god,* he prayed, *don't let it be my time among the Borg. I couldn't bear to be Locutus once again.* He cast off his fears, however, and faced his opponent defiantly. "You must be getting old, Q," he said. "You're starting to repeat yourself."

To his surprise, Q began to look more uncomfortable than Picard, as though the relentless puppeteer was genuinely reluctant to proceed now that the moment of departure had arrived. "Oh, Picard," he sighed, "how I wish we were merely sightseeing in your own insignificant existence, but I'm afraid it's not your disreputable past we must examine, *mon capitaine,* but my own." He took a deep breath, quelling whatever trepidations he possessed, then gave Picard a devil-may-care grin. "Starting now."

The mist converged on Picard, swallowing him up. For what could have been an instant or an eternity he found himself trapped in a realm of total, blank sensory deprivation—until the universe returned. Sort of.

Where am I? Picard wondered. *What am I?*

There was something wrong with his eyes, or, if not wrong precisely, then different. He could see from three distinct perspectives simultaneously, the disparate views blending to grant him a curiously all-inclusive image that made ordinary binocular vision seem flat by comparison. He searched his surroundings, finding himself seemingly adrift amid the blackness of space. An asteroid drifted by, its surface pitted with craters and shadows, and he glimpsed a blazing yellow sun in the distance, partially eclipsed by an orbiting planet. *I don't understand,* he thought. *How can I be surviving in a vacuum? Am I wearing a pressure suit, or did Q not bother with that?* It was hard to tell; he couldn't feel his arms or his legs. He tried to look down at his body, but all he could see was a bright white glare. What had Q done to him?

"Q!" he shouted, but what emerged from his throat was a long, sibilant hiss. Make that throats, for, to his utter shock, he felt the vibrato of the hiss in no less than three separate throats. *This is insane,* he thought, struggling not to panic. Over the years, he had almost grown accustomed to being miraculously transported here and there throughout the universe by Q's capricious whims, but he had never been transported out of his own body before—and into something inhuman and strange. "Q?" he hissed again, desperate for some sort of answer.

"Right behind you, Jean-Luc," Q answered. Picard had never been so relieved to hear that voice in his entire life. Somehow, merely by thinking about it, he managed to turn around and was greeted by an astounding yet oddly familiar sight:

A three-headed Aldebaran serpent floated in the void only a few meters away. A trio of hooded, serpentine bodies rose from a glowing silver sphere

151

about which smaller balls of light ceaselessly orbited. The heads, which each resembled Earth's king cobra, faced Picard. Strips of glittering emerald and crimson scales alternated along all three of the snakelike bodies. Three pairs of cold, reptilian eyes fixed Picard with their mesmerizing stare. A threesome of forked tongues flicked from the serpentine faces. "Welcome," the snakes said in Q's voice, "to the beginning."

Of course, Picard thought. Not only did he recognize the triple serpent, an ancient mythological symbol dating back to well before the onset of human civilization, but he recalled how Q had once assumed this form before, at the onset of his second visit to the *Enterprise.* But this time, it seemed, Q had done more than merely transform himself into the fantastical, hydra-headed creature; he had somehow mutated Picard as well. Straining the unfamiliar muscles of his outermost necks, Picard turned his eyes on himself. Even though he had already guessed what he would find, it still came as a terrible shock when he saw, from two opposing points of view, two more serpentine heads rising from the radiant globe that was now his body. For a second, each of his outer heads looked past the central serpent so that Picard found himself staring directly into his own eyes—and back again. The jolt was too much for his altered nervous system to endure and he quickly looked away to see the other hydra, Q, hovering nearby. "So what do you think of your new body, Captain?" he asked. "Tell me, are three heads truly better than one?"

"Good Lord, Q," Picard exclaimed, trying his best to ignore the peculiar sensation of speaking through three sets of jaws, "what have you done?" He had to pray that his unearthly transformation was only a temporary joke of Q's, or else he would surely go mad. Good god, did he now have three separate brains, three different minds to lose?

"Merely trying to inject a note of historical verisimilitude into our scenic tour of my past," Q stated. "Relatively speaking, that is. Understand this, Picard: there is no way your primitive consciousness can truly comprehend what it means to be part of the Q Continuum, so everything I show you from here on has been translated into a form that can be perceived by your rudimentary five senses. It's a crude, vastly inadequate approximation of my reality, but it is the best your mind can cope with." Q drifted closer to Picard, until the transformed starship captain could see the individual scales overlapping each other along the lengths of each extended throat. The flared hoods behind each head puffed up even larger. "Anyway," Q went on, "it seemed more appropriate, and more accurate, to take these shapes during this stage of our excursion, given that the evolution of the humanoid form is still at least a billion years away at this point. In fact, this was one of my favorite guises way back in the good old days, before you overreaching humanoids came down from the trees and started spreading your DNA all over the galaxy."

"Billions of years?" Picard echoed, too stunned at Q's revelations to even register the usual insults and patronizing tone. "Where . . . when . . . are we?"

"Roughly five billion years ago, give or take a few dozen millennia." Q's leftmost head nipped playfully at the head next to it. "Ouch. You know, sometimes I surprise even myself." The central head snapped back while the head on the right continued speaking. "Tell me the truth, Jean-Luc, don't you get tired of Data's painfully precise measurements? How refreshing it must be to deal with someone—like myself, say— who is quite comfortable rounding things off to the nearest million or so."

Picard watched his own heads nervously, unsure when or how he might start turning on himself. There was something horribly claustrophobic about being trapped in this inhuman form, deprived of his limbs and hands and all the normal physical sensations he was accustomed to after sixty-plus years of existence as a human being. He felt a silent scream bubbling just beneath the thin surface of his sanity. "Q, I find this new form . . . very distracting."

It was possibly the greatest single understatement in his life.

"Oh, Jean-Luc," Q sighed, sounding disappointed, "I had hoped you were more flexible than that. After all, you coped with being a Borg for a week or two. Is a tri-headed serpent god all that much harder?"

"Q," Picard pleaded, too far from his own time and his own reality to worry about his pride. "Please."

"If you insist," Q grumbled. "I have important things to show you and I suppose it wouldn't do to have you fretting about your trivial human body the whole time. You might miss something." The triple necks of the Q-serpent wrapped themselves around each other until the three heads seemed to sprout from a single coiled stalk. Picard was briefly reminded of Quetzalcoatl, the serpent deity of the ancient Aztecs. *Quetzalcoatl . . . Q? Could there be a connection?*

He might never know.

"Pity," the triune entity continued, "you hadn't begun to scratch the possibilities of this identity." A flash of light illuminated the darkness for a fraction of a second, and then Q appeared before Picard in his usual form, garbed in what looked like a simple Greek chiton fastened over his left shoulder. A circlet of laurel leaves adorned his brow. Simple leather sandals rested upon nothing but empty space.

Picard's trifocal vision coalesced into a single point of view. Gratefully, he looked down to see his human body restored to him. So relieved was he to have arms and legs again, he barely noted at first that he was now attired in an ancient costume similar to the one Q now wore. He remained floating in space, of course, protected from the deadly vacuum only by Q's remarkable powers, but that was a level of surreality that he felt he could cope with. *Just permit me to be myself,* he thought, *and I'm ready for whatever Q has up his sleeves.*

"Happy now?" Q pouted. He wiggled his fingers in front of his face and scowled at the sight. "I hope you realize what a dreadful anachronism this is. Be it on your head, and you a professed archaeologist!"

"I feel much better, thank you," Picard answered, regaining his composure even while conversing in open space. He glanced down at his own sandaled feet and saw nothing but a gaping abyss extending beneath him for as far as his eyes could see. He was not experiencing a null-gravity state, though; he knew what that felt like and this was quite different. Q was somehow generating the sensation of gravity, so that he felt squarely oriented despite his surroundings. Up was up and down was down, at least for the moment. He fingered the hem of his linen garment, noting the delicate embroidering along the border of the cloth. *God is in the details,* he thought, recalling an ancient aphorism, *or was that the devil?* "What is this?" he asked, indicating the chiton. "Another anachronism?"

"A conceit," Q said with a shrug, "to give a feel of antiquity. As I explained before, and I hope you were paying close attention, this is nothing like what I really looked like at this point in the galaxy's history, but simply a concession to your limited human understanding."

"And the Aldebaran serpent?" Picard pressed. "Was that your true form?"

Q shook his head, almost dislodging his crown of leaves. "Merely another guise, one better suited to a time before you mammals began putting on airs."

"If anyone can be accused of putting on airs," Picard replied, "it's you. You've done little but flaunt your alleged superiority since the time we first encountered you. Frankly, I'm not convinced."

"Yes, I recall your little speech right before we departed the bridge," Q said. "Would you be surprised to know that I share some of your opinions about the more . . . shall we say, heavy-handed . . . tendencies of the Continuum?"

"I know that you've been on the outs with your own kind at least once," Picard answered, "which gives me some hope that the Continuum itself might be rather more mature and responsible." It dawned on him, not for the first time, that almost everything he knew about the rest of the Q Continuum had come from Q's own testimony, hardly the most reliable of sources. He resolved to question Guinan more deeply on the subject, if and when he ever had the opportunity. "Well?" he asked, surveying this desolate section of space. On the horizon, the eclipsing planet no longer passed between himself and the nearest sun, permitting him an unobstructed view of the seething golden orb, which he registered as a typical G-2 dwarf star, much like Earth's own sun. It was a breathtaking sight, especially viewed directly from space, but he was not about to thank Q for letting him see it. "Why are we here?" he demanded. "What is it you wish to show me?"

"The beginning, as I said," Q stated. With a wave of his arm, he and Picard began to soar through the void toward the immense yellow sun. The hot solar wind blew in his face as the star grew larger and larger in his sight. It was a thrilling and not entirely unpleasant experience, Picard admitted to himself. He felt like some sort of interstellar Peter Pan, held aloft by joyous spirits and a sprinkling of pixie dust.

"Picture yourself in my place," Q urged, "a young and eager Q, newly born to my full powers and cosmic awareness, exploring a shiny new galaxy for the first time. Oh, Picard, those were the days! I felt like I could do anything. And you know what? I was right!"

At that, they plunged into the heart of the roaring sun. Picard flinched automatically, expecting to be burnt to a crisp, but, as he should have known, Q's omnipotence protected them from the unimaginable heat and brilliance. He gaped in awe as they descended first through the star's outer corona as it hurled massive tongues of flame at the surrounding void, not to mention, Picard knew, fatal amounts of ultraviolet light and X-rays. Listening to the constant crackle and sizzle of the flames, he could not help recalling how the *Enterprise* had nearly been destroyed when Beverly, in command while he and the others were being held captive by Lore, had flown the ship into another star's corona in a daring and ultimately successful attempt to escape the Borg. Yet here he was, without even the hull of a starship to shield him against the unleashed fury of the sun's outer atmosphere.

Next came the chromosphere, a thin layer of fiery red plasma that washed over Picard like a sea of hot blood, followed by the photosphere, the visible surface of the sun. Picard had thoroughly studied the structure of G-2 stars at the Academy, of course, and subjected hundreds of stars to every variety of advanced sensor probe, but none of that had prepared him for the reality of actually witnessing the surface of a sun firsthand; he gawked in amazement at churning energies that should have been enough to incinerate him a million times over. Not even the legendary lake of fire within the Klingon homeworld's famed Kri'stak Volcano compared to the raging inferno that seemed to consume everything in sight except him and Q.

Despite Q's protective aura, Picard felt as if he were standing naked in a Vulcan desert at high noon. Sweat dripped from his forehead while rivers of perspiration ran down his back, soaking the simple linen garment he wore. *Humidity on the surface of a sun?* It was flagrantly impossible; he had to assume that Q had inflicted this discomfort on him purely for the sake of illusion. Picard was none too surprised to note that Q himself looked perfectly cool and comfortable. "I get the idea, Q," he said, wiping more sweat from his brow and flinging it toward his companion. Tiny droplets evaporated instantly before reaching their target. "It's very hot here. Do you have anything less obvious to teach me?"

"Patience," Q advised. "We've barely begun." He dabbed his toe in the boiling gases beneath their feet and Picard felt whatever was supporting him slip away. He began to sink even deeper into the bright yellow starstuff. A mental image of himself being dipped into hot, melted butter leaped irresistibly to the forefront of his consciousness. Reacting instinctively, he held his breath as his head sank beneath the turbulent plasma, but he needn't have bothered; thanks to Q, oxygen found him even as he drowned in the sun.

They dropped through the photosphere until they were well within the convection zone beneath the surface of the sun. Here rivers of ionized gas, not unlike those that composed the Calamarain, surged throughout the outer third of the sun's interior. Picard knew the ambient temperature around him had to be at least one million degrees Kelvin. They dived headfirst into one of the solar rivers and let the ferocious current carry them ever deeper until at last, like salmon leaping from white water, they broke through into the very heart of the star.

Now he found himself approaching the very center of a stellar furnace that beggared description. Here untold amounts of burning hydrogen atoms, transformed into helium by a process of nuclear fusion, produced a temperature of more than fifteen million degrees Kelvin. Not even the warp core aboard the *Enterprise* was capable of generating that much heat and raw energy. The visual impression Picard received was that of standing in the midst of a single white-hot flame, and the heat he actually felt was nearly unbearable. Every inch of exposed skin felt raw and dry and sunburnt. Acrid chemical fumes stung his eyes, nose, and throat. The crackle of the spurting flames far above him gave way to a constant pounding roar. Overall, the intense gravitation and radiation at the solar core were so tremendous that they practically overwhelmed his senses, and yet somehow he was still able to see Q, who looked rather bored until his eyes lit on something *really* interesting. "Look, there I am," he announced.

Brushing tears away from his eyes, Picard stared where Q was pointing, but all he could see was a faint black speck in the distance, almost imperceptible against the dazzling spectacle of the core. They flew closer to the point of darkness and soon he discerned an individual figure sitting cross-legged in the middle of the gigantic fusion reaction. He seemed to be toying with a handful of burning plasma, letting the ionized gas stream out between his fingers. "Another golden afternoon," Q sighed nostalgically, seemingly oblivious of Picard's intense discomfort. "How young and inexperienced I was."

Picard coughed harshly, barely able to breathe owing to the caustic fumes and searing heat. The choking sounds jarred Q from his reminiscing and he peered at Picard dubiously. "Hmm," he pronounced eventually, "perhaps there is such a thing as too much verisimilitude." He snapped his fingers, and Picard felt the awful heat recede from him. He gulped down several lungfuls of cool, untainted air. It still felt warm all around him, but more like a sunny day at the beach than the fires of perdition. "I hope you appreciate the air-conditioning," Q said, "although it does rather spoil the effect."

The effect be damned, Picard thought. He was here as an abductee, not a tourist. He gave himself a moment to recover from the debilitating effects of his ordeal, then focused on the individual Q had apparently brought him here to see. *A young and inexperienced Q?* This he had to see.

Picard flew close enough to discover that the figure did indeed resemble a more youthful version of Q, one not yet emerged from adolescence. To his surprise, something about the teen reminded Picard of Wesley Crusher, another wide-eyed young prodigy, although this boy already had a more mischievous twinkle in his eye than Wesley had ever possessed. "Portrait of the artist as a young Q," Picard's companion whispered with a diabolical chuckle. "Beware." As he and Picard looked on, the young man, dressed as they were in the garb of ancient Greece, isolated a ribbon of luminous plasma, stretching it like taffy before imbuing it with his own supernatural energies so that it shimmered with an eldritch radiance that transcended conventional physics. He pulled his new creation taut, then flung it free. The fiery ribbon shot like a rubber band toward the ceiling of the core and soon passed out of sight. "I had forgotten about that!" Q marveled. "I wonder whatever happened to that little energy band?"

With a start, Picard remembered the inexplicable cosmic phenomenon that had driven Tolian Soran to madness—and, in more ways than one, claimed the life of James T. Kirk. Surely Q couldn't be claiming to have created it during an idle moment in his boyhood, could he? "Q," he began, shocked and appalled at the implications of what he suspected, "about this energy band?"

"Oh, never mind that, Jean-Luc," Q said, dismissing the question with a wave of his hand. "Do try not to get caught up in mere trivia."

Only Q could be so blasé, Picard thought, about the genesis of a dangerous space-time anomaly, and so negligent as to the possible consequences of his actions. He opened his mouth, prepared to read Q the riot act, when the boy came up with a new trick that rendered Picard momentarily speechless. Miniature mushroom clouds sprouted from the teen Q's fingers and he hurled them about with abandon, paying no heed to either Picard or the older Q. A toy-sized nuclear blast whizzed by Picard, missing his head by a hair. "Can he see us?" Picard asked, ducking yet another fireball.

"If he wanted to, of course," Q answered. A nuclear spitwad passed through him harmlessly. "But he has no reason to even suspect we are here, so he doesn't."

I suppose that makes sense, Picard thought. He could readily accept that the older Q was more adept at stealth and subterfuge than his youthful counterpart. He wondered if Q felt the least bit uncomfortable about peeking in on his past like this. "Aren't you at all tempted," Picard asked, "to speak to him? To offer some timely advice, perhaps, in hopes of changing your own past?"

"If only I could," Q said in a surprisingly melancholy tone. Picard was disturbed to see what appeared to be a genuine look of sorrow upon his captor/companion's face. *What kind of regrets,* Picard mused, *can plague such as Q?*

The moment passed, and Q regained his characteristic smugness. "You're not the only species, Jean-Luc, that worries incessantly about preserving the sanctity of the timeline. If changing one human life can start a historical chain reaction beyond any mortal's powers to predict, imagine the sheer universal chaos that could be spawned by tampering with a Q's lifetime." He shuddered, more for effect than because of any actual chill. "Remind me to tell you sometime about how your own Commander Riker owes his very existence to a momentary act of charity by one of my contemporaries. It's quite a story, although completely irrelevant to our present purposes."

Picard hoped that Q was exaggerating where Will Riker was concerned, but he saw Q's point. Various ancient theologians throughout the galaxy, he recalled, had argued that even God could not undo the past. It was comforting to know that Q recognized the same limitation, at least where his own yesterdays were concerned. Picard took a closer look at the adolescent figure not too far away. "What is he . . . you . . . doing now?"

Before their eyes, the teen Q rose to his feet, dusted some stray solar matter from his bare knees, and stretched out his arms. Suddenly he began to grow at a catastrophic rate, expanding his slender frame until he towered like a behemoth above his older self and Picard. He seemed to grow immaterial as well, so that his gargantuan form caused nary a ripple in the ongoing thermonuclear processes of the star. Soon he eclipsed the great golden sun itself, so that its blazing corona crowned his head like a halo. His outstretched hands grazed the orbits of distant solar systems.

"I don't understand," Picard said. "How can we be seeing this? What is our frame of reference?" The gigantic youth loomed over them, yet he was able to witness the whole impossible scene in its entirety. He tore his gaze away from the colossal figure to orient himself, but all he could see was the sparkle of stars glittering many light-years away. Somehow they had departed from the sun completely without him even noticing. "What is this place? Where are we now?"

"Shhh," Q said, raising a finger before his lips. "You must be quite a pain at a concert or play, Picard. Do you always insist on examining the stage and the curtains and the lighting before taking in the show?" He quietly applauded the boy's grandiose dimensions. "Just go with it. That which is essential will become clear."

I hope so, Picard thought, feeling more awestruck than enlightened. *There must be some point to this, aside from demonstrating that Q was as flamboyant and egotistic in his youth as he is in my own time.*

The boy Q inspected his own star-spanning proportions and laughed in delight. It was an exuberant laugh, Picard noted, but not a particularly malevolent one. Picard was reminded of the optimistic, idealistic, young giants in H. G. Wells's *The Food of the Gods,* a novel he had read several times in his own boyhood.

Most unexpectedly, he found himself liking the young Q. *Pity he had to grow into such a conceited pain-in-the-backside.*

"I was adorable, wasn't I?" Q commented.

Is that what he wants me to know? Picard thought. *Merely that he was once this carefree boy?* "Even Kodos the Executioner was once a child," he observed dryly. "Colonel Green is said to have been a Boy Scout."

"And Jean-Luc Picard built ships in bottles and flew kites over the vineyards," Q shot back. "Evidence suggests that he may have briefly understood the concept of fun, although some future historians dispute this."

Picard bristled at Q's sarcasm. "If this is some misguided attempt to reawaken my sense of fun," he said indignantly, "might I suggest that your timing could not be worse. Snatching me away while my ship is in jeopardy is hardly conducive to an increased appreciation of recreation. Perhaps you should postpone this little pantomime until my next scheduled shore leave?"

Q rolled his eyes. "Don't be such a solipsist, Jean-Luc. I told you before, this isn't about you. It's about me." His head tilted back and he stared upward at the Brobdingnagian figure of his younger self. "Look!" he exclaimed. "Watch what I'm doing now!"

Without any other warning except Q's excited outburst, the teen Q began to shrink as swiftly as he had grown only moments before. His substance contracted and soon he was even smaller than he had been originally, less than half the height of either Picard or the older Q. But his process of diminution did not halt there, and he quickly became no larger than a doll. Within seconds, Picard had to get down on his knees, kneeling upon seemingly empty space, and strain his eyes to see him. The boy Q was a speck again, as he had been when Picard had first spied him across the immeasurably long radius of the solar core.

A heartbeat later, he vanished from sight. Picard looked up at the other Q, who had a devious smile on his face. "Well?" Picard asked, frustrated by all this pointless legerdemain. "He's gone."

"Au contraire, mon capitaine," Q said, waving a finger at the puzzled human. "To Q, there is no zero," he added cryptically. "Let's go see."

In a blink, Picard was somewhere else. It was a strangely colorless realm, a shapeless world of stark black and white without any shading in between. The utter darkness of space had been supplanted by an eerie white emptiness that seemed to extend forever, holding nothing but flying black particles that zipped about ceaselessly, tracing intricate patterns in the nothingness. A slow-moving particle arced toward Picard and he reached out to pluck it from its flight. The black object streaked right through his outstretched hand, however, leaving not a mark or a tingle behind, leaving Picard to wonder whether it was he or the particle that was truly intangible.

He hoped it was the particle. Certainly, he thought, patting himself for confirmation, he felt substantial enough. He could hear his own breathing, feel his heart beating in his chest. He felt as tangible, as real, as he had ever been.

But where in all the universe was he now?

Total silence oppressed him. There were no sounds to hear and no odors to smell. Not even the limbo where Q had first transported him, with its swirling white mists, had seemed quite this, well, vacant. For as far as his eyes could see, there were only three objects that seemed to possess any color or solidity: himself, Q, and a now-familiar young man cavorting among the orbiting particles. Picard watched as the adolescent Q did what he had not been able to do and caught on to one of the swooping particles with his bare hands. Compared with the youth, it looked about the size of a type-1 phaser and completely two-dimensional. It dangled like a limp piece of film from his fingertips.

Picard looked impatiently at the Q he knew. "What are you waiting for? Explain all this, or do you simply enjoy seeing me confused and uncertain?"

"There is nothing simple about that joy at all, Jean-Luc, but I suppose I do have to edify you eventually. This," he said grandly, "is the domain of the infinitesimal. What you see buzzing about you, smaller than the very notion of sound or hue, are quarks, mesons, gluons, and all manner of exotic subatomic beasties. Or rather, to be more exact, they are the *possibilities* of micro-micro-matter, discrete units of mathematical probabilities following along the courses of their most likely speeds and directions. Whether they actually exist at any one specific time or place is open to interpretation."

"Spare me the lecture on quantum theory," Picard said, doing his best not to sound impressed. He hated to give Q the satisfaction of watching him play the dumbstruck mortal, but, if Q was in fact telling the truth about their present location, if they were actually existing on a subatomic level, then it was hard not to marvel at the sights presented to him. "Is that really a quark?" he asked, pointing to the young Q's immaterial plaything. The boy was peering into the thin black object as if he saw something even smaller inside it.

"Cross my heart," his older self said, "a honest-to-goodness quark, not to be confused with that grasping barkeep on you-know-where."

Picard had no idea whom Q was referring to, and he didn't really care. Perhaps the greatest challenge posed by Q, he reflected, was to see past his snideness to the occasional tidbits of actual revelation. Picard took a moment just to bask in the wonder of this uncanny new environment, one never before glimpsed by human eyes. It was sobering to think that, ultimately, everything in existence was composed of these phantom particles and their intricate ballet.

"The cloud-capped towers, the gorgeous palaces, the solemn temples, the great globe itself," he recited, recalling his precious Shakespeare. "Yea, all which it inherit, shall dissolve; and like this insubstantial pageant faded, leave not a rack behind. We are such stuff as dreams are made on."

"My goodness, Picard," Q remarked, "are you moved to poetry?"

"Sometimes poetry is the only suitable response to what the universe holds for us," Picard answered. The essential building blocks of matter darted around him like flocks of birds on the wing. "This is fascinating, I admit, but I fail to see the relevance to your earlier warnings and prohibitions. What has this to do with my mission to the galactic barrier?"

"More than you know," Q stated. An hourglass materialized in his hands and he tipped it over, letting the sands of time pour down inexorably. "Keep watching. Here's where things start to get messy."

The boy Q held the quark up in front of him, like a scrap of paper, then thrust his arm into the quark up to his elbow. His hand and lower arm disappeared as if into a pocket-sized wormhole. He dug around inside the quark for a moment, the tip of his tongue poking out of the corner of his mouth in his concentration, until he seized hold of something and yanked it back toward his body. It looked to Picard like he was turning the quark inside-out.

Instantly, the entire submicroscopic realm changed around them all, becoming a sort of photo-negative version of its prior self; Picard looked about him to see a dimension of total blackness, lightened only by flying white particles. Black was white and white was black and the young Q gazed goggle-eyed at what he had wrought. "I don't understand," Picard said. "What's happening?"

"Quiet," Q shushed him, his gaze fixed on his younger self, who was whooping and hollering in triumph. He appeared very pleased with himself, unlike the curiously somber Q standing next to Picard. Clearly, this memory held no joy for Q, although Picard could not tell why that should be so. *Am I missing something?* Picard wondered.

"Q!" a booming Voice exploded out of the darkness, startling both Picard and the adolescent Q, but not, conspicuously, the Q Picard was most accustomed to. He knew exactly what was coming.

"WHAT HAVE YOU DONE?" the Voice boomed again.

The boy glanced about guiltily, dropping the now snow-white quark like a hot potato. He struck Picard as the very portrait of a child caught with his hand in the proverbial cookie jar. The inverted quark flopped like a dead thing at the boy's feet, and he tried to kick it away casually, but it stuck to the sole of his sandal. "Um, nothing in particular," he replied to the Voice, trying unsuccessfully to shake the quark from his foot. "Why do you ask?"

"YOU KNOW WHY. YOU ARE TOO YOUNG TO TRIFLE WITH ANTIMATTER. WHY HAVE YOU DEFIED THE EDICTS OF THE CONTINUUM?"

The Voice sounded familiar to Picard, although its excessive volume made it hard to identify. *Where have I heard it before?* he thought. *And what was that about antimatter?* He surveyed his surroundings another time; was all of this actually antimatter? He was used to conceiving of antimatter as a fairly abstract concept, something tucked away at the heart of warp engines, safely swaddled behind layers of magnetic constriction. It was difficult to accept that antimatter was all around him, and that, contrary to the fundamental principles of physics, no explosive reaction had resulted from his contact with this realm. Antimatter, in any form, was intrinsically dangerous.

Small wonder the rest of the Continuum frowned on the young Q's impulsive experiments.

Sheepishness gave way to defiance as the teen Q realized there was no way to escape the blame. "It's not fair!" he declared. "I know what I'm doing. Look at this!" He snatched the telltale quark from his foot and waved it like a flag. "Look all around! I did this—me!—and nothing got hurt. Nothing important, anyway."

"THE WILL OF THE CONTINUUM CANNOT BE FLOUTED."

Without any fanfare, the quantum realm reversed itself, returning to its original monochromatic schema. Once again, inky particles glided throughout a blank and silent void. "I liked it better the other way," the boy Q muttered to himself. Picard glanced at his companion and saw that the older Q was quietly mouthing the same words.

"YOU MUST BE DISCIPLINED. YOU ARE REQUIRED TO SPEND THE NEXT TEN MILLION CYCLES IN SOLITARY MEDITATION."

"Ten million!" the boy protested. "You have to be joking. That's practically forever!" He flashed an ingratiating smile, attempting to charm his way out of hot water. "Look, there's no harm done. How about I just promise not to do it again?"

"THE JUDGMENT OF THE CONTINUUM CANNOT BE QUESTIONED. TEN MILLION CYCLES."

"But I'll be ancient by then!" the young Q said.

"Ouch!" his future self responded.

MAKE IT SO, the Voice declared, and Picard suddenly realized whom the Voice reminded him of. *Me. The Voice sounds like me.* Was that why Q had always delighted in provoking him, he speculated, or was the similarity merely an unusually subtle joke on Q's part? Either way, it appeared obvious that Q had developed a grudge against authority figures at a very early age.

"Just you wait," the boy vowed bitterly, more to himself than to his oppressor. "One of these days I'll show you what I can really do, you wait and see."

"THE TEN MILLION CYCLES BEGIN NOW," the Voice stated, apparently unimpressed by the youth's rebellious attitude. *Do I really sound that pompous?* Picard had to wonder. *Surely not.*

Staring sullenly at his feet, the young Q vanished in a twinkle of light. Picard could not tell if he had transported himself willingly or if he had been yanked away by the Continuum. He supposed it didn't matter much.

"Believe me, Jean-Luc," Q said, gazing mournfully at the spot his earlier self had occupied, "when I was that young, ten million cycles really did feel like an eternity."

Picard found it hard to sympathize, especially when he was being held against his will while the *Enterprise* faced unknown dangers. "Was this extended flashback really necessary?" he asked. "It comes as no surprise to learn that you started out as a juvenile delinquent."

"Says the man who was nearly expelled from Starfleet Academy—twice," Q replied. "And we're not done yet." He flipped over the hourglass once more, reversing the flow of sand. "This was only the beginning."

There's more? Picard thought. How much longer did Q intend to keep him away from his ship? "No more," he began to protest, but his angry words were swallowed up by another flash of supernatural light, leaving the quarks to continue alone their endless and invisible pavanes.

He was on his way again—to only Q knew where.

Interlude

LIEUTENANT REGINALD BARCLAY did his best to ignore the ceaseless hum of the Calamarain as he inspected the battered probe, but that was easier said than done. He was all too aware that the steady drone in the background emanated from the same entities, called the Calamarain according to Chief La Forge, that had inflicted the damage he was now evaluating. If they could do this to the molded duranium-tritanium casing, what could they do to ordinary human flesh-and-blood?

Barclay shuddered, glad that no one was present to witness his attack of nerves. Sometimes his imagination was just a little too vivid for his own peace of mind, even if Counselor Troi tried occasionally to convince him that his rich imagination could be a source of strength rather than a liability, provided he managed to control it rather than the other way around. Unfortunately, that was about the only eventuality he couldn't imagine.

And who wouldn't be worried, now that the captain

was missing, too? Abducted by Q, from what Chief La Forge said. Barclay had a great deal of faith in Captain Picard's ability to keep the ship intact despite the numerous—too numerous, as far as Barclay was concerned—hazards encountered in deep space, but how could the captain extricate them from this crisis if he wasn't even aboard? It was enough to make even a Klingon nervous . . . maybe.

The probe, plucked from the Calamarain's grasp moments before its imminent destruction, rested on the floor of Transporter Room Five. Approximately four meters in length, it was a conical, metallic object with a bulbous, multifaceted head constructed of triple-layered transparent aluminum. The matte black finish of the probe was scorched and dented while the once transparent head, resembling the eye of an enormous insect, appeared to have been partially melted by whatever forces had assailed the probe. The formerly clear sensor windows had clouded over, turning opaque and milky. A fissure along the right side of the cone revealed a sliver of charred circuitry beneath the ruptured hull.

A full-color, three-dimensional picture of a similar crevice opening up along the length of the *Enterprise* itself forced its way into Barclay's mind, but he pushed it away as fast as he could. *That's the way,* he told himself. *Just focus on the job.* He scanned the probe with his tricorder, detecting no significant residual radiation, before gingerly laying his hands on the blasted surface of the mechanism. To his surprise, it felt slightly warm to the touch, despite having been beamed in straight from the cold of interstellar space. He consulted his tricorder again and observed that the metals composing the hull remained agitated at an atomic level, although the degree of ionic activity was swiftly falling off as the disrupted matter restabilized. He recorded the data into the memory of the tricorder and charted its progress for several seconds. The forced acceleration of the atoms within the alloy, along with the resulting stresses of its molecular bonds, were consistent with the sort of tachyon overload La Forge had suggested he look out for. Tachyons definitely seemed to be the Calamarain's weapons of choice, but what kind of harm could they impose on Federation technology, not to mention innocent Starfleet officers?

Convinced that he had learned as much as he could from the torn and toasted exterior of the probe, he proceeded to the next stage of the autopsy, wincing slightly at the more alarming connotations of that term. First, he confirmed that the deuterium microfusion propulsion unit at the rear of the probe was indeed deactivated; fortunately, class-2 sensor probes were not equipped with warp capacity, so he didn't have to worry about any loose particles of antimatter poking a hole into reality as he knew it. Next, using a delicate phaser scalpel, he peeled off a section of the burnt outer casing, exposing the intricate navigational and sensory apparatuses within.

The probe's innards did not look much better than its supposedly protective sheath. Most of the circuitry was fused and useless now. Still, he chipped the carbon scoring away from one of the output ports and plugged a palm-sized data-retrieval unit into the central memory processor in hope of rescuing whatever scraps of information might have survived the tachyon barrage. *There's probably not much left,* he thought glumly, *but here goes nothing.*

Unexpectedly, the retrieval unit whirred to life at once and began humming almost as loudly as the Calamarain themselves. "Hey!" he said out loud to the empty transporter room. Maybe the internal damage wasn't as bad as it looked.

He waited until the unit had recorded all available data onto an isolinear chip, then began dissecting the entire mechanism, methodically extracting the coprocessors one at a time, scanning every component with his tricorder to record the extent of the damage (if any), then moving on to the next one. It was slow, laborious work and Barclay soon found himself wishing that Chief La Forge had been able to spare another engineer to assist him at the task.

Not that he was all too eager to return to Engineering, not while there was still a chance he might run into Lem Faal again. That distinguished and ever-so-intimidating scientist still gave him dirty looks every time Barclay had to come by Faal's temporary workstation to check with Mr. La Forge about something or another. *I can't believe I almost wrecked the pulse generator,* he thought, reliving those awful, endless seconds for the one thousandth time. His cheek still burned where Faal *almost* hit him. Barclay knew that he had completely thrown away any chance he had of taking part in the historic experiment, even assuming the Calamarain let the operation proceed as planned. *Another wasted opportunity,* he thought, the latest in a long string of self-administered wounds to his Starfleet aspirations. Counselor Troi insisted that his reputation among his peers wasn't nearly as bad as he feared, but sometimes he wondered if she was just being nice.

At times like this, he thought, his mind wandering somewhat, it was very tempting to sneak away to the nearest holodeck and escape from the stress and humiliations of the real world. Perhaps he could relive some of his greatest holovictories, like defeating Baron Diabolis in Chapter Twenty-Three of *The Quest for the Golden Throne* or outwitting Commander Kruge before the Genesis Planet completely self-destructed. The latter was one of his proudest moments; after seventy-three tries, he'd actually managed to save Spock without sacrificing the original *Enterprise,* which was even better than the real Kirk had been able to do. Perhaps next time he could save David Marcus, too. . . .

No, he thought, shaking his head to clear his mind

of past and future fantasies. He had worked too hard to get a handle on his holodiction problem to back-slide now, especially when Chief La Forge and the others were depending on him. He refocussed all his concentration on job at hand, using the phaser scalpel to separate two fused coprocessors, then gently pulled a melted chip out of its slot.

A glint of blue flame peeked out from beneath the slot and Barclay scooted backward on his knees, half-expecting the entire probe to explode in his face like a defective torpedo. When nothing of the sort occurred, he crept back toward the probe, his tricorder out-stretched before him. *Funny,* he noted; the tricorder wasn't reporting any excess heat or energy.

There was definitely something there, though: an incandescent blue glow that seemed to come from somewhere deeper within the inner workings of the perhaps-not-totally lifeless probe. Not entirely trust-ing his instruments, Barclay held up his open palm in front of the mysterious radiance. His skin didn't detect any heat either, but he thought he felt a peculiar tingling along his nerve endings. He might be imagining the sensations, he reminded himself, pain-fully aware of his own tendency toward hypochon-dria. He still remembered, with excruciating accu-racy, that time last month when he paged Dr. Crusher in the middle of the graveyard shift, thoroughly convinced that he was dying from an accidental overdose of genetronic radiation and in immediate need of massive hyronalyn treatments, only to discov-er that there was nothing wrong with him except a slight case of heartburn. Maybe it was best, he con-cluded, to reserve judgment on the whole question of whether he was really feeling something or not.

But what was causing that glow? It wasn't very intense, more like the bioluminescent gleam of a Rigelian firefly, but he couldn't account for what might be producing the light. *Wait a sec,* he thought, a hypothesis forming in his mind. Maybe bioluminescence was precisely what he was looking at. Excitement overcoming his trepidations, he reached down with both hands and pried out an entire shelf of singed isolinear coprocessors, then looked back eagerly into the cavity he had exposed. There, beneath the discarded rows of coprocessors, was the source of the lambent blue sheen: the newfangled bio-gel packs that were rapidly becoming the next generation of Starfleet data-processing technology. The organic memory cells, designed to accelerate the transfer and storage of information from the probe's sensors, looked surprisingly undamaged compared with the rest of the probe's entrails; they were laid out in a sequence of finger-sized sacs connected by semipermeable silicate membranes that appeared to have remained intact despite the pummeling endured by the probe. Now that the preceding layer of circuitry had been removed, he could see that all of the gel packs were imbued with the same strange, unaccountable incandescence that had first attracted his attention.

Even though the bio-organic technology was relatively new, having been introduced on the ill-fated *U.S.S. Voyager* before that ship ended up in the Delta Quadrant, Barclay knew the packs didn't ordinarily glow this way; they were intended to store information, not energy. Something must have happened to them during the probe's interrupted voyage to the barrier. *You know,* he thought, *the light from the packs kind of looks like the glow of the galactic barrier.*

Inspiration struck him like the blast of a holographic disruptor beam (set well within conventional safety parameters). He quickly scanned the gel-filled sacs to confirm that the curious glow was not an aftereffect of a tachyon overload. This had nothing to do with the Calamarain then, and perhaps everything to do with the probe's brief proximity to the barrier itself.

According to the latest scientific theories, which Barclay had studiously reviewed before getting kicked off the wormhole project, the energies that composed the galactic barrier were largely psychokinetic in nature. He had not programmed his tricorder to scan for any psionic traces before, but now he recalibrated the sensor assemblies to detect emanations along the known psychic frequencies and checked out the probe again.

Voilà, he thought, feeling much as he had when he found the (holographic) lost Orb of the Prophets; there they were, distinct pockets of psionic energy contained within the shining gel packs. Obviously, the bio-neural material within the packs had somehow absorbed small quantities of psionic energy from the barrier. *Is that why the Calamarain attacked the probe,* he wondered. It was even possible that the borrowed psionic power had helped protect the organic components of the probe from the Calamarain's tachyon bombardment.

This is amazing, he thought. Who knew what the full implications of his discovery might be? He couldn't wait to tell Mr. La Forge. Even the thought of facing Professor Faal again didn't seem as daunting as before, at least in the abstract. He double-checked his tricorder readings one more time, then headed for the exit. "Wow," he murmured to himself, proud of his accomplishment and wondering if this heady feeling was what Mr. La Forge or Commander Data felt whenever they made some startling scientific breakthrough. Reality, he discovered, could be even more satisfying than a holodeck.

Who would have thought it?

Chapter Twelve

THE STORM WAS WELL and truly upon them.

The wrath of the Calamarain could be felt all over the bridge, much more viscerally than before. The unremitting hum of the plasma cloud had grown into the rumble of angry thunder that battered the ears of everyone aboard. On the main viewer, lightning arced across the prow of the saucer section, striking violently against the forward deflector shields. Riker gritted his teeth as the impact slammed him back into his seat. Sparks flew from the tactical station behind him, singeing the back of his neck, and he spun his chair around in time to see Leyoro snuff out the flames with her bare hands. "Shields down to fifty-one percent," she reported, rerouting the deflector readings through the auxiliary circuitry even as she extinguished the last white-hot spark beneath the heel of her palm.

Riker scowled at the news, the smell of burning circuitry irritating his nostrils. Their defenses were almost halfway down already, and they hadn't even begun to fight back. Hell, they still didn't know why they were under attack. "What in blazes did we do to provoke this?" he asked out loud.

"I am afraid I cannot yet determine that, Commander," Data answered from his station at Ops, "although I believe I am making progress in adapting the Universal Translator to the transmissions from the Calamarain." Deanna stood at the android's side, between Ops and the conn, her hands cupped over her ears in a futile attempt to screen out the roar of the thunder. How could she be expected to sense anything, Riker thought, in the middle of a tempest like this? "The counselor's impressions are proving quite informative," Data stated nonetheless.

"How much more time do you need?" Riker asked. Given a choice, he'd rather talk with the Calamarain than engage them in battle, but the *Enterprise* couldn't take this pummeling much longer. There was only so long he was willing to turn the other cheek.

"That is difficult to estimate," Data confessed. "The intensity of the barrage is now such that it is extremely problematic to filter out what might be an attempt at communication, much like trying to listen to a whistled melody in the midst of a hurricane."

"Give me your best guess," Riker instructed.

Data cocked his head to one side as he pondered the problem. "Approximately one-point-three-seven hours," Data concluded after only a few seconds of contemplation. "As a best guess," he added.

"Thank you, Mr. Data," Riker said, although he would have preferred a significantly smaller figure. At the rate the storm outside was eating away at their shields, the *Enterprise* might not last another hour, unless they started giving as good as they got. *Who knows?* he thought. *Maybe the Calamarain are like the Klingons, and only respect aliens who fight back.*

Then again, he reminded himself, it took the Federation close to a hundred years to come to terms with the Klingon Empire. . . .

A new thunderbolt rocked the ship, tilting the bridge starboard. Next to Data, Deanna staggered and grabbed on to the conn station to maintain her balance. Riker felt a shudder run along the length of the bridge, and possibly the entire starship, before their orientation stabilized. "We have damage to the starboard warp nacelle," Ensign Schultz reported from the aft engineering station.

"Casualties reported on Decks Twelve through Fourteen," another officer, Lieutenant Jim Yang, called out from the environmental station. "No fatalities, though."

Not yet, Riker thought grimly.

"Commander," Leyoro spoke up, echoing his own thoughts, "we can't wait any longer."

"Agreed," Riker said, hitting the alert switch on the command console. He regretted that yet another first-contact situation had to lead to a show of force, but the Calamarain hadn't given them any other choice except retreat. *Let's see what happens when we bite back,* he thought. "All crew to battle stations."

Baeta Leyoro, for onc, was raring to go. Her white teeth gleamed wolfishly as she leaned over the tactical controls. "All weapons systems primed and ready," she announced. "Awaiting your command."

"Start with a midrange phaser burst," he ordered. "Maximum possible dispersal." The wide beams would weaken the burst's total force, but Riker saw no obvious alternative. *How the hell,* he thought, *do you target a cloud?*

"Yes, sir!" Leyoro said, pressing down on the controls. Phaser arrays mounted all along the ship's surface fired at once, emitting a unified pulse that spread out from the *Enterprise* in every possible direction. On the screen, Riker saw the pulse emerge as a wave of scarlet energy that disappeared into the billowing, churning mass of the Calamarain. He wasn't sure, but he thought the turbulent cloud became even more agitated when and where it intersected with the phaser burst. The roiling gases swirled furiously, throwing off electrical discharges that crackled against the *Enterprise*'s shields. A clap of thunder rattled Riker all the way through to his bones.

"I sure felt that," he said, raising his voice to be heard over the din. "The question is: did they feel us?" He peered over at Deanna, who had taken her seat beside him the minute he sounded the battle alert. "Any response from out there?"

Deanna shook her head. "I'm not sure. I don't think so. They're already so upset, it's hard to tell."

He nodded. *In for a penny,* he thought, *in for a pound.* "Another burst. Increase phaser intensity to the next level." There was no turning back now. He hoped he could avoid actually killing one or more of the Calamarain, but their alien nature made it impossible to gauge the ultimate effect of the phaser beams. He had no intention of going to maximum strength before he had to, but, one way or another, he was going to make these strange, bodiless beings think twice about attacking this ship.

"Here goes nothing," Leyoro muttered as she fired again. A second burst of directed energy, even more dazzling than before, met the fury of the Calamarain. Once again, it was absorbed into the accumulated plasma almost instantaneously.

The cloud's reaction was just as immediate.

With a howl even louder than any Riker or the others had heard before, the Calamarain shook the *Enterprise* savagely. Riker held on tightly to the armrests of the captain's chair while keeping his jaw firmly set to avoid biting down on his tongue. All about the bridge, crew members bounced in their seats, their minds and bodies jangled by the brutal quaking. Even Data appeared distracted by the disturbance; he looked up from his console with an impatient expression upon his golden face, as if he was anxious for the shaking to cease so he could continue with his work. Riker knew just how he felt.

Mercifully, the worst of the battering subsided after a few moments, although the sentient tempest still raged upon the screen and the thunder reverberated ominously behind every buzz and beep from the bridge apparatus. Riker felt his temples begin to pound in concert with every resounding peal. He searched the bridge to make sure that no one had been injured seriously, then looked back at Deanna. The counselor's face was pale, her eyes wide with alarm.

"They felt that," she gasped. Obviously, she had shared at least a part of the Calamarain's pain.

"I got that impression," he said.

Barclay had hoped that Mr. La Forge would be alone when he reached Engineering, but no such luck. The first thing Barclay saw as soon as he got off the turbolift was the chief engrossed in a heated discussion with Lem Faal, who was the last person Barclay wanted to run into right now. The red alert signals flashing all around the engineering section only added to his trepidation, as did the all busy Starfleet officers hard at work in response to the alert.

Engineering was abuzz with activity, much more so than usual. Every duty station was manned, sometimes by more than one individual. His fellow engineers shouted instructions and queries back and forth to each other as they hastily adjusted and/or monitored illuminated instrumentation panels all along engineering. Yellow warning signals blinked upon the tabletop master systems display, indicating problems with at least half a dozen vital ship systems, while a whole team of crew members, led by Sonya Gomez, clustered around the towering warp engine core, carefully manipulating the enclosed matter/antimatter reaction. Ordinarily, Barclay could have expected a friendly greeting upon entering Engineering, but at the moment his colleagues were too intent upon their assigned tasks to take note of his arrival. Even Lem Faal seemed too busy with Chief La Forge to spare Barclay another dirty look.

Maybe this isn't the best time, Barclay thought, his previous enthusiasm cooling in the face of the irate Betazoid scientist. He wanted to talk to Mr. La Forge about his discovery in Transporter Room Five, but the chief looked like he had his hands full with the red alert, not to mention Professor Faal. The visiting scientist was obviously upset. He held on to a duranium pylon for support while he argued with La Forge. "I don't understand," he said. "We can't cancel the experiment now. It's ridiculous."

"We're under attack," La Forge pointed out, looking past Faal at the cutaway diagram of the *Enterprise* on the master situation monitor, his attention clearly divided between Faal and the ongoing crisis. "It's a shame, but I'm sure Commander Riker knows what he's doing." He started to turn away from the irate physicist. "Now, you'll have to excuse me while I see what's the matter with our warp engines. You should go back to your quarters."

"This is more than a shame," Faal objected, a faint whistle escaping his throat with every breath. La Forge had discreetly briefed the engineering team on the physicist's medical problems, and Barclay felt sorry for the man despite the bad blood between them. Iverson's disease, like all manner of illnesses and medical threats, terrified Barclay. Even though he knew Iverson's disease was caused by a genetic disorder and was by no means contagious, listening to Faal's tortured breathing still gave him the creeps.

"I've devoted years to this project. It's my last hope for . . . well, I suppose you'd call it immortality." His knuckles whitened as he held on to the pylon with what looked like all his strength. "Your Commander Riker has no right to make this decision. I'm in charge of this experiment. Starfleet specifically told your captain to cooperate with my experiment!"

La Forge shrugged impatiently. "I don't know much more than you do, but I know we can't pull this off in the middle of a combat situation, especially with the captain missing." He hurried over to the master systems display, where Ensign Daniel Sutter stepped aside to permit La Forge access to the primary workstation. La Forge continued to speak to Faal as he simultaneously ran a diagnostic on the graviton polarity generators. "Maybe the Calamarain will go somewhere else and we can try again. Or maybe you'll have to try another section of the barrier."

"No," Faal said, following closely behind La Forge. He sounded ever more sick and distraught. "This is the ideal location. All our sensor readings and calculations prove that. We have to break through the barrier now. I might not get another chance. I don't have much time left. . . ."

Barclay was getting tense just listening to this conversation. He seriously considered turning around and coming back later. *But what if the way the bio-gel packs in the probe absorbed some of the barrier's energy turns out to be important?* He'd never forgive himself if the *Enterprise* got destroyed and it was all his fault; it was bad enough that he'd infected the entire crew with that mutagenic virus a couple years ago. *Don't live in the past,* Counselor Troi always told him. *Show people what you're capable of.*

Mustering up all his courage, Barclay stepped closer to the chief and Faal. The Betazoid genius spotted him approaching and gave him a murderous look; clearly, he hadn't forgotten the incident with pulse generator. Or forgiven.

"Excuse me, sir," Barclay said to La Forge. He

could feel Lem Faal's baleful glare burning into the back of his neck. "But when you've got a moment, I'd like to talk to you about something I found in that probe you asked me to look at."

La Forge sighed, as if the rescued probe was just one more thing for him to worry about. Barclay immediately regretted bringing it up. "Can this wait, Reg?" he asked with a slight edge of irritation in his tone. "There's an emergency with the warp engines *and* the deflectors."

"Yes. No," he answered. "I mean, I don't know."

Professor Faal lost his patience entirely. "What are you doing, wasting time with this idiot?" Saliva sprayed from his mouth as he gasped out the words. "This is intolerable! I want to speak to Commander Riker!"

Before La Forge could respond, a tremendous clap of thunder echoed through Engineering, drowning out even the constant thrum of the warp core. The floor swayed beneath Barclay's feet and he found himself stumbling down a sudden incline that hadn't existed an instant before, bumping awkwardly into no less than Professor Faal himself. *Just kill me now,* he thought.

La Forge frowned as the floor gradually leveled out again. "This isn't good," he said. Circuit patterns rotated in his ocular implants as he concentrated on the tabletop display, taking stock of the situation. "I can't waste any more time with this. Reg, make sure the professor gets back to his quarters okay, then head back here. We'll talk about the probe later." Without a backward glance, he stalked across Engineering toward the warp core, issuing orders as he went. "Sutter, divert impulse power to the subspace field amplifiers. Ortega, keep an eye on the EPS flow. . . ."

Why me? Barclay thought, left alone with Lem Faal. *Couldn't someone else—anyone else—escort Faal? He already hates me enough.* But La Forge was in charge; he had to keep his eyes on the big picture. "Yes, sir,"

Barclay said dutifully, if less than enthusiastically. "Please come with me."

Faal ignored him entirely, chasing after Geordi. "You can't do this, La Forge," he said, his wheezing voice no more than a whisper. "The barrier is bigger than some pointless military exercise. We can't lose sight of that. The experiment is all that matters!"

But La Forge, determined to inspect the warp engine power transfer conduits, would not be distracted. "Reg," he called out, exasperated, "if you could take care of this?"

I can't let Mr. La Forge down, Reg thought, taking Faal gently but firmly by the arm. "Please come along, Professor." Part of him felt guilty about bullying a sick man; another part was greatly relieved that Faal wouldn't be able to put up much resistance.

Physically, that is. The scientist's vocal indignation showed no sign of abating. "Let go of me, you incompetent cretin! I insist on seeing Commander Riker."

Barclay had no idea where Riker was. On the bridge, he assumed, coping with the latest ghastly emergency. *There you go again,* he chastised himself, *leaping to the worst possible conclusion.* But he couldn't help it. The flashing red alert signals and blaring sirens ate away at his nerves like Tarcassian piranha. A dozen nightmarish scenarios, ranging from an uncontrolled plasma leak to a full-scale Q invasion, raced through his mind. He tried to dismiss his fears as irrational and unfounded, but with only partial success. *An angry Q could do anything,* he thought, *anything at all.* Still, he somehow managed to get the professor away from La Forge and into the turbolift. *Let me just get Faal stowed away safely. Then I can report my findings on the probe.* "Which deck are your quarters on?" he asked.

"Seven," Faal said grudgingly, still visibly incensed. Unable to stand upright on his own, he had to lean back against the wall of the lift. Something wet and clotted gurgled in his lungs. Barclay tried not to stare at the silver hypospray Faal removed from his pocket. *It's not contagious,* he kept reminding himself. *It's not.*

The turbolift came to a stop and the doors whooshed open, revealing an empty corridor leading to the ship's deluxe guest quarters, the ones reserved for visiting admirals and ambassadors. *Nothing but the best for the winner of the Daystrom Prize,* Barclay thought, wondering how much larger the suite was than his own quarters on Level Eleven. "Here we are," he announced, grateful that Faal had not raised more of a fuss once they left Engineering. *I'll just drop him off, then hurry back to Mr. La Forge.* He still needed to tell the chief about the psionic energy the probe had picked up.

"Just give me a minute, Lieutenant," Faal said. His hypospray hissed for an instant, and the debilitated scientist grabbed on to the handrail for support. His chest rose and fell slowly as he choked back a rasping cough. Barclay looked away so as not to embarrass the professor.

The next thing he knew a pair of hands shoved him out of the lift compartment into the hall. Surprised and befuddled, he spun around in time to see the doors sliding shut in front of his face. For one brief instant, he glimpsed Faal through the disappearing gap in the door. The Betazoid grinned maliciously at him. The doors came together and the lift was on its way.

Oh no! he thought. He immediately called for another lift, which arrived seconds later, and he jumped inside. *I can't believe I let him do that. I can't even keep track of one sickly Betazoid.* He didn't know how he was ever going to look Geordi La Forge in the eyes again. *Just when I thought I was really on to something, what with the probe and all, I have to go and do something like this!*

"Destination?" the turbolift inquired when Barclay

didn't say anything at first. The prompt jogged his mind. Where could Professor Faal have run off to? Back to Engineering? Boy, was Chief La Forge going to be annoyed when Faal showed up to pester him again. "Engineering," he blurted, and the lift began to descend. *Maybe I can still stop him before he gets to Mr. La Forge.*

But, wait, he recalled. Hadn't Faal kept demanding to see Commander Riker? Suddenly, he knew what the professor's destination had to be.

The bridge.

"Stop. Cancel previous order. Take me to the bridge. Nonstop."

Please let me get there before Faal can bother the commander too much.

"Fire phasers again," Commander Riker ordered. "Take us up another notch, Lieutenant."

"With pleasure, sir," Leyoro said. A burst of high-intensity phaser beams leaped from the emitter arrays to sting the alien cloud-creatures enclosing the *Enterprise*. As before, the Calamarain reacted with a thunderous roar that caused the starship to rock like an old-fashioned sailing vessel adrift on a stormy sea.

The floor of the command area rolled beneath Riker's feet as yet another tremor jarred the bridge, reminding him forcibly of the Great Alaskan Earthquake of 2349. *Back on Earth,* he thought, *that would have been at least a five-point-two.* Thank heavens the *Enterprise*-E had been constructed as soundly as it had; otherwise, he'd be expecting the roof to cave in at any moment.

His mind swiftly reviewed the situation. They had hurt the Calamarain with that last phaser burst, but not enough, apparently, to make the vaporous aliens let go of the ship; frothing, luminescent fog still filled the screen of the main viewer. So far, it seemed, all they had done was make the Calamarain even more angry. *That's progress, I guess,* he thought, wondering briefly what Jean-Luc Picard would do in these circumstances before pushing that thought out of his mind. The captain was gone. Riker had to rely on his judgment and experience, as he had many times before. "Tactical status?" he inquired.

"Shields at forty-six percent," Leyoro briefed him. "Phasers armed and ready. Quantum torpedoes locked and loaded."

Riker acknowledged her report with a nod. He wasn't sure what good the torpedoes would do against a living cloud of plasma, especially one located at such close quarters to the *Enterprise,* but it might be worth finding out. "Ensign Berglund," he ordered the officer at the primary aft science station, "locate the area of maximum density within the Calamarain cloud formation."

Ordinarily, he'd assign Data a task like that, but he didn't want to divert the android's concentration from his work with the Universal Translator. Sondra Berglund, a blond Canadian officer with a specialty in advanced stellar spectroscopy, could handle the job just as well with the sensors assigned to her science console. *If we're going to target anywhere,* he decided, *we might as well aim for the highest concentration of Calamarain.*

"Um, I'm afraid that would be us," she reported after a few seconds. "The plasma is most dense around the *Enterprise* and diminishes in volume and intensity the farther the distance from the ship."

That was no good then, Riker realized. He had a vivid mental image of hundreds, if not thousands, of gaseous Calamarain swarming over and around the Sovereign-class starship. *They're ganging up on us, all right,* he thought, *and pounding on the walls.* There was no way he could detonate a quantum torpedo against the Calamarain while the ship remained at the heart of the cloud; they'd be caught within the blast-hazard radius. For all they knew, the matter/antimatter reaction set off by a standard torpedo could harm the *Enterprise* more than the Calamarain.

He'd have to hold back on the torpedoes until he put some distance between the ship and its noncorporeal adversaries.

On the main viewer, riotous swells of ionized gas convulsed between the ship and open space. Riker didn't remember the cloud looking anywhere near this stirred up the first time the *Enterprise* encountered the Calamarain several years ago. He still didn't understand what they had done to agitate the amorphous entities. Q wasn't even aboard anymore!

His temples throbbed in time with the thunder outside. His gaze darted over to Deanna, who looked like she was having an even harder time. Her eyes were shut, her face wan and drawn. He assumed she was still in touch with the Calamarains' pain and anger, and it tore at his heart to see her under such strain. Between the tumult on the bridge and the damage they had inflicted back on their foes, Deanna was getting lambasted from both sides.

Hold on, imzadi, he thought. *No matter what happens next, this can't go on much longer.*

Her lids flickered upward and she met his eyes. A thin smile lifted her lips. Riker knew that even if his actual words hadn't gotten across to her, his message definitely had. There was a Klingon term, he recalled, for such an instance of wordless communication in the midst of battle, but what exactly was the word again? *Tova'dok.* That was it, he recalled. He and Deanna were sharing a moment of *Tova'dok.*

Their private communion did not last long. With renewed ferocity, the unleashed power of the Calamarain slammed into the ship, causing the bridge to lurch to port. Behind him, at the engineering station, Ensign Schultz lost his balance and tumbled to the left, smacking his head into the archway over a turbolift entrance. Berglund hurried to assist him.

"Everyone okay back there?" Riker called out over the crashing thunder.

"I think so," Schultz answered. Riker glanced back

over his shoulder to see a nasty cut on the young man's scalp. A trickle of blood leaked through his fingers as he held his hand to his head. Undaunted, Schultz headed back to his post. Riker admired his spirit, but saw no reason to risk the ensign unnecessarily.

"Report to sickbay, mister," Riker ordered. "Berglund, take over at engineering." The overhead lights dimmed momentarily, more evidence of the duress imposed on the ship by the Calamarain; Ensign Schultz wasn't the only resource on the *Enterprise* that had been knocked out of commission.

"Shields at forty-one," Leyoro updated him as Schultz took the turbolift from the bridge. Riker wished he could have sent someone with the wounded ensign to insure that he got to sickbay, but he couldn't spare anyone from the bridge while they remained besieged by the Calamarain.

"Understood," he said. No warp engines. Minimal shields. And, so far, no significant damage to the Calamarain. Their situation was getting worse by the moment. "Data, how are you doing on that translator?"

Data looked up from his computations. "Significant headway has been made; in fact, I believe I have identified a specific wave pattern that translates to something close to an expression of pain." His voice acquired a regretful tone. "Unfortunately, I estimate that I still require as much as one-point-two-zero hours before I can reliably guarantee actual communication with the Calamarain."

That might not be good enough, Riker thought.

Before he could open his mouth, though, he heard the turbolift whish open behind him. At first, he thought it might be Robert Schultz, stubbornly refusing to abandon his post, but then he heard the impassioned voice of Professor Faal. "What's happening?" he asked frantically. "What are you doing?"

Damn, Riker thought. This was the last thing he needed. Deanna looked distressed as well by the Betazoid scientist's unexpected arrival. He peeked at Deanna, recalling her concerns about the doctor's stability and motives. She raised one hand before her face, as if to fend off the disruptive emotions emanating from Faal. *No surprise there,* Riker thought. He imagined that the professor was throwing off plenty of negative feelings.

A moment later, the turbolift doors opened again, revealing an abashed Reg Barclay. "I'm s-sorry, Commander," he stammered, his Adam's apple bobbing nervously, "but the professor insisted, sort of." His eyes bulged and his jaw fell open as his gaze fell upon the frothing plasma storm upon the main viewer.

"Yes," Faal seconded. His face was flushed, his wild brown eyes crazed with anxiety. "I have to talk to you, Commander. It's more important than you can possibly realize."

"Commander?" Leyoro asked, still determined to engage the enemy despite the lack of any tangible results. The nonstop reverberations of the Calamarain rolled over the bridge like a series of sonic booms. The red alert signals flashed like beacons in the night.

Riker decided to get the confrontation over with; Faal wasn't going to like what he had to say, but perhaps he could be made to see reason. He rose from the captain's chair to face the celebrated physicist. Faal's body was trembling so hard that Riker feared for his health. The man's breathing was shallow and rapid, and he seemed to be having trouble standing; Faal tottered unsteadily on shaky feet. Riker's hand drifted over his comm badge, ready to summon Dr. Crusher if necessary.

"I regret to inform you, Professor, that I've made the decision to abandon the experiment due to hostile activity on the part of the Calamarain." He saw no reason to alarm the doctor by detailing the full particulars of their danger; instead, he reached out to brace up the ailing scientist. "I'm sorry, but that's the only prudent choice under the circumstances."

Faal batted Riker's arm away. "You can't do that!" he snapped. "It's completely unacceptable. I won't hear of it. The captain's orders came straight from Starfleet Command." A fit of coughing attacked Faal, bending him all the way over. Faal dosed himself with his ubiquitous hypospray, then staggered over to the empty chair Riker usually occupied and collapsed down onto it. "The barrier," he gasped. "That's all that matters."

The floor beneath Riker's boots tilted sharply, nearly knocking him off balance. Lightning flashed through the storming plasma cloud upon the main viewer, the glare of the thunderbolt so bright that it overloaded the safety filters on the screen and made him squint. "The Calamarain seem to disagree."

"Then destroy them!" Faal urged from the chair, squinting at the control panel in front of him as if he was determined to launch a volley of photo torpedoes himself. Wet, mucous noises escaped from his lungs. "Disintegrate them totally. This is a Federation starship. You must be able to dispose of a pile of stinking gases!"

Riker was shocked by the man's bloodthirsty ravings. "That's not what we're here for," he said forcefully, "and that's not what this ship is about." He pitied Faal for his failing health and frustrated ambitions, but that didn't condone advocating genocide. "Mr. Barclay, return Professor Faal to his quarters."

"No!" Faal wheezed. He tried to stand up, but his legs wouldn't support him. Barclay hurried around to Faal's side, but Faal just glared at him before shouting at Riker again. "I won't go! I demand to be heard!"

"Shields down to thirty-four percent," Leyoro interrupted. "Shall I call Security to remove the professor?"

"Do it," Riker ordered. Lieutenant Barclay, wringing his hands together, looked like he wanted to sink through the floor. Riker turned his back on both the irate scientist and the embarrassed crewman. He had more important things to deal with.

Like saving the *Enterprise*.

Chapter Thirteen

COOL NIGHT AIR BLEW against Picard, chilling him. Far beneath him, moonlight from no less than two orbiting satellites reflected off the shimmering surface of a great expanse of water. *Where am I?* he thought, trying to orient himself.

He and Q were no longer in the subatomic realm they had exited only a heartbeat before, that much was certain. Without even knowing where he truly was, he could tell that this was more like reality as he knew it. The coolness of the breeze, the taste of the air, the comforting tug of gravity at his feet, all these sensations assured him that he was back in the real world once more. But where and, perhaps more important, when?

He quickly took stock of his surroundings. He, along with Q, appeared to be standing on some sort of balcony overlooking a precipitous cliff face that dropped what looked like a kilometer or so to the still black waters of an enormous lake or lagoon. The balcony itself, as green and lustrous as polished jade, seemed carved out of the very substance of the cliff. As Picard leaned out over the edge of a waist-high jade railing, intricately adorned with elaborate filigree, he saw that similar outcroppings dotted the face of the precipice, each one packed with humanoid figures, some looking out over the edge as he was, others dining comfortably at small tables as though at some fashionable outdoor café. A sense of excitement and anticipation, conveyed by the hubbub of a hundred murmuring voices, permeated the atmosphere. Picard got the distinct impression that he and Q had arrived just in time for some special occasion.

Jade cliffs. Two moons. A gathering of hundreds in caves dug out of the face of a great, green cliff. The pieces came together in his mind, forming a picture whose implications left him reeling. *"Mon dieu!"* he gasped. "This is Tagus III. The sacred ruins of the ancient cliff dwellers!"

"Well, they're not exactly ruins at the moment, Jean-Luc," Q said casually, "nor are they really all that ancient." Picard's self-appointed tour guide sat a few meters behind him at a circular table set for two. Q sipped a bubbling orange liquid from a translucent crystal goblet and gestured toward the empty seat across from him. A second goblet rested on the jade-inlaid tabletop, next to a large copper plate on which were displayed strips of raw meat, swimming in a shallow pool of blue liquid that could have been sauce or gravy or blood for all Picard knew. He didn't recognize the delicacy, nor did he expect to if this alien time and place was truly what it appeared to be.

The jade pueblos of Tagus III, he marveled, *as they must have been nearly two billion years ago.* He had studied them for years, even delivered the keynote speech at an archaeological conference devoted to the topic, but he had never expected to witness them in person, let alone in their original condition. The Taguans of his own time had strictly forbidden any outsiders to visit the ruins, keeping them off-limits to archaeologists and other visitors ever since the Vulcans conducted their own ill-fated dig on the site over a decade before. The ban had frustrated a generation of scholars and historians, including Picard himself, for whom the celebrated ruins remained one of the foremost archaeological mysteries in the Alpha Quadrant. Possibly the oldest evidence of humanoid civilization in the galaxy, at least prior to the ground-breaking and still controversial work of the late Professor Richard Galen, the ruins on Tagus III had provoked literally millennia of debate and speculation. Before the Taguans decided to deny the site to offworlders, there had been at least 947 known excavations, the first one dating back to 22,000 years ago, almost 18,000 years before the rise of human civilization on Earth. The legacy of the ancient beings who first made their mark on this very cliff had puzzled and intrigued the galaxy since before human history began.

And here he was, visiting in the flesh a wonder of immeasurable age that he had read about ever since he was a small child in Labarre. Picard recalled that once before Q had offered to show him the secrets of Tagus III, the night before Picard was to speak at that prestigious archaeological conference. Seldom had he ever been so tempted by one of Q's insidious propositions, although he had ultimately found the strength to reject Q's offer, both out of respect for the Taguans' deeply held convictions and his own habitual suspicions as to Q's true motives. He'd be lying to himself, however, if he didn't admit just how enticing the prospect of actually setting foot on the site had been.

Now that he really was here, he could not resist trying to absorb as many sights and sounds as he was able. No matter the circumstances of his arrival, and despite his compelling desire to return to his ship as expeditiously as possible, the archaeologist in him could have no more turned away from this once-in-a-lifetime opportunity than the starship captain could have accepted a desk job at the bottom of a gravity well. He had to witness all there was to see.

Besides, he rationalized, the Taguans' twenty-fourth-century mandate against visiting aliens would not go into effect for a couple of billion years or so. . . .

He took a closer look at the people crowding the balconies beside and below him. Whether the Taguans of his own time were actually descended from those who had left their presence marked upon these cliffs, as they steadfastly maintained, or whether they represented a subsequent stage of immigration or evolution, as suggested by the findings of the Vulcan expedition of 2351, was a question greatly debated in the archaeological community. Indeed, it was this very issue that had inspired the modern Taguans to close off the ruins to outsiders, in an attempt to protect their vaunted heritage from the "lies and fallacies" of non-Taguan researchers.

Judging from what he saw now, it appeared that the Vulcans were correct after all. The Taguans he knew were characterized by turquoise skin and a heavy layer of downy white fur. In contrast, the figures populating this historical vista, clad in revealing silk garments of diverse hues, looked quite hairless, with smooth, uncovered flesh whose skin tones ranged from a pale yellow to a deep, ruddy red. Their faces were remarkably undifferentiated from each other, bearing only the essential basics of humanoid features, without much in the way of distinguishing details. Two eyes, a nose, a mouth, a vague suggestion of lips and ears. The vague, generalized visages looked familiar to Picard, but it took him a moment to place them.

Of course, he realized after a quick search through his memory. The inhabitants of ancient Tagus bore a distinct resemblance to the unnamed humanoids who had first spread their genetic material throughout the galaxy some four billion years before his own era. He well remembered the holographic image of the original, ur-humanoid who had greeted him at the completion of his quest to finish the work of Professor Galen. Could it be that the people of the jade cliffs were the direct descendants of those ancient beings who had indirectly contributed to the eventual evolution of the human race, the Klingons, the Vulcans, the Cardassians, and every other known form of humanoid life? If so, then the ruins on modern-day Tagus were even more important than he had ever believed.

A thought occurred to him, and he turned from the railing to address Q, who took another sip from his goblet. "Why aren't they noticing us?" Picard asked. He explored his own very human features with his hand. They felt unchanged. Looking down, he felt relieved to see that his Grecian garments had been replaced by his familiar Starfleet uniform. "We must stand out in the crowd. In theory, Homo sapiens has not even evolved yet."

"To their eyes, we look as they do," Q explained. He drained the last of his drink, then refilled the cup simply by looking at it. "Given your own limited ability to adapt to new forms, I'm letting you stick with the persona you're accustomed to. I hope you appreciate my consideration."

"But this is what the ancient Taguans looked like?" Picard asked, gesturing at the crowds swarming over the cliff face.

"Actually, they called themselves the Imotru," Q stated, "but, yes, this is no illusion or metaphor. Aside from you and I, you're seeing things exactly as they were." Q's face remolded itself until he looked like another Imotru. Only the mischievous glint in his eyes remained the same. "See what I mean?" He blinked, and his customary features returned.

The peal of an enormous gong rang across the night, and a hush fell over the scene as the buzz of countless conversations fell silent. Picard could feel a sense of acute expectation come over the scene, drawing him back to the railing overlooking the great lake. Something was obviously about to happen; the teeming throng of Imotru assembled along the cliff were waiting eagerly for whatever was to come.

A spark of light way down upon the surface of the lagoon caught his attention. Picard heard a hundred mouths gasp in anticipation. A moment later, a string of torches ignited above the black, moonlit water, their flames reflected in a series of mirrors arranged around the torches, which formed a hexagonal pattern, cordoning off an open stretch of water, about seventy meters across, in the direct center of the dark lake. The polished mirrors reflected the light inward so that this single swatch of rippling water was illuminated as if by the afternoon sun, while the rest of the lagoon remained cast in shadow. A single swimmer, holding aloft the glowing brand she must have used to light the torches, floated amid the brightly lit pool she had created. With a dramatic flourish, she doused the brand to a smattering of cheers and stamping feet.

Was that it? Picard thought, peering down at the lighted hexagon demarcated by the torches and mirrors. Based on the crowd's reaction, he suspected not. There was still that keen sense of anticipation in the air, an almost palpable atmosphere of mounting excitement. Somehow he knew that what he had just witnessed was merely a prelude, not the main event.

Most of the assembled Imotru, he observed, were now looking upward, eagerly searching the moonlit sky for . . . what? An image from an ancient jade bas-relief, meticulously reproduced in the Federation database, popped into his head just as a thrilling possibility presented itself. *No,* he thought, disbelieving his own good fortune, *surely we couldn't have arrived in time for that!*

A roar rose from the crowd. Dozens of seated

Imotru leaped to their feet, including Q, who joined Picard by the railing. "Look up, Jean-Luc," he whispered. "Here they come."

Picard needed no urging. He strained his eyes to spot the sight that had electrified the assemblage, the sight whose true nature he could scarcely bring himself to believe. *It must be them,* he thought. *It couldn't be anything else, not here in this place and time.*

Sure enough, his eyes soon discerned a flock of winged figures on the horizon, soaring toward them. The Imotru cheered and stomped their feet so heavily that Picard feared for the safety of the jade balconies, even though he knew that some of them had endured even into the twenty-fourth century. He found himself stamping his own boots, caught up in the fervor of the crowd. The winged figures drew ever nearer, much to the delight of the onlookers upon the cliff. "They've been gliding for two full days," Q commented, "since taking flight from the peak of Mount T'kwll."

Picard no longer doubted what he was about to behold. He could only marvel at the amazing twist of fate that had granted him this unparalleled chance to see a timeworn legend made flesh. "The fabled Sky Divers of Tagus III," he whispered, his voice hushed. If this was no mere trick of Q's, then he was about to make the most astounding archaeological discovery since Benjamin Sisko found the lost city of B'hala on Bajor.

Within moments, the fliers were near enough that he could see that, as he had hoped, they were in fact dozens of youthful Imotru men and women, borne aloft by artificial wings strapped to their outstretched arms. Silver and gold metallic streamers trailed from their wrists and ankles, sparkling in the moonlight. Were the wings made of some unusual gravity-resistant substance, Picard wondered, or were the Imotru lighter than they appeared, perhaps gifted with hollow bones like birds? Either way, they presented a spectacular sight, silhouetted against the twin moons or glittering in the night like humanoid kites.

The Sky Divers soared overhead, swooping and gliding in complex feats of aerial choreography. Each flier, he saw, gripped a shining blade in one hand, just as they did on the fragmentary bas-relief Picard now recalled so well. Despite the graceful ballet taking place above, his gaze was invariably drawn back to the dark waters at the base of the cliff—and the lighted regions within the radiance of the torches and mirrors. He felt his heart pounding, knowing what had to come next. His eyes probed the rippling surface of the lake, hunting for some sign of what lurked beneath. *Perhaps that part of the legend is just a myth,* he thought, unsure whether to feel disappointed or relieved. Professor Galen, he recalled, had theorized that the Sky Divers were no more than a symbolic representation of cultural growth and entropy.

Then it began. A single flier, chosen through some process Picard could only guess at, used his silver blade to sever the straps binding him to his wings while the crowd below bellowed its approval. The shed wings drifted away aimlessly, slowly spiraling down like falling leaves, as the young Imotru plunged toward the water below with frightening speed.

Trailing golden ribbons behind him, the diver splashed headfirst into the lake below, landing squarely within the brightly lit boundaries of the hexagon. On a hundred balconies, Imotru whooped and stamped wildly. Things had clearly gotten off to a good start as far the crowd was concerned. Down in the hexagon, the triumphant diver kicked to the surface and impulsively embraced the lone swimmer who had waited there. His joy and exuberance were obvious to Picard even from more than a kilometer away.

One by one, following some prearranged signal or sequence, more gliders fell from the sky. The second diver used her arms and legs to guide her descent, also landing safely within the torch-lit target zone. The audience cheered again, although slightly less whole-heartedly than they had before. Still, the woman joined the other two Imotru in their celebration, splashing happily within the golden glow of reflected light.

The third diver looked less fortunate, his downward trajectory carrying him away from the charmed hexagon. Too late, he threw out his arms and legs, striving to alter his course, but his efforts were in vain. The entire crowd held its breath, and, for a second or two, Picard feared the young man would be scorched by the dancing flames of the torches.

Before he came within reach of the flames, however, an enormous serpentine head broke the surface of the black waters and snapped at the falling youth. Water streamed off its scaly hide and a slitted yellow eye fixed on the falling youth. A forked, sinuous tongue, larger than a man's arm, flicked at the sky. Ivory fangs flashed in the moonlight and Picard saw a splash of azure blood burst from the diver before both predator and prey disappeared beneath the waves churned up by the creature's shocking appearance.

Just like on the jade artifact, Picard thought, saddened but not too surprised by what had transpired. Apparently the myth of the Sky Divers was all too true, up to and including the Teeth of the Depths. *So much for mere symbolic interpretations,* he thought.

And still the gliders cut their wings free, undeterred by the grisly fate of their cohort. Toward the waiting lake they dropped like Icarus, some attempting to steer their falls, others simply trusting to fate. Looking carefully, Picard saw more reptilian heads rising from the murky waters outside the protective torches, drawn no doubt by the scent of blood and the splashing of the defenseless bodies. Only within the illuminated hexagon did the divers appear to be safe. Those who hit the water within its confines floated merrily, crowing and cavorting as only those who have barely escaped death can rejoice. Those who plummeted beyond the light of the torches were quickly dragged under by the voracious predators.

"The trick," Q said casually, as though discussing some minor athletic competition, "is to miss the flames and the snapping jaws. The faster the fall, the greater the risk—and the glory." He applauded softly, whether for the divers or the serpents Picard was afraid to guess. "Like I told you a few years back, they really knew how to have fun here back in the good old days." Wandering back toward the table, Q plucked a strip of raw meat from the copper plate and tossed it over the edge of the balcony. As Picard watched aghast, similar scraps flew from balconies all around him, so it looked like it was raining blue, bleeding strips of meat. "The treats are to distract the snakes from the divers," Q explained, "or to incite the snakes to an even greater frenzy. I can't remember which."

Rather than watch the fierce serpents claim their prey, Picard focused on the jubilant survivors within the hexagon. "They're safe now," he said, "but how will they escape from the lake?"

"Oh, the snakes are strictly nocturnal," Q told him. "They'll be able to swim to shore in the morning, after what will undoubtedly be the greatest night of their lives."

Picard was unable to tear his gaze away from the barbaric spectacle. Before his eyes, what seemed like an unending string of young people gambled with their lives, some joining the riotous celebration within the six-sided sanctuary, others torn asunder by the hungry serpents. To cope with the awful and awe-inspiring pageant, he forced himself to think like an archaeologist. "What is this?" he asked. "A religious sacrifice? An initiation rite? A means of population control?" Turning away from the rail, he confronted Q. "What in heaven's name is the purpose of this appalling display?"

"Don't be so stuffy, Jean-Luc," Q said, offering

Picard a strip of meat dripping with blue gore. Picard refused to even look at the edible. With a sigh, Q tossed it off the balcony himself. "They do it for the thrill. For the sheer excitement. It's all in fun."

Picard tried to grasp the notion. "You're saying this is simply some form of sports or theater? A type of public entertainment?"

"Now you're getting closer," Q confirmed. "Think of the matadors or bull dancers of your own meager history. Or the *'Iwghargh* rituals of the Klingons. With a slightly higher body count, of course."

It was almost too much to digest. Deep in thought, Picard pulled out a chair and sat down opposite Q. "This is fascinating, I admit, and, you're right, no worse than various bloodthirsty chapters of early human history. The gladiatorial violence of the Roman coliseums, say, or the human sacrifices of the ancient Aztecs. I can't say I regret having viewed this event. Still, seeing it in person, it's hard not to be appalled by the profligate waste of life."

"But you short-lived mortals have always taken the most extraordinary and foolish risks to your brief existences," Q said. "Diving off cliffs, performing trapeze acts without a net, flying fragile starships into the galactic barrier . . ."

Q's coy reference to the *Enterprise* jolted Picard, yanking the status of his ship back into the forefront of his consciousness. Never mind this time-lost scenario, what was happening to Riker and his crew back in his own era, and how soon was this game of Q's likely to end? "Is that why we're here?" he asked, thinking that perhaps he had seen through Q's current agenda. "It seems rather a roundabout way to make your point."

"If only it were that easy," Q replied, "but that diverting little entertainment out there is far from the most important event transpiring at this particular moment in time. Permit me to call your attention to that individual dining on that balcony over there." Q pointed past Picard at a jade outcropping located several meters to the left, where he saw a solitary Imotru watch in fascination as the Sky Divers tempted fate with their death-defying descents. "Recognize him?"

What? Q's question puzzled Picard. How could he be expected to recognize a being who had died billions of years before he was born? "He's Imotru, obviously, but beyond that I don't see anything familiar about him."

Q looked exasperated. "Really, Picard, you can be astonishingly dim sometimes." He rolled up his sleeves and extended both hands toward the figure on the other balcony. He wiggled his fingers as if casting a spell. "Perhaps this will make things easier."

Wavy brown hair sprouted from the Imotru's shining skull, but he appeared not to notice. His features remolded themselves, becoming more human in appearance, even as he continued to observe the divers as if nothing were happening. His eyebrows darkened, his lips grew more pronounced, until Picard found himself staring at a very familiar acquaintance, albeit one still clad in Imotru garb. "It's you," he said to Q. "You were disguised as an Imotru."

"I'm disguised every time we meet," Q pointed out. "Surely, you understand that my true form no more resembles a human being than it does an Imotru."

So we're still exploring Q's own past, Picard realized. Examining the scene, he saw that the other Q looked noticeably younger than the Q who had brought him here, although not nearly as youthful as the boyish Q who had toyed with antimatter in the micro-universe. This Q had left adolescence behind and seemed in the first full flush of adulthood, however those terms applied to entities such as Q. He appeared utterly riveted by the grisly extravaganza put on by the Imotru, lifting a scrap of blue meat from his plate and nibbling on it experimentally while his eyes tracked each and every plunge. The expression on his face, Picard discerned, looked wistful and faintly envious.

"This was the first time I had ever seen anything like this," the older Q said, "but not the last. I came every year for millennia, until their civilization crumbled, the Imotru gradually succumbed to extinction, and the Sky Divers became nothing more than a half-forgotten myth." He watched himself watching the divers. "But it was never quite the same."

"Did you always come alone?" Picard asked. It occurred to him how seldom the young Q seemed to interact with others of his kind. *When I was his age, relatively speaking,* he thought, *I thrived on the company of my friends: Marta, Cortin, Jenice, Jack Crusher . . .*

"Funny you should mention that, Jean-Luc," Q responded, throwing their last shred of blue meat to the serpents. He snapped his fingers and both he and Picard were gone before the bloody scrap even reached the water.

Interlude

THE RED ALERT ALARMS did not go off in the guest quarters, so as not to panic unnecessarily any civilian passengers, but Milo Faal did not need to see any flashing colored lights to know that something was happening. He could sense the tension in the minds of the crew, as he could see the raging plasma storm outside his window and feel the tremors every time the thunder boomed around them.

Milo did his best not to look or think afraid in front of his little sister. Kinya was too young to understand all that was occurring. The little girl stood on her tiptoes, her nose and palms glued to the transparent window, captivated by the spectacular show of light and sound. Milo couldn't look away from the storm, either. He stood behind Kinya with one hand on the arm of a chair and the other one on his sister's shoulder, just in case she lost her balance, while he tried to figure out what was going on.

Most of the crew members whose thoughts he latched on to did not know much more than he did about the churning cloud outside, but he got the idea from some of them that the cloud was actually alive. Did that mean the storm was shaking them around on purpose? He could not repress a shudder at the thought, which transferred itself empathically to Kinya's tiny frame, which begin to tremble on its own, even if the little girl was not consciously aware of the source of the anxiety. "Milo," she asked, looking back over her shoulder, "what's wrong?"

"Nothing," he fibbed, but another sudden lurch said otherwise. A half-completed jigsaw puzzle, featuring a striking illustration of a Klingon bird-of-prey, slid off a nearby end table, the plastic pieces spilling onto the carpet. Milo had spent close to an hour working on the puzzle, but he barely noticed the undoing of his efforts. He had more important things to worry about.

Where are you, Dad? he called out telepathically. Lightning flashed on the other side of the window, throwing a harsh glare over the living room. *Dad?* he called again, but his father might as well have been back on Betazed for all the good it did.

Taking Kinya by the hand, and stretching his other arm out in front of him to break any falls, he led her across the living room toward the suite's only exit. If his father would not come to them, he thought, then he was getting pretty tempted to go find their dad. The *Enterprise* was a huge ship, he knew, but it couldn't be too hard to locate Engineering, could it? Anything was better than just sitting around in the quaking guest quarters, wondering what to do next.

He and Kinya approached the double doors leading outside, but the heavy metal sheets refused to slide apart. "Warning," the voice of the ship's computer said. "Passengers are requested to stay within their quarters until further notice. In the event of an emergency, you will be notified where to proceed."

Milo stared in disbelief at the frozen doors. *In the event of an emergency . . . ?* He glanced back at the seething mass of destructive plasma pounding against the hull. If this wasn't an emergency, then what in the name of the Sacred Chalice was it? And how come Dad wasn't stuck here, too?

"Dad?" Kinya picked up on his thoughts. "Where's Daddy, Milo?"

I wish I knew, he thought.

Chapter Fourteen

IT TOOK PICARD A SECOND or two to realize that he and Q had relocated once again, although none too far. The jade cliffs remained intact. The Sky Divers continued their daring plunges to salvation or doom. Even the cool of the evening breeze felt much the same as before. Then he observed that their vantage point had shifted by several degrees; they now occupied another balcony, one perched about ten or eleven meters above their previous locale. "I don't understand," he told Q. "Why have we moved? What else is there to see here?"

"Ignore the floor show," Q advised, "and look at the audience." He lifted an empty saucer from the table and set it glowing like a beacon in the night, using it as a spotlight to call Picard's attention to one specific balcony below them. There Picard saw once more the solitary figure of the youthful Q, enraptured by the life-and-death drama of the ancient Imotru ritual. Before Picard could protest that he had already witnessed this particular episode in Q's life, the beam shifted to another balcony, where Picard was stunned to see both himself and the older Q watching the younger Q intently. "Look familiar?" his companion asked. Speechless, Picard could now only nod numbly. *What is it about Q,* he lamented silently, *that he so delights in twisting time into knots?*

But Q was not finished yet. The spotlight moved once again, darting over the face of the cliff until it fell upon a young Imotru couple dining on a balcony several meters to the right of Picard and Q's new whereabouts. Or at least they looked like Imotru; the harsh white glare of the searching beam penetrated their attempt at camouflage, exposing them to be none other than the young Q one more time, as well as a female companion of similarly human appearance. "It's you," Picard gasped, "and that woman." Although noticeably younger than Picard recalled, the other Q's companion was manifestly the same individual who had recently visited the *Enterprise,* two billion years in the future.

Picard's mind struggled to encompass all he was confronted with. Counting the smirking being seated across from him, there were, what, *four* different versions of Q present at this same moment in time? Not to mention at least two Picards. He kneaded his brow with his fingers; as captain of the *Enterprise,* he had coped with similar paradoxes before, including that time he had to stop himself from destroying the ship, but that didn't make them any easier to deal with. The human mind, he was convinced, was never designed with time travel in mind.

Still, he had no choice but to make the best of it. "What are you and she doing over there?" he asked, contemplating the couple highlighted by the glow of the spotlight.

"If you're referring to my future wife," the Q at his table said, "her name is Q." He beamed at the oblivious couple. "As for what is transpiring, can't you recognize a romantic evening when you see one?"

"I'm not sure I'm prepared to cope with the concept of you dating, Q," Picard said dryly. "Why are we here? Is it absolutely imperative that I share this moment with you?"

"Trust me, Jean-Luc," Q assured him, "all will become clear in time." Another goblet of liquid refreshment occupied the center of the table. Q finished off a cup of orange elixir, then placed the crystal goblet on the tabletop between him and Picard. He tapped the rim of the cup, producing a ringing tone. "Let's listen in, shall we?"

A pair of voices rose from the cup, as though the goblet had somehow become some sort of audio receiver. The voice of the younger Q was unmistakable, although surprisingly sincere in tone. Picard heard none of the self-satisfied smugness he associated with the Q of his own time.

He (eagerly): "Isn't it amazing? Didn't I tell you how wondrous this is? Primitive, corporeal life, risking everything for one infinitesimal moment of glory. Look, the snakes got another one! Bravo, bravo."

She (faintly scandalized): "But it's so very aboriginal. You should be ashamed of yourself, Q. Sometimes I wonder why I associate with you at all."

He (disappointed): "Oh. I was sure you, of all Q's, would understand. Don't you see, it's their very primitiveness that makes it so moving? They're just sentient enough to make their own choices, decide their own destinies." He stared gloomily into his own cup. "At least they know what they want to do with their lives. Nothing's restraining them except their own limitations as a species."

She (conciliatory): "Well, maybe it's not entirely dismal. I like the way the moonlight sparkles on the reptiles, especially when their jaws snap." She placed a hand over his. "What's really bothering you, Q? You're young, immortal, all-powerful . . . a touch undisciplined, but still a member of the Continuum, the pinnacle of physical and psychic evolution. What could be better?"

He (wistful): "It's just that . . . well, I feel so frustrated sometimes. What's the good of having all this power, if I don't know what to do with it? Merely maintaining the fundamental stability of the multiverse isn't enough for me. I want to do something bold, something magnificent, maybe even something a little bit dangerous. Like those foolish, fearless humanoids out there, throwing themselves into gravity's clutches. But every time I try anything the least bit creative, the Continuum comes down on me like a ton of dark matter. 'No, no, Q, you mustn't do that. It's not proper. It's not seemly. It violates the Central Canons of the Continuum. . . .' Sometimes the whole thing makes me sick."

For a second, Picard experienced a twinge of guilt over eavesdropping on the young Q's this way. It felt more than a little improper. Then he remembered how little Q had respected his own privacy over the years, even spying on his romantic encounters with Vash, and his compunctions dissolved at a remarkable rate.

She (consoling, but uncertain): "Every Q feels that way at times." A long pause. "Well, no, they don't actually, but I'm sure you do." She made an effort to cheer the other Q up, looking out at the plummeting Imotru. "Look, two reptiles are fighting over that skinny specimen over there." She shuddered and averted her eyes. "Their table manners are utterly atrocious!"

He (appreciative, aiming to lighten the mood): "You know, I don't think you're half as shocked as you make yourself out to be. You've got an unevolved streak as well, which is why like you."

She (huffily): "There's no reason to be insulting." She spun her chair around and refused to look at him.

He (hastily): "No, I didn't mean it that way!" Materializing a pair of wineglasses out of thin air, along with a bottle of some exotic violet liqueur, he poured the woman a libation and held it out to her. Glancing back over her shoulder, her slim back still turned on Q, she inspected the gift dubiously. Q plucked a bouquet of incandescent yellow tulips from the ether. "Really, Q, you know how much I respect and admire you."

She (ominously, like one withdrawing a hidden weapon): "Just me?"

He (uncomfortably): "Um, whatever do you mean?"

She (going in for the kill): "I mean that cheeky little demi-goddess out by Antares. Don't think I didn't hear about you and her commingling on the ninth astral plane. I am omniscient, you know. I wasn't going to mention it, presuming I was above such petty behavior, but since you think I'm so unevolved . . . !"

He (defensive): "What would I be doing on the ninth astral plane? This has to be a case of mistaken cosmology. It wasn't me, it was Q. Why, I barely know that deity."

She (unconvinced): "And a fertility spirit, no less! Really, Q, I thought you had better taste than that."

He (desperate): "I do, I do, I promise. I was only trying to broaden my horizons a bit, explore another point of view. . . ." He offered her a strip of succulent meat. "Here, why don't you try feeding the serpents?"

She (chillingly): "I think I want to go home."

Picard laughed out loud. It was almost worth traveling back in time to hear Q put on the spot like this. "That reminds me," he said to the Q sitting across from him, "back during that business in Sherwood Forest, you gave me quite a bad time about my feelings for Vash. You described love as a weakness, and berated me constantly about being 'brought down by a woman,' as I believe you put it." He cocked his head toward the quarreling couple on the next balcony. "I must confess I find your own domestic situation, both here and back on the *Enterprise,* more than a little ironic."

"Don't be ridiculous," the older Q retorted. "You can't possibly compare your farcical mammalian liaisons with the communion, or lack thereof, between two highly advanced intelligences. They're entirely different situations."

"I see," Picard said skeptically, contemplating the scene on the adjacent balcony, where the female Q had just conspicuously turned her back on her companion. "As we ridiculous mammals like to say, tell me another one."

The voices from the goblet argued on, lending more credence to Picard's position. He savored the sound of the younger Q losing ground by the moment.

He: "Fine, go back to the Continuum. See if I care!"

She: "You'd like that, wouldn't you? More time to spend with that pantheistic strumpet of yours. No, on second thought, I'm not going anywhere. And neither are you."

He: "Try and stop me."

She: "Don't you dare!"

Picard eyed Q across the jade tabletop. "Advanced intelligences, you said? I am positively awestruck by your spiritual and intellectual communion. You were quite correct, Q. This excursion is proving more illuminating that I ever dreamed."

"I knew this was a bad idea," Q muttered, a saturnine expression on his face. "I could hardly expect you to sympathize with the perfectly excusable follies of my youth."

Picard showed him no mercy. "I have to ask: what did your ladyfriend over there think of your short-lived partnership with Vash?"

"That?" Q said dismissively. "That lasted a mere blink of an eye by our standards. It was nothing. Less than nothing even." He shrugged his shoulders, remembering. "She was livid."

More livid than she sounds now? Picard wondered. That was hard to imagine.

He: "I should have known you wouldn't appreciate any of this. None of you can."

She: "Maybe that's because the rest of us are perfectly happy being Q. But if that's not good enough for you, then I don't belong here either."

With an emphatic flash, the female Q vanished from the scene, leaving the young Q just as alone as his even younger counterpart a few balconies below. "Our first fight," an older Q explained, "but far from our last."

The abandoned Q looked so dejected that, despite Picard's well-earned animosity toward the being sitting opposite him, he felt a touch of sympathy for the unhappy young Q. "No one understands," he muttered into his cup, completely unaware that his private heartbreak was being transmitted straight to Picard's table. "Just once, why can't I meet someone who understands me?"

His older self looked on with pity and regret. "I believe you mortals have a saying or two," he observed, "about the danger of getting what you wished for." He sighed and pushed the talking goblet away from him. "Too bad you wouldn't coin those little words of wisdom for another billion years or so."

A moment later, the balcony was empty.

Chapter Fifteen

LEM FAAL WAS NOT ABOUT to leave the bridge quietly. "I'm warning you, Commander Riker, you'll regret interfering with this operation. My work is my life, and I'm not going to let that go to waste because of a coward who doesn't have guts enough to fight for our one chance to break through the barrier."

"Perhaps," Riker answered, losing patience with the Betazoid physicist despite his tragic illness, "you should worry more about the safety of your children and less about your sacred experiment."

Summoned by Lieutenant Leyoro, a pair of security officers flanked Faal, but the scientist kept protesting even as they forcibly led him toward a turbolift. Claps of thunder from the Calamarain punctuated his words. "Don't lecture me about my children, Riker. Sometimes evolution is more important than mere propagation."

What exactly does he mean by that, Riker wondered. Surely he couldn't be saying what Riker thought he was implying? *Faal's starting to make my*

217

dad sound like father of the year. Even Kyle Riker, hardly the most attentive of parents, never seemed quite so eager to sacrifice his children's well-being on the altar of his overweening ambition. Riker refused to waste any further breath debating the man. If it weren't for the failure of the warp engines, they would have already been long gone by now, whether Faal liked it or not.

The turbolift doors slid shut on Faal and his grim-faced escorts. Riker breathed a sigh of relief. "Mr. Barclay, please take over at the engineering station." Riker wasn't sure what precisely Barclay had to do with Faal's unexpected arrival on the bridge, but now that Barclay was here he might as well replace the injured Schultz.

Faal had no sooner left, however, when a blinding flare at the prow of the bridge augured the sudden return of the baby q. A second flare, instants later, brought the child's mother as well. "Sir?" Barclay asked uncertainly.

"You have your orders, Lieutenant," Riker said, aggravated by yet more unwanted visitors. When had the bridge of the *Enterprise* turned into the main terminal at Spacedock? "Can I help you?" he asked the woman in none too hospitable a tone. *Blast it, I was hoping we'd seen the last of these two.*

The toddler stared wide-eyed at the swirling colors of the Calamarain as they were displayed on the main viewer. "Frankly, I was in no hurry to revisit this ramshackle conveyance," the woman said disdainfully, "but little q insisted. He simply adores fireworks. Perhaps you could fire your energy weapons again?"

"Our phasers are not here to entertain you!" Leyoro snapped, offended by the suggestion. She took her weapons very seriously.

Riker didn't blame her. This was no laughing matter, although he hardly expected a Q to appreciate that. Things kept getting worse, no matter what they tried. A crackle of lightning etched its way across the screen, throwing off discharges of bright blue Cerenkov radiation wherever the electrical bursts intersected with the ship's deflector shields. The rattle of thunder was near-constant now; it almost seemed to Riker that the persistent vibrations had been with them forever. His determined gaze fell upon the female Q and her child. *Hmmm*, he thought. Both Barclay and Geordi seemed to find the malfunction in the warp nacelles pretty inexplicable. Well, he could think of few things more inexplicable than a Q.

He rose from his chair and strode toward the woman. "There wouldn't be any fireworks at all if we weren't dead in the water," he accused. "Is this your doing?"

"You mean your petty mechanical problems?" she replied. "Please, why would I want to go mucking about with the nuts and bolts of this primitive contrivance?" A Calamarain-generated earthquake shook the bridge, and q squealed merrily. "We're simply here as spectators."

Riker considered the female Q. Since her previous visit to the bridge, she had discarded her antique sports attire for a standard Starfleet uniform, as had the little boy. He wondered briefly what they had done in the interim. Did infant Q's require naps? More important, why would this Q want to prevent the *Enterprise* from leaving? The other Q had done nothing but encourage them to turn back.

"Maybe so," he conceded. It was entirely possible that the Calamarain were responsible for the failure of the *Enterprise*'s warp drive, in which case it was even more urgent that they find a way to communicate with the cloud-beings. "But you must know something about Captain Picard. What has your husband done with him?"

"Oh, not that again!" she said in a voice filled with exasperation. "First the doctor, now you. Really, can't you silly humanoids do without your precious captain for more than an interval or two? You'd think that none of you had ever flown a starship on your own."

"We don't want to do without the captain," Riker insisted, ignoring the woman's ridicule. She was sounding more like her mate every minute. "Wherever Q has taken him, he belongs here, on this ship at this moment."

The woman made a point of scanning the entire bridge, as if looking for some sign of Captain Picard's presence, then returned her attention to Riker. "That doesn't seem to be the case," she said with a smirk.

"Shields down to twenty-seven percent," Leyoro reported. A few meters away from Leyoro, a small electrical fire erupted at the aft science station. Ensign Berglund jumped back from the console just as the automatic fire-suppression system activated. A ceiling-mounted deflector cluster projected a discrete force-field around the flickering blaze, simultaneously protecting the surrounding systems from the flames and cutting off the fire's oxygen supply. Within seconds, the red and yellow flames were snuffed out and Berglund cautiously inspected the damage.

At least something's working right, Riker thought, grateful that the fire had been taken care of so efficiently. Now if he could only get the warp nacelles functioning again . . . ! *Maybe if we shoot our way out of here,* he thought, *without holding anything back?* "Lieutenant Leyoro, target the phaser beam directly in front of us, *maximum* intensity." He had held back long enough; the Calamarain needed to learn that they could not threaten a Starfleet vessel without risking serious repercussions. "If you can disengage from contact with the enemy, Counselor, now would be the time to do it."

She nodded back at him, acknowledging his warning. "Just give me a second," she said, closing her eyes for a heartbeat or two, then opening them once more. "Okay, I'm as prepared as I'll ever be."

"Fire when ready, Lieutenant," Riker ordered. He glared at the turbulent vapors upon the viewer. "I want to see the stars again."

"My feelings exactly," Leyoro agreed. A neon-red phaser beam ploughed through the seething chaos of the Calamarain, cutting an open swath through the iridescent vapors. Riker winced inwardly, hoping he was not burning through scores of Calamarain individuals. *Am I killing separate entities, or merely diminishing the mass of the whole?* He would have to ask Deanna later; right now he didn't want to know. Beside him, Troi bit down on her lower lip as the beam seared past swollen clouds filled with angry lightning, and gripped her armrests until her knuckles whitened; obviously, she had not been able to cut herself off entirely from the emotions of the Calamarain.

"Ooh!" q exclaimed, pointing enthusiastically at the screen. He stuck out his index fingers like gun muzzles, as little boys have done since the invention of firearms across the universe, and red-hot beams leaped from his fingertips to sear two burning holes in the visual display panel. Riker jumped out of his seat to protest, terrified that the playful child would create a hull breach beyond the screen. *Blast it,* he thought. *This is the last thing I need right now.*

Thankfully the female Q was on top of things. With a snap of her fingers, she squelched the child's imitative phaser beams and repaired the damage to the main viewer. "Now, now, darling," she cooed to the boy, "what have I told you about pointing?" Thus chastened, q meekly hid his tiny hands behind his back.

Blast it, Riker thought angrily. The last thing he needed right now were the two Q's and their antics, even though he seemed to be stuck with them. He sank back into the captain's chair and concentrated on the *Enterprise*'s efforts to carve out an escape route. As he had requested, Riker soon saw the welcoming darkness of open space at the far end of the tunnel the phasers had cut through the Calamarain. *Now there's a sight for sore sensors,* he thought. "Straight ahead, Mr. Clarze. Full impulse."

"Yes, sir!" the pilot complied, sounding more than anxious to leave the sentient thunderstorm behind. Riker was gratified to see the distant stars grow brighter as the unscratched viewscreen transmitted images from the ship's forward optical scanners. *Here goes nothing,* he thought, crossing his fingers. Once they were clear of the clouds, perhaps their warp engines would function again.

"Riker to Engineering," he barked, patting his comm badge. "Prepare to engage the warp drive at my signal."

"Acknowledged," Geordi responded. "We're ready and willing."

But the Calamarain would not release them so easily. Thick, viscous vapors flowed over and ahead of the ship's saucer section, encroaching on the channel before them. Lightning speared their shields repeatedly, giving them a rough and bumpy ride. To his dismay, Riker saw their escape route narrowing ahead, the gathering cloud front eating away at that tantalizing glimpse of starlight. "Keep firing!" he urged Leyoro, despite an almost inaudible whimper of pain from Deanna. *Hang on,* he told her wordlessly, lending her whatever support his own thoughts could provide. *We're almost out.*

A single scarlet beam shot from the saucer's upper dorsal array. Two hundred and fifty linked phaser emitter segments contributed to the awesome force of the beam, striking out at the enveloping throng of the Calamarain. On the screen, heavy accumulations of ionized plasma steamed away beneath the withering heat of the phaser barrage.

And still the furious cloud kept coming. Despite the unchecked power of the *Enterprise*'s phasers, a roiling flood of incandescent gas poured over them as fast as

Leyoro could boil it off with her phasers, if not faster. Riker couldn't help being amazed by the sheer immensity and/or quantity of the creature(s) pursuing them; even on full impulse, it was taking several moments to fly clear of them. He felt like he was trying to outrace an animated nebula.

The choppiness of their headlong flight increased every second. Riker was thrown from one side of the chair to the other as he struggled to ride out the violent squall. There was no way he could have shouted out any additional orders even if he had wanted to; it would have been like trying to converse during the downward plunge of a roller coaster. His stomach rushed up into his throat as the *Enterprise* executed a full 360-degree barrel before stabilizing, more or less, on an even keel.

Additional fires broke out around the bridge, more than the automated system could cope with. Smoke and the smell of burning plastic tickled Riker's nose. At the operations console, Data dealt with a small blaze swiftly and effectively by opening a flap in his wrist and spraying the flames with some of his own internal coolant. Other crew members followed his example, more or less, by resorting to the handheld fire extinguishers stored beneath each console. Riker took pride in the bridge crew's performance; they had coped with the outbreak of electrical fires without even a single command from him. *You can't beat Starfleet training,* he thought.

Through it all, the baby q appeared to be having the time of his life. He squealed happily as the *Enterprise* careered through the gap in the Calamarain at close to the speed of light. Defying gravity, the boy turned somersaults in the air, occasionally blocking Riker's view of the screen. *Enjoy this ride while you can,* he thought, *because we're not doing this again.*

The child's mother just shook her head in obvious disdain. "Barbaric," she muttered. "Utterly barbaric."

Sorry we couldn't provide a smoother trip, Riker thought sarcastically. Frankly, the female Q's low opinion of the ship was the least of his concerns.

Instead, his attention was focused on the rapidly shrinking opening ahead of them. He could barely see the stars now, only a small black hole in the substance of the Calamarain that looked scarcely large enough for the Sovereign-class starship to squeeze through. *C'mon,* he thought, *faster, faster,* spurring the *Enterprise* on with his mind even though he knew that they could not possibly accelerate any further without their warp capacity. Would they make it through the gap before it closed entirely? It was going to be close.

Ultimately, the ship tore through the advancing edges of the tunnel, leaving frayed tendrils of glowing mist behind it. Staring at the main viewer, Riker saw a vast expanse of interstellar space, bisected briefly by their own crimson phaser beam before Leyoro ceased fire. For the first time in hours, he could no longer hear the discordant thunder of the Calamarain, although that blessed silence would not last long unless they left their gaseous foes far behind them. Riker didn't need to see the input from the rear sensors to know that the Calamarain had to be hot on their heels.

"Riker to La Forge," he ordered, hoping that the damping effect on their warp engines did not extend beyond the boundaries of the Calamarain. "Give me everything you've got."

Chapter Sixteen

YEARS OF BEAMING to and from the *Enterprise* had accustomed Picard to instantaneous travel. Even so, the ease and speed with which Q switched settings remained disconcerting.

The jade cliffs were gone, replaced by crumbling gray ruins that seemed to stretch to the horizon. Toppled stone columns, cracked and fractured, leaned against massive granite blocks that might once have composed walls. Dry gray powder covered the ground, intermixed with chips of broken glass or crystal. Gusts of wind blew the powder about, tossing it against the desolate landscape, while the breeze keened mournfully, perhaps longing for the bygone days when the ancient structures had stood tall and proud. No sign of life, not even vermin, disturbed the sere and lonely ruins.

What is this place? Picard wondered. That which he saw about him reminded him of what was left of the Greek Parthenon after the Eugenics Wars, except on a vastly larger scale. Piles of stone debris blocked his

225

view in most every direction, but he could tell that the original structure or structures had been huge indeed. The ruins seemed to extend for kilometers. He looked upward at an overcast sky, through which a cool, twilight radiance filtered. If ever a ceiling had enclosed any part of the ruins, no trace of it remained, except perhaps in the hundreds of tiny crystal shards that sparkled amid the dust.

Picard blinked against the wind as it cast the sand into his face, and he stepped behind the shattered stump of a colossal stone column for shelter from the gritty powder. The climate felt different from Tagus III: the air more dry, the temperature cooler, the gravity slightly lighter. He suspected he wasn't even on the same planet anymore, although his and Q's latest destination seemed M-class at least. "Where are we now?" he asked Q, who stood a few meters away, heedless of the windblown powder. He was getting damned tired of asking that question, but there seemed to be no way around it. He was merely a passenger on this tour, without even the benefit of a printed itinerary. "And when?"

"Don't you recognize this place?" Q challenged him. He kicked the gray powder at his feet, adding to the airborne particulates. "Surely, a Starfleet officer of your stature has been informed of its existence? We're still a couple million years in the past, to be fair, but this particular locale looks much the same in your own tiny sliver of history."

Intrigued despite himself, Picard inspected his surroundings, searching for some clue to his present whereabouts. The sky above was no help; the heavy cloud cover concealed whatever constellations might have been visible from the surface. He contemplated the truncated column before him, running his hand over its classic Ionic contours and leaving a trail of handprints in the dust. The wandering aliens who had once posed as gods to the ancient Greeks had left similar structures throughout the Alpha Quadrant;

this could be one of any of a dozen such sites discovered since Kirk first encountered "Apollo" close to a century ago, or another site as yet uncharted by Starfleet. Was Q about to claim kinship to those ancient Olympians who had visited Earth in the distant past? Picard prayed that wasn't the case. The last thing he wanted to do was give Q credit for any of the foundations of human civilization. *If I had to pick Q out of the Greco-Roman pantheon, though,* he thought, *I'd bet a Ferengi's ransom that he was Bacchus or maybe Pan.*

None of which gave him a clue where in the galaxy he was.

"Stumped?" Q asked, savoring the mortal's perplexity. "Do let me know if this is too difficult a puzzle for your limited human mind."

Picard opened his mouth to protest, to ask for more time, then realized he had fallen into playing Q's game. *The fewer minutes we waste, the sooner I'll return to my ship.* "Yes, Q," he admitted freely. "I'm at a complete loss. Why don't you illuminate me?" *And with all deliberate speed,* he added silently.

Q scowled, as if irked by Picard's ready surrender, but he wasn't ready to abandon the game just yet. "Perhaps a slight alteration in perspective will refresh your memory."

Picard felt an abrupt sense of dislocation. His surroundings seemed to rush past him and, in the space of a single heartbeat, he found himself standing elsewhere within the same ruins. He staggered forward, dizzy from the rush, and braced himself against a fragment of a fallen wall. *I think I like Q's usual teleportation trick better,* he thought, steadying himself until the vertigo passed. He lifted his gaze from the gravel at his feet—and spotted *it* at once.

What from the side had appeared to be just more jutting granite rubble was now revealed to be a lopsided stone torus about three meters in diameter. Its asymmetrical design looked out of place among the scattered evidence of ancient architecture. Green patches of corrosion mottled its brownish gray surface, although the torus appeared more or less intact. Q waved at him through the oblong opening at the center of the torus, but Picard was too stunned to respond. Suddenly, he knew exactly where he was.

"The Guardian," he breathed in awe. He had never seen it in person, but, Q was correct, he was of course familiar with its history. More precisely known as "the Guardian of Forever," it was the oldest known artifact in the universe, believed to date back at least six billion years. Since its discovery by the crew of the original *Enterprise,* the Guardian had been subject of intensive study by Starfleet yet had remained largely an enigma. Picard glanced about him at the dilapidated stone ruins that surrounded the Guardian; archaeological surveys conducted in his own century had proven conclusively that the crumbling masonry was little more than a million years old. The Guardian predated the other ruins by countless aeons, having already been incalculably ancient before the temples or fortresses that rose up around it were even conceived. *Here,* he thought, *was antiquity enough to daunt even Q . . . perhaps.*

But its age was not its only claim to fame. The Guardian, he recalled, was more than merely an inanimate relic of the primordial past. Although it appeared inactive now, it was supposedly capable of opening up a doorway to any time in history, past or future. Picard briefly wondered if he could use the portal to return to his own era without Q's cooperation, but, no, that was probably too risky. More likely he would simply strand himself upon an unknown shoal of time with no more appealing prospect than to hope for rescue at Q's hands. *Better to stay put for the time being,* he concluded. Matters had not grown that desperate yet.

Brushing the clingy powder from his palms, Picard shielded his eyes with one hand while he scanned the vicinity. He and Q appeared to be the only beings alive in the ruins, excluding the Guardian, which was said to possess at least a pseudo-life of its own. "Shouldn't we be expecting your younger self any time now?" he asked Q. At this point, Picard felt he had a fairly good idea of the nature, if not the purpose, of their extended trek through time. "That is why we're here, I assume."

"A brilliant deduction, Jean-Luc," Q said, his sarcastic tone belying his words. "Even Wesley could have figured that out by now." He strutted across the rubble-strewn plain toward Picard, skirting around the Guardian. "But I'm afraid you're mistaken. My irrepressible earlier incarnation is not coming. He's already here. He's been here all along, only not in any form you can perceive." He pointed at a solitary cornerstone that had survived beyond the edifice it had once supported. "Cast your eyes over there while I adjust the picture for the metaphysically impaired."

In a blink, another Q, looking not much older than the one who had been so taken by the bloody spectacle at the jade cliffs, appeared, sitting cross-legged atop the great granite block. His chin rested upon the knuckles of his clasped hands as he stared moodily into the empty space within the Guardian. Clad in a stark black sackcloth robe that struck Picard as ostentatiously severe, he presented an almost archetypal portrait of disaffected youth, trapped on the cusp between adolescence and maturity. "A rebel without a cosmos," the older Q recalled, climbing marble steps that no longer led to anything recognizable. He swept the top step free of dust and sat down a few meters away from Picard. "I really had no idea what to do with myself back then."

Some of us still don't know what to do with you, Picard thought, refraining from saying so aloud lest he initiate another pointless war of words. The lighting itself had changed when the young Q became visible, throwing deep red and purple shadows upon the angst-ridden youth and his barren backdrop. Tilting his head back, Picard saw that the sky was now filled with an astonishing display of surging colors that put Earth's own aurora borealis to shame. Flashes of vibrant red and violet burst like phaser fire through what only moments before had been a dull and lifeless canopy. The dazzling pyrotechnics reminded Picard of the legendary firefalls of Gal Gath'thong on Romulus, but the pulsating, vivid hues above him were, if anything, even more luminous. "What's happening?" he asked Q. "Where did . . . that . . . come from?"

"Now you're seeing as a Q sees," the other explained. "What you call the Guardian produces ripples in space-time that extend far beyond this planet's atmosphere. Think of them as fourth-dimensional fireworks," he suggested breezily.

The young Q seemed unimpressed by the unparalleled light show unfolding overhead. His gaze fixed straight ahead, he yawned loudly. A listless forefinger traced the outline of the Guardian in the air, and a miniature replica of the stone torus materialized out of nothingness, hovering before his face. Q examined his creation without much enthusiasm. "At least our ancestors *made* things," he muttered sulkily.

Atop the immense cornerstone, young Q twirled his index finger and the model Guardian rotated for his inspection. He thrust the single digit into the tiny orifice of his toy and watched sullenly as it disappeared up to the bottom knuckle. Apparently unsatisfied by this diversion, he retrieved his finger, then dispatched the replica back into the ether with a wave of his hand. Leaping impatiently to his feet, his simple sandals kicking up a flurry of dust, he confronted the genuine Guardian. "Show me something!" he demanded.

"WHAT DO YOU WISH TO BEHOLD?" the Guardian asked, hundreds of centuries before it ever spoke to Kirk or Spock, its sonorous voice echoing off the accumulated wreckage of its former housing. An inner light flashed with each syllable of its query, rendering the weathered surface of the portal momentarily translucent. Scientists still debated, Picard recalled, whether the Guardian actually possessed sentience or merely a highly sophisticated form of interactive programming. Was it more or less alive, he wondered, than his ship's computer, the fictional characters that came to life in a holodeck, or even Data? That was a question better suited to philosophers, he decided, than a timelost Starfleet captain.

"Anything!" the young Q cried out in boredom. "Show me anything. I don't care."

"AS YOU WISH," the Guardian replied. A pristine white mist began to descend from the upper arch of the great torus, filling the vortex at its center. Through the falling vapor, Picard glimpsed images appearing, rushing swiftly by like a holonovel on fast-forward. Visions of the past, Picard wondered, or of untold ages to come? Despite the haze produced by the mist, the procession of images summoned up by the Guardian looked more real and tangible than any he had ever seen on a conventional viewscreen. Picard felt he could reach out and touch the people and places pictured therein, then remembered that he probably could. Gaping in amazement, he tried to capture each new vision as it played out before him:

A tremendous explosion cast immeasurable quantities of matter and energy throughout creation; vast clouds of gas collapsed until they ignited into nuclear fire; drifting elemental particles clumped together, forming moons and planets, asteroids and comets; single-celled organisms swam through seas of unimaginable breadth and purity; limbless creatures flopped onto the land and almost instantly (or so it appeared to Picard) evolved into a bewildering variety of shapes and sizes; humanoids appeared, and non-humanoids, too, creatures with tentacles and feelers and antennae and wings and fins, covered with fur and feathers and scales and slime. Civilizations rose up and collapsed in a matter of seconds; for an instant, Picard thought he spotted the ancient D'Arsay in their ceremonial masks and rites, and then the cascade of history rushed on, leaving them behind. Machines were born, sometimes surpassing their makers, and fragile life-forms dared the void between worlds in vessels of every description, leaving their tracks on a thousand systems before shedding their physical forms entirely to become numinous beings of pure thought. There were the Organians, Picard realized, and the Metrons and the Thasians and the Zalkonians and the Douwd . . .

"No, no," Q exclaimed, not content with the ongoing panorama of life and the universe. "I've seen all this before! I want to see something else. I want to *be* somewhere else."

"WHERE DO YOU WISH TO JOURNEY?" The Guardian flashed its willingness to convey Q wherever he desired.

The black-garbed youth stamped his foot impatiently, sending yet another fissure through the massive block beneath him. "If I knew that, I wouldn't be here in the first place, you pretentious doorframe." He hopped off the stone, raising a cloud of gray powder where he landed, and approached the Guardian. "Show me more," he commanded. "Show me what's new, what's different!"

"Here we go," his older self sighed. He rose to his feet and took Picard by the elbow, leading him over to just behind where young Q now stood. "Get ready," he warned Picard, his words unheard by the youth only a few centimeters away, who quivered with unfocused energy.

Again? Picard thought, readying himself for another change of venue. He'd been on whirlwind tours of the Klingon Empire that had moved at a more leisurely pace.

Within the Guardian, images zipped past so speedily that he could barely keep up with them. He caught only quick, almost subliminal fragments of random events, of which only the smallest fraction could he even begin to identify: a mighty sailing ship sinking beneath the waves, a glistening Changeling dissolving into a golden pool, a dozen Borg cubes converging on a defenseless world, a shuttlecraft crashing into a shimmering wall of light . . .

"What now?" Picard asked, unable to look away from the rapid-fire parade of images. "What does he intend to do?"

"Stick a pin in a map," his companion stated. "Entrust his future to the fickle whims of chance." He shrugged apologetically. "It seemed like the only thing to do at the time."

The young Q glanced back over his shoulder, and, for a second, Picard thought they had been exposed. But the youth was merely giving the lifeless ruins one last look before taking a deep breath, closing his eyes, crossing his fingers, and hurling himself forward into the mist-draped opening of the time portal. Picard had only an instant to register the young Q's disappearance before the other Q's hands shoved him roughly from behind, propelling him straight into the waiting maw of the Guardian of Forever.

Chapter Seventeen

ACCORDING TO STANDARD Starfleet guidelines, it took zero-point-three-five seconds to go from impulse flight to warp travel. According to Riker's chronometer on the bridge, Geordi and his engineering crew did it in zero-point-two.

It wasn't nearly fast enough.

Riker felt a momentary surge of acceleration that trailed off almost immediately as the Calamarain hit them from behind like the front of a hurricane. The ship's inertial dampers were tested to the limit as its propulsive warp field collapsed instantaneously, causing the vessel to skid to a halt through friction with the cloud's billowing mass. The storm enveloped them at once, much to the delight of little q, who clapped his tiny hands in synch with the thunder.

Riker was considerably less amused. *Dammit,* he thought. *It's not fair!* He was no Betazoid, but he could practically feel the distress and disappointment permeating the bridge. Baeta Leyoro swore and slammed a fist into her open palm. Lieutenant Barclay poked at the engineering controls rather frantically, as if hoping to reverse their readings. Only Data appeared unaffected by the dashing of their hopes of escape, looking preoccupied with his repairs to the operations console. "Let me guess," Riker said bitterly. "No more warp drive."

Barclay swallowed nervously before confirming the awful truth. "I'm afraid not, Commander. Something's interfering with the field coils again."

"If this is typical of your expeditions," the female Q sniffed, "it's a wonder that you humans ever got out of your own backwoods solar system."

If we'd known the likes of you were waiting for us, Riker mused, *we might have had second thoughts.* Outwardly, he disregarded the Q's needling, preferring to address the problem of the Calamarain, who at least refrained from waspish gibes. He was starting to wonder, though, whether this was truly a new entity at all, or if the original Q had simply had a sex change. Granted, he had already seen both Q and his alleged mate at the same time, but somehow he suspected that materializing in two places simultaneously was not beyond Q's powers.

"Shall I go to impulse, sir?" Ensign Clarze asked.

Riker gave the matter a moment's thought. Was there any way they could outrace the Calamarain? Given that they had previously encountered the cloud-creatures in an entirely different sector several years ago, he could only deduce that the Calamarain were capable of faster-than-light travel on their own, assuming that these were indeed the very same entities that had attacked Q aboard the *Enterprise* during the third year of their ongoing mission. Certainly, the storm had managed to keep pace with them at impulse speed.

"No, Mr. Clarze," Riker declared evenly. They were running low on options, but he was determined to maintain a confident air for the sake of the crew's morale. "Well, Mr. Data?" Riker asked, addressing the android. "It's looking like you're our best hope at the moment."

If all else failed, he thought, he would have to order a saucer-separation maneuver, dividing the *Enterprise* into two independent vessels. The Calamarain appeared to clump together as one cohesive mass; possibly they could not pursue two ships at the same time. In theory, he could distract the sentient cloud with the battle section while the majority of the crew escaped in the saucer module. Naturally, he would remain aboard the battle bridge until the bitter end—and hope that Captain Picard eventually returned to command the saucer.

Apparently tired of standing upon the bridge, the female Q and her little boy had, without even thinking of asking anyone's permission, occupied Riker's own accustomed seat, to the right of the captain's chair. The child sat on his mother's lap, sucking his thumb and watching the main viewer as if it were the latest educational holotape from the Federated Children's Workshop. Riker didn't waste any breath objecting to the woman's brazen disregard of bridge etiquette and protocol. Why bother arguing decent manners with a Q? *I wonder how long they'll choose to stick around if I have to separate the saucer,* he wondered. *Would they transfer to the battle bridge as well, and stay all the way to the ship's final annihilation?*

Before he sacrificed one half of the *Enterprise,* however, along with the lives of the bridge and engineering crew, Riker intended to exhaust every other alternative, which was where Data came in.

And the Universal Translator.

"I believe I have," Data stated, "successfully developed a set of algorithms that may translate the Calamarain's tachyon emissions into verbal communication and vice versa, although the initial results may be crude and rudimentary at best."

"We don't want to recite poetry to them," Riker

said, "just call a truce." He stared grimly at the luminescent fog stretching across the main viewer. Jagged bolts of electricity and incessant peals of thunder rocked the ship. "Say hello, Mr. Data."

The android's fingers manipulated the controls at Ops faster than Riker's eye could follow them. "I am diverting power to the primary deflector dish," he explained, "in order to produce a narrow wavelength tachyon stream similar to those the Calamarain appear to use to communicate. If my calculations are correct, our tachyon beam should translate as a simple greeting."

"I hope you're right, Data," Riker said. "It would be a shame if we accidentally insulted them by mistake."

"Indeed," Data replied, cocking his head as if the possibility had not previously occurred to him, "although it is difficult to imagine how we could conceivably make them more hostile than they already appear to be."

You've got a point there, Riker admitted, given that the Calamarain had spent the last several hours dead set on shaking the *Enterprise* apart. The sharp decline in the strength of the ship's deflector shields testified to the force and severity of the Calamarain's assault. *Perhaps now we can finally learn why they attacked us in the first place.*

"Greeting transmitted," Data reported. The tachyon emission was invisible to the naked eye, yet Riker peered at the viewer regardless, looking for some sign that the Calamarain had received their message. All he saw, though, were the same churning mists and flashes of discharged energy that had besieged the *Enterprise* since before the captain disappeared.

Troi abruptly sat up straight in her chair. "They heard us," she confirmed, her empathic senses once more linked to the Calamarain. "I feel surprise . . . and confusion. They're not sure what to do."

"Good work, Mr. Data," Riker said, hope surging

inside him for the first time in nearly an hour, "and you too, Deanna." Was he just deluding himself or had the oppressive thunder actually subsided a degree or two in the last few moments? They weren't out of the woods yet, but maybe the Calamarain had stopped hammering them long enough to contemplate Data's greeting. *Go ahead,* he thought to his amorphous foes. *Think it over some. Give us another chance to make contact!*

"Commander," Data alerted him, "short-range sensors detect an incoming transmission from the Calamarain, using the same narrow wavelength they applied earlier."

Hope flared in Riker. Thanks to Data, they still had a prayer of turning this thing around. *Too bad Captain Picard isn't here to speak with the Calamarain. He's probably the best diplomat in Starfleet.* "Put them through, Mr. Data."

"Yes, Commander," Data said. "Our modified translator is interpreting the transmission now."

A genderless, inhuman voice emerged from the bridge's concealed loudspeakers. The voice lacked any recognizable inflections and sounded as though it were coming from someplace deep underwater. "We/singular am/are the Calamarain," it stated.

"I apologize for the atonal quality of the translation," Data commented, "as well as any irregularities in syntax or grammar. Insufficient time was available to provide for nuance or aesthetics."

"This will be fine," Riker assured him. "Can the computer translate what I say into terms the Calamarain can understand?"

"Affirmative, Commander," Data said. "You may speak normally."

Riker nodded, then took a deep breath before speaking. "This is Commander William T. Riker of the *Starship Enterprise,* representing the United Federation of Planets." He resisted an urge to straighten his uniform; the Calamarain were not likely to appreciate any adjustment in his attire, even if they could see him, which was unlikely. Their senses were surely very different from his own. "Do I have the honor of addressing the leader of the Calamarain?"

There was a lag of no more than a second while Data's program translated his words into a series of tachyon beams; then that chilling voice spoke again. "We/singular speak from/for the Calamarain," it said in its muffled, watery tones.

What precisely did it mean by that? Was more than one individual addressing him at once, Riker wondered, or was it merely a verbal conceit, like the royal "we" once employed by Earth's ancient monarchs? Or could it be that the Calamarain genuinely possessed a collective consciousness like the Borg? He repressed a shudder. Anything that reminded him of the Borg was not good news. Riker decided to take the speaker at its word, whoever it or they might be.

"We come in peace," he declared, going straight to the heart of the matter. "Why have you attacked us?"

After another brief pause, the eerie voice returned. "Mote abates/attenuates. No assistance/release permitted. Stop/eliminate."

What? Riker gave Data a quizzical look, but the android could do nothing but shrug. "I am sorry, Commander, but that is the closest translation," he said.

"Deanna?" Riker whispered, hoping she could decipher the Calamarain's cryptic explanation.

"I sense no deception," she said. "They are quite sincere, very much so. Whatever they're trying to tell us, it's very important to them." She bowed her head and massaged her brow with both hands, clearly striving to achieve an even greater communion with the enigmatic aliens. "Beneath their words, I'm picking up that same mixture of fear and anger."

Why would the Calamarain be afraid of us? Riker couldn't figure it out. If the events of the last hour or so had proved anything, it was that the *Enterprise* could not inflict any lasting harm on the Calamarain. *If only I knew what they meant,* he thought. "I don't understand," he said, raising his voice. "What do you want of us?"

"Preserve/defend mote," the Calamarain insisted obscurely.

Interlude

WHAT IS THAT? the spider asked. *That is what?*

Something was there, on the other side, that he could not quite identify, something at the center of it all. The smoke surrounded the bug, and bug surrounded *It*, but what was *It*, glowing within the entrapped insect like a candle in a skull? Sparking like a quark in the dark?

There was something Q-ish about it, but different, too. Not the Q, nor a Q, but flavored much the same. *It is new,* the spider realized with a shock. *Newer than new. Q-er than Q.*

New . . . For the first time it occurred to the spider to wonder how much might have changed, there on the other side. But that would depend on how long he'd been outside, wouldn't it, and that would be . . . ? *No! Not! No!* His mind scuttled away from the question, unable to face the answer that loomed just past his awareness.

Change, change, he chanted, calming himself. *Change on the range into something quite strange.* Change could be good, especially his own. He could make changes, too, and he would, yes indeed, just as soon as he could.

Everything changes, and will change even more. . . .

Chapter Eighteen

SOMEONE WAS SINGING in the snow.

Picard had little time to orient himself. An instant ago he had inhabited the arid ruins encircling the Guardian of Forever. Now he seemed to be located amid a frozen wasteland, his boots sinking into the icy crust, cold and distant stars shining in the dark sky far above him. The rime-covered plain stretched about him in all directions. Like Cocytus, he thought, the ninth and lowest level of hell. His breath misted before him, but he did not feel in any danger of freezing to death. Q's work, no doubt. The cold, dry air felt chill against Picard's body, nothing more. *Very well then,* he thought, disinclined to question his lack of hypothermia. He had more important mysteries to solve, like where was that infernal singing coming from?

The voice, rich and resonant, carried through the glacial cold:

"She was a kind-hearted girl, a lissome fair daughter,
Who always declined the gifts that I brought her. . . ."

Still unaware of his two humanoid observers, the young Q looked similarly intrigued by the robust voice crooning through the frigid air. Deterred not at all by the forbidding landscape, he trudged across the frosty tundra in search of the source of the melody. Picard and the older Q followed closely behind him, sometimes stepping in his sunken footprints. Starlight trickled down through the endless night, but not enough to truly light their way. Defying logic and conventional means of combustion, Q whipped up a torch, which he held out in front of him. Lambent red flames flickered above his fist, casting an eerie crimson glow upon their frozen path. The sleeves of Q's charcoal robe flapped slowly in the biting winter wind, and Picard found himself wishing that Starfleet uniforms came complete with gloves and a scarf. Although no new snow fell from the cloudless sky, the breeze tossed loosely packed white flakes into the air, making vision difficult. The icy bits pelted his face, melting against his reddened cheeks and brow.

"But pity's the thing, so I begged for cool water,
And then led her away like a lamb to a slaughter. . . ."

They marched for several minutes, during which time Picard observed the utter absence of any signs of animation. Nothing moved upon or above the ice except the windblown particles of snow. Picard wondered if any form of life existed beneath the permafrost, such as that found in Antarctica. Perhaps, if he could place this planet by means of the constellations overhead, it might be worth bringing the *Enterprise* by to check? Then he recalled that all of this was taking place millions of years in the past. Any lifeforms that might exist here and now would most likely be long extinct when he returned to his own time. *For all I know, this entire planet and star system may not even exist in the twenty-fourth century.*

The soles of his boots crunched through the snow. No, he knew instinctively, there was no life here. This was a dead place, devoid of vitality, empty of possibility. Save for the singing voice, and the soft hiss of the burning torch, the icy plain was locked in silence. *Much like the old Klingon penal colony on Rura Penthe,* he mused, *known to history as the "aliens' graveyard."* Surely, that icebound planetoid could have been no more bleak and inhospitable than this.

"Like a lamb to slaughter, yes, like a lamb to the slaughter. . . ."

The echoing refrain grew louder as they neared its origin. Soon Picard spied the figure of a man, human in appearance, sitting upon a granite boulder covered by a thick veneer of frost. He appeared larger than either Q, and his stout frame was draped in heavy clothing that looked as though it had seen better days yet nonetheless retained a semblance of faded glory. His heavy fur coat was frayed around its sleeves and along its hem while his high black boots were scuffed and the heels worn down to the sole. Rags were wrapped around his hands and boots to hold on to his heat, and a ratty velvet scarf protected his throat. A wide-brimmed hat, drooping over his brow, and tattered trousers completed his outfit, giving him an archaic and faintly dispossessed air.

"Who is this?" Picard asked. "I don't recognize him."

"Of course not," Q retorted impatiently. "Your ancestors weren't even a gleam in creation's eye yet."

It wasn't that foolish an observation, Picard thought, considering the timelessness of Q and his ilk. "Is this what he genuinely looked like," he asked his guide, wanting to fully understand what he was witnessing, "or are we dealing in metaphor again?"

"More or less," Q admitted. "In fact, he resembled a being not unlike a Q, whose true form would be patently incomprehensible to your limited human senses."

So this is your interpretation of how he first appeared to you, Picard thought. *He must have made quite an impression.* Although worn and ragged, the stranger presented an intriguing and evocative figure. Singing to himself, he was engaged in what looked like a game of three-dimensional solitaire. Oversized playing cards were spread out on the snow before him, or floated in fixed positions above the mud-slick ground, arranged in a variety of horizontal, vertical, and diagonal patterns. He looked engrossed in his game, meticulously shifting cards from one position to another, until the flickering, phosphorescent light of Q's torch fell upon the outermost row of cards. He looked up abruptly, fixing gleaming azure eyes on the young Q, his face that of a human male in his mid-forties, with weathered features and heavy, crinkly lines around his eyes and mouth. "Say, who goes there?" he said, sounding intrigued rather than alarmed.

Q faltered before the stranger's forthright gaze, taking a few steps backward involuntarily. "I might ask you the same," he retorted, his brash manner failing to conceal a touch of obvious apprehension. He thrust out his chest and chin to strike a less nervous pose.

"You must understand," his older self whispered in Picard's ear, "this was the first time since the dawn of my omniscience that I had encountered anything I didn't understand. A little healthy trepidation was only natural under the circumstances."

Picard was too entranced by the unfolding scene to respond to Q's excuses. "Well said!" the stranger laughed lustily. "And you're more than welcome, too. I was starting to think I was the only preternatural deity stuck in the middle of this irksome Ice Age."

"W-who are you?" Q stammered. Fog streamed from his lips; another artistic touch, Picard guessed, courtesy of the other Q. "What are you?"

"Call me 0," he said, doffing his hat to reveal unruly orange hair streaked with silver. "As to where I'm from, it's no place you've ever heard of, I promise you that."

"That's impossible," young Q said indignantly, his pride stung. "I'm Q. I know everything and have been everywhere."

"Then where are you now?" the stranger asked.

The simple question threw Q for a loop. He glanced around, feigning nonchalance (badly), and seemed to be searching his memory. Taking his own inventory of their surroundings, Picard noted a trail of deep, irregularly paced footprints stretching away in the opposite direction from the way they had come. As far as he could see, the tracks extended all the way to the horizon. How long, he wondered, how the stranger been wandering through this wintry Siberian waste-land?

"Er, I'm not sure," Q confessed finally, "but I'm quite certain it's no place worth remembering. Other-wise, I would recognize it at once, as I would your own plane of origin."

The individual who called himself 0 did not take offense at this challenge to his veracity. He simply chuckled to himself and shook his head incredu-lously. "But there's *always* someplace else, no matter how far you've been. Some unknown territory beyond the horizon, across the gulf, or hidden beneath a hundred familiar layers of what's real and everyday. There has to someplace Other or why else do we roam? We might as well just plant ourselves in one cozy cosmos or another and never budge." He clapped his gloved, rag-swaddled hands together, and a curved glass bottle, filled with an unknown liquid of pinkish tint, appeared in his grasp. He wrenched the stopper from the spout and spit it onto the hoarfrost at his feet. Roseate fumes poured from the mouth of the bottle.

"For myself," he said, after taking a swig from the carafe, "I don't much care whether you believe me or not, but if I'm not from the parts you know, then where did this come from? Answer that."

He offered the bottle to Q, who looked uncertain what to do. "How do I know you aren't trying to poison me?" he said, striving for a light, jokey tone.

0 grinned back at him. "You don't. That's the fun of it." He shoved the bottle at Q. "Come now, eternity's too short not to take a chance now and then. Caution is for cowards, and for those who lack the gaze and the guts to try something new."

"You really think so?" Q asked. Despite his earlier misgivings, he was clearly curious about the rakish stranger. It struck Picard that 0's professed philosophy was a far cry from the conservative limits imposed on the young Q by the Continuum.

"I *know* so," 0 declared. He wagged the bottle in front of Q's face, then started to withdraw it. "But maybe you don't agree. Perhaps you're one of those timid, tentative types who never do anything unexpected. . . ."

Impulsively, Q grabbed the carafe by its curved spout and gulped down a sizable portion of the bottle's contents. His eyes bugged out as the drink hit his system like a quantum torpedo. He bent over coughing and gasping. "By the Continuum!" he swore. "Where did you find that stuff?"

0 slapped Q on the back while deftly retrieving the bottle from Q's shaking hand. "Well, I'd tell you, friend," he said, "but then you don't believe in places you've never laid eyes on."

Next to Picard, across the ice from the young Q and his new acquaintance, an older-but-arguably-wiser Q confided in the starship captain. "It's true, you know," he said, a wistful melancholy tingeing his voice, "I've never tasted anything like it ever again. I've even tried re-creating it from scratch, but the flavor is never quite right."

Only Q, Picard thought, *could get nostalgic about something that happened millions of years in the past.* Still, he thought he could identify with some of what Q was experiencing. He felt much the same way about the *Stargazer,* not to mention the *Enterprise*-D.

By now, the young Q had recovered from the effects of the exotic concoction. "That was fantastic!" he blurted. "It was so . . . different." He said that last word with a tone of total disbelief, then regarded the stranger with new appreciation. "I don't understand. How did you get here, wherever here is? And are there others like you?"

0 held up his hand to quiet Q's unleashed curiosity. "Whoa there, friend. I'm glad you liked the brew, but it seems to me you have the advantage on me. Where are you from, exactly?" His icy blue eyes narrowed as he looked Q over. "And what's this Continuum you mentioned a couple moments ago?"

"But surely you must have heard of the Q Continuum?" Q said, all his misgivings forgotten. "We're only the apex of sentience throughout the entire . . . I mean, the *known* . . . multiverse."

"You forget, I'm not from around your usual haunts," 0 said. "Nor have I always been camped out in this polar purgatory." He swept his arm to encompass his Arctic domain. "A bit of a wrong turn there, I admit, but that's what happens sometimes when you strike out for parts unknown. You have to accept the risks as well as the rewards." He regarded Q with a calculating expression, brazenly assessing the juvenile superbeing. Picard didn't like the avid gleam in the stranger's eyes; 0 seemed more than simply curious about Q. "Perhaps you'd care to show me just how you got here?"

His game abandoned, 0 began to sweep his playing cards together, combining them into a single stack.

Picard peeked at the exposed faces of the cards, and was shocked to see what looked like living figures moving about in the two-dimensional plane of the cards. The suits and characters were unfamiliar to him, bearing little resemblance to the cards used in *Enterprise*'s weekly poker games, but they were definitely animated. He spotted soldiers and sailors, balladeers and falconers and dancing bears among the many archetypes represented upon the metal cards, and apparently crying out in fear as 0 shuffled them together. Although no sounds escaped the deck, the figures shared a common terror and state of alarm, their eyes and mouths open wide, their arms reaching out in panic. "What in heaven's name," Picard started to ask Q, but 0 patted the cards into place, then dispatched the deck to oblivion before Picard could finish his question. Snow-flecked air rushed in to fill the empty void the stack of cards had formerly occupied.

Had the young Q noticed the unsettling nature of the cards? Picard could not tell for certain, but he thought he discerned a new wariness entering into the immature Q's face and manner. Or maybe, he speculated, 0 simply seemed a shade too eager to uncover Q's secrets.

"How I got here?" young Q repeated slowly, displaying some of his later self's cunning and evasiveness. "Well, that's a terribly long and complicated story."

"I've got time," 0 insisted. He clapped his hands and another ice-coated boulder appeared next to his own. He gestured for Q to take a seat there. "And there's nothing I like better than a good yarn, particularly if there's a trace of danger in it." He looked Q over from head to toe. "Do you like danger, Q?"

"Actually, I think I should be going," Q stated, taking a few steps backward. "I have an appointment out by Antares Prime, you see? Q is expecting me, as well as Q and Q."

His retreat was short-lived, for 0 simply rose from his polished stone resting-place and advanced on Q, dragging his left leg behind him. His infirmity caught the young Q by surprise, freezing him in his tracks upon the tundra; Picard guessed he'd never seen a crippled god before. "Not so fast, friend," 0 said, his voice holding just a trace of menace, a hint of a threat. "As you can plainly see, I can't get around as quickly as I used to." He leaned forward until his face was less than a finger's length from Q, his hot breath fogging the air between them. "Don't suppose you know an easy exit out of this oversized ice cube, do you, boy?"

Picard struggled to translate what he was witnessing into its actual cosmic context. "His leg," he asked Q. "What is the lameness a metaphor for?"

"Just what he said," Q answered impatiently, unheard by the figures they observed. "Must you be so bloody analytical all the time? Can't you accept this gripping drama at face value?"

"From you, never," Picard stated. He refused to accept that an entity such as 0 appeared to be would actually limp, at least not in a literal human sense.

Q resigned himself to Picard's queries. "If you must know, he could no longer travel at what you would consider superluminal speeds, at least in the sort of normal space-time reality you're familiar with." He directed Picard's gaze back to the long-ago meeting upon the boreal plain. "Not that I fully understood all that at the time."

"Can't you leave on your own?" the young Q asked, apparently reluctant to divulge the existence of the Guardian to the stranger. Picard admired his discretion, even if he doubted it would last. He knew Q too well.

"Sort of a personal question, isn't it?" 0 shot back indignantly. "You're not making light of my handicap, are you? I'll have you know I'm proud of every scrape and scar I've picked up over the course of my travels. I earned every one of them by taking my

251

chances and running by my own rules. I'd hate to think you were the kind to think less of an entity because he's a little worse for wear."

"Of course not. Not at all!" Q replied and his older self groaned audibly. His perennial adversary, Picard observed, was not enjoying this scene at all. He shook his head and averted his eyes as his earlier incarnation apologized to 0. "I meant no offense, not one bit."

"That's better," 0 said, his harsh tone softening into something more amiable. "Then you won't mind if I hitch a ride with you back to your corner of the cosmos?" He flashed Q a toothy grin. "When do we leave?"

"You want to come with me?" the young Q echoed, uncertain. Events seemed to be proceeding far too fast for him. "Er, I'm not sure that's wise. I don't know anything about—I mean, you don't know anything about where I come from?"

"True, but I'm looking to learn," 0 said. He tapped the large rock behind him with the heel of his boot and both boulders disappeared, leaving the frozen plain devoid of any distinguishing features. "Trust me, there's nothing more to be seen around here. We might as well move on."

When did they become "we," Picard wondered, and the young Q might have been asking himself the same question. "I don't know," he murmured, lowering his torch to create a little more space between him and 0. "I hadn't really thought—"

"Nonsense," 0 retorted. His robust laughter produced a flurry of mist that wreathed his face like a smoking beard. He threw his arm around Q's shoulders, heedless of the youth's blazing torch. "Don't tell me you're actually afraid of poor old me?"

"Of course not!" Q insisted, perhaps too quickly. Picard recognized the tone immediately; it was the same one the older Q used whenever Picard questioned his superiority. "Why should I be?"

Next to Picard, the older Q glowered at his past. "You fool," he hissed. "Don't listen to him."

But his words fell upon literally deaf ears. Breaking away from 0, the younger Q snuffed out his torch in the snow; then, displaying the same supreme high-handedness that Picard had come to associate with Q, he traced in silver the oddly shaped outline of the time portal. "Behold," he said grandly, as if determined to impress 0 with his accomplishment, "the Guardian of Forever."

0 stared greedily at the beckoning aperture, and Picard did not require any commentary from the older Q to know that the younger was on the verge of making a serious mistake. Picard had not reached his advanced rank in Starfleet without learning to be a quick judge of character, and this 0 character struck him as a bold, and distinctly evasive, opportunist at the very least. In fact, Picard realized, 0 reminded him of no one so much as the older Q at his most devious. "You should have trusted your own instincts," he told his companion.

"Now you tell me," Q grumped.

Chapter Nineteen

PRESERVE THE MOTE? What the blazes did that mean?

Riker's fists clenched in frustration. This was like trying to communicate with the Tamarians, before Captain Picard figured out that their language was based entirely on mythological allusions. *We rely too damn much on our almighty Universal Translator,* he thought, *so we get thrown for a loop when it runs into problems.* He signaled Data to switch off the translation program while he conferred with the others. "'Preserve/defend mote,'" he echoed aloud. "What mote are they talking about? A speck of spacedust? A solitary atom?" Could this refer to some primal metaphor, such as the Tamarians employed? What was that old quote about "a mote in your eye" or something?

Or, looking at it from a different angle, couldn't "mote" also be used as a verb? Yes, he recalled, an archaic form of the word "might," as in "So mote it be." Preserve might? Preserve possibilities? Riker's

254

spirit sagged as he considered all the diverse interpretations that came to mind.

"Maybe they don't mean mote," Leyoro suggested, "but moat, as in a circle of water protecting a fortress."

Spoken like a security officer, Riker thought, but maybe Leyoro was on to something here. A moat, a ring of defense . . . *Of course,* he realized. "The barrier. The Calamarain don't think in terms of solids, like walls or fences. To them, the galactic barrier is a big moat, circling the entire Milky Way!"

"That is a most logical conclusion," Data observed. "As you will recall, they first attacked when the probe attempted to enter the barrier."

"'Moat abates/attenuates,'" Troi said, repeating the Calamarain's original pronouncement. "Perhaps they're referring to the weaknesses in the barrier that Professor Faal detected."

"That makes sense," Riker declared, convinced they had found the answer. He would have to remember to commend Lieutenant Leyoro in his report, assuming they all came out of this alive. "They're protecting the barrier from us. 'No assistance/release permitted.' Maybe that means they don't want us to escape—or be 'released' from—the galaxy."

That sounds just presumptuous enough to be right, he thought. Lord knows this wouldn't be the first time some arrogant, "more advanced" life-form had tried to enforce limits on Starfleet's exploration of the universe. Just look at Q himself, for instance. It was starting to seem like the Calamarain had a lot in common with the Q Continuum. He glanced sideways at the strange woman and child seated at his own auxiliary command station. She appeared to be flipping through a magazine titled simply *Q,* materialized from who-knows-where, while q watched the tempest visible on the viewscreen. The other Q, he recalled, had warned the captain not to cross the barrier. Could it be that Q and the Calamarain had been on the same side all along?

"This might not be the most judicious occasion to argue the point," Data stated with characteristic understatement.

"Shields down to twenty-one percent," Leyoro confirmed.

Riker saw the wisdom in what they were saying. As much as he resented being dictated to by a glorified cloud of hot gas, he was perfectly willing to withdraw from the field of battle this time, provided that the Calamarain could be persuaded to release the *Enterprise* long enough to let them go home. "Put me through to them again," he instructed Data.

"This is Commander Riker to the Calamarain," he said in a firm and dignified manner. "We respect your concerns regarding the . . . moat . . . and will not tamper with the moat at this time. Please permit us to return to our own space."

The entire bridge, he knew, waited anxiously for the aliens' response. With any luck at all, they would soon be able to abort their mission with no fatalities and only minimal damage to the ship. *That's good enough for me,* he thought. Any first-contact situation where you could walk away without starting a war was at least a partial success in his book. Besides, for all they knew, the Calamarain had a legitimate interest in the sanctity of the galactic barrier. That was something for the scientists and the diplomats to work out in the months to come, if the Calamarain proved willing to negotiate.

Right now, he mused, *I just want to bury the hatchet so we can concentrate on finding the captain.*

Then the voice of the Calamarain spoke again, crushing all his hopes: "*Enterprise* is/was chaoshaven. Deceit/disorder. No permit trust/mercy/escape. Must preserve/enforce moat. *Enterprise* is/to be dissipated."

"I do not think they believed you, Commander," Data said.

"I got that impression, Data," Riker affirmed. There was no audible menace in that uninflected voice, but the essence of its message was clear. The Calamarain did not trust them enough to let the ship go free. "Guilt by association," he realized. "All they know about us is that we've harbored Q in the past, shielding him from their retribution. That's what they mean by 'chaos-haven.' They think we're accomplices."

Now, there's a bitter twist of fate, he thought. *Will the* Enterprise *end up paying the price for Q's crimes?*

"I don't get it," Ensign Clarze said, scratching his hairless dome. "What do they mean, dissipated?"

Baeta Leyoro translated for the younger, less experienced crewman. "Destroyed," she said flatly. "They intend to destroy the entire ship."

"Touchy creatures," the female Q remarked, sounding quite unconcerned about the starship's imminent obliteration. "I never much cared for them."

Riker was inclined to agree.

Chapter Twenty

THE OBLONG PORTAL SHIMMERED beneath the ice-cold
sky. Young Q had not summoned the entire stone
framework of the Guardian to 0's Arctic realm, but
merely the aperture itself, which hovered above the
frozen tundra like a mirage. The same white mist
began to seep from the portal, turning to frost as it
came into contact with the surface of the snow-
covered plain; through the fog, Picard glimpsed the
dusty ruins from which they had entered this glacial
waste.

"Come along, Picard," Q instructed, heading for
the spuming portal. "What transpires next is best
witnessed from the other side."

Picard followed without argument. In truth, he
would be happy to leave the barren ice behind; even
with Q's powers to protect him from the cold, he
found this frigid emptiness as desolate and dispiriting
as Dante must have found the frozen lake of sinners at
the bottom of the Inferno. Still, he had to wonder
what was yet to occur. Was the young Q actually going

258

to introduce 0 to Picard's own universe even with everything they didn't know about the mysterious entity? Picard, for one, would have liked to know a lot more about what precisely 0 was—and how he came to be stranded amid the drifting snow.

"Après vous," the older Q said to Picard, indicating the frothing aperture. Holding his breath involuntarily, Picard rushed through the fog, and found himself back among the dusty wreckage of the ancient ruins surrounding the Guardian of Forever, beneath a sky transformed by luminous time ripples. Moments later, his all-powerful guide emerged from the gateway as well. He joined Picard a few meters away from the Guardian. Their uniforms, Picard noted with both surprise and relief, were totally warm and dry despite their recent exposure to snow and ice. "Now what?" the captain asked.

"Now," Q said glumly, "you get a firsthand view of one of my more dubious achievements."

"One of many, I imagine," Picard could not resist remarking.

"Don't be ill-mannered, Jean-Luc," Q scolded. "I'm reliving this for your benefit, don't forget."

So you say, Picard thought, although he had yet to deduce what exactly Q's youthful exploits, millions of years in the past, had to do with himself or the *Enterprise,* unless 0 or his heirs somehow posed a threat in his own time. That seemed unlikely given the enormous stretches of time involved, but where Q and his sort were concerned, anything was possible.

"Here I come," Q stated, as his younger self indeed leaped out of the mist. The callow godling spun around on his heels and looked back the way he had come. Picard was unable to interpret the apprehensive expression on his face. Was the young Q worried that 0 would not be able to follow him through the portal—or that he would?

"Couldn't you have simply closed the door behind you?" Picard asked the other Q.

"Why, Captain," Q answered, looking aghast at the very suggestion, "I'm shocked that you would even propose such a cowardly ploy. That would have hardly been honorable of me, and, as you should know by now, I always play fair."

That's debatable, Picard thought, but saw no reason to press that point right now. Peering past both Q's, he spotted the silhouette of 0's stocky frame appearing within the foggy gateway. He held his breath, anticipating the stranger's arrival, but then something seemed to go wrong. Travel through the Guardian had always been instantaneous before, but not for 0 apparently. He strained against the opening as though held back by some invisible membrane. Reality itself seemed to resist his entrance. "Help me," he called out to Q, a single arm stretching beyond the boundaries of the portal. "For mercy's sake, help me!"

The older Q shook his head dolefully, but his earlier incarnation wavered uncertainly. He stepped forward to grip 0's outstretched hand, then hesitated, chewing his lower lip and wringing his hands together. "I don't know," he said aloud.

Perhaps responding to his indecision, the Guardian itself weighed in with its own opinion. "CAUTION," it declared, "FOREIGN ENTITY DOES NOT CONFORM TO ESTABLISHED PARAMETERS FOR THIS PLANE."

"Q!" 0 cried, his face pressed furiously against the membrane, his voice distorted by the strain. "Help me through, will you? I can't do it without you."

"CAUTION," the Guardian intoned. "THE ENTITY DOES NOT BELONG. YOU CANNOT INTERFERE."

"Don't listen to it, Q," 0 urged. His words came through the portal even if his physical form could not. "You can make your own rules, take your own chances. You and me, we're not the kind to play it safe. What's the good of living forever if you never take a risk?"

For a second, Picard entertained the hope that 0 would not be able to break through the unseen forces that held him back. Unfortunately, the Guardian's solemn warnings had exactly the opposite effect on the young Q as intended. "No one tells me what to do," the youthful Q muttered, and in his defiant tone Picard heard uncounted centuries of resentment and stifled enthusiasm, "not Q, not the Continuum, and especially not some moldering keyhole with delusions of grandeur."

Leaving all his doubts behind, he leapt forward and grasped 0's wrist with both hands. "Hold on!" he shouted. "Just give me a second!"

"ENTRY IS DENIED," the Guardian proclaimed. "INTERFERENCE IS NOT PERMITTED."

"Oh, be quiet," 0 urged him, eliciting a bark of laughter from his young, would-be liberator. His face flattened against the invisible barrier that barred his way, 0 kept pushing forward, gaining a millimeter or two. "You can do it, Q. I know you can!"

"You're quite right," Q said, grunting with effort. "I *can* do anything. And I will." Digging his heels into the dusty ground, he pulled on 0's arm with all his might. Perspiration speckled his brow and the veins on his hands stood out like plasma conduits. Picard tried to imagine the cosmic forces at work behind this façade of human exertion. Despite his better judgment, he had to admire the young being's tenacity and determination. Too bad they weren't being applied to a less questionable purpose. . . .

Smoke poured from the Guardian as it sought to restrain the stranger from beyond, defying the combined strength of both Q and 0. For a few fleeting instants, Picard could actually see the membrane, stretched over 0's thrusting head and shoulders like a layer of adhesive glue and glowing with white-hot energy so intense it made his eyes water. A network of spidery black cracks spread rapidly over the luminescent surface of the membrane and then, with a crash that sounded like a thousand stained-glass windows collapsing into broken shards, the barrier winked out of existence and 0 came tumbling onto the rubble-strewn ground, knocking Q onto his back.

"What was I thinking of?" the older Q said, looking on mournfully. "Would you have ever guessed I could be arrogant, so rash and presumptuous?"

Picard refrained from comment, more interested in observing the ongoing saga than in engaging in more fruitless banter with Q.

The young Q, exhilarated by his triumph, leaped to his feet, the back of his robe thoroughly dusted with gray powder. He looked no more frosted than Picard or his older counterpart. "Let's hear it for Q," he gloated, shaking his fist at the defeated Guardian, "especially this Q."

0 rose more slowly. Panting and pale, he clambered onto shaky legs and inspected his new surroundings, scowling somewhat at the obvious evidence of age and decay. "Looks like this locality has seen better days," he said darkly. "Please tell me this seedy cemetery is *not* the celebrated Q Continuum."

"What, this old place?" Q replied. He appeared much more confident now that he was back on familiar ground. "The Continuum exists on a much higher level than this simple material level." He laughed at the other's error. "You have a lot to learn about this reality, old fellow."

"No doubt you'll be happy to show me around," 0 said slyly. He stretched his limbs experimentally, looking mostly recovered from the duress of his transition. His bones cracked like tommyguns in a Dixon Hill mystery. "Ah, but it's good to breathe warm air again, and see something beside that endless, infernal ice." He limped over to Q. "Where to next, young man?"

"Next?" Q scratched his head. His plans had obviously not proceeded that far. Now that 0 had arrived safely, Q looked uncertain what to do with him.

"Well, um, there's kind of an interesting spatial anomaly a few systems away. Some entities find it amusing." He pointed toward a distant patch of turbulent, rippling sky. "See, over by those quasars there, just past the nebula." He tugged on the fabric of his robe to shake off some of the dust. "Race you there?" he proposed.

"Sounds good to me," 0 agreed, "but I'm afraid it's been a long time since I moved faster than a sunbeam, at least through plain, ordinary space." He gave his bad leg a rueful pat. "I don't suppose a bright young blade like you knows any convenient shortcuts in this vicinity?"

"A shortcut?" Q mulled the matter over while 0 looked on expectantly, far too keenly for Picard's liking. Bad enough that Q had let this unknown quantity into reality as he knew it, he didn't want young Q to give 0 free rein throughout the physical universe. Alas, inspiration struck Q, much to Picard's dismay. "The Continuum itself is the ultimate shortcut, linking every time and place in a state of constant, ineffable unity. I'll bet you could use the Continuum to go anywhere you pleased."

"There's an idea!" 0 crowed, slapping Q on the back. "That's positively brilliant. I knew I could count on you." Beneath the silent gaze of the Guardian, 0 circled the young and relatively inexperienced Q like a lion that had just separated an antelope from the herd. "Now then," he said in an insinuating manner, "about this Continuum? I can hardly wait to lay my eyes on such an auspicious establishment." He limped across the arid landscape, conspicuously favoring his weaker leg. "If you don't mind giving me a lift, that is."

"I suppose," Q answered absently, "although I could as easily transport us straight to the anomaly."

"Time enough for that later," 0 assured him, an edge in his voice belying the courteous phrasing. Was the young Q aware, Picard wondered, of just how intent the stranger was on his goal? 0's single-mindedness was obvious enough to Picard, even if his full motives remained obscure. "The Continuum first, I think."

"Oh yeah, right," Q mumbled, looking around the forlorn ruins. "I suppose there's no reason to stick around here anymore." He cast a guilty, sidelong glance at the brooding edifice of the Guardian, perhaps only now wondering if he really should have heeded the ancient artifact's warnings. "Unless you'd like to look around here some more? There's a nearly intact temple over on the southern continent that was built by some of my direct organic precursors."

"The Continuum will do just fine," 0 insisted. He stopped limping around the other being and lowered his head to look Q directly in the eye. "Now if you please."

Q shrugged, apparently deciding not to cry over spilled interdimensional membranes. "Why not?" he declared, and Picard felt an unaccountable chill run down his spine even though he knew that all of these events had transpired millions of years before his own time. "Get ready to feast your senses on possibly the pinnacle of existence, a plane of reality never before glimpsed by anyone but Q." He summoned an expectant drumroll from the ether. "Q Continuum, here we come!"

Picard saw a wily smile creep over 0's weather-beaten visage an instant before both Q and his new friend departed the abandoned ruins in a single burst of celestial light. He and the older Q were left alone amid the crumbling pillars and shattered stones. "Now what?" Picard asked his self-appointed travel director, although he suspected he knew what was coming next.

Q shrugged. "Whither they goest, we goest." He smirked at Picard. "I'd tell you to hold on to your hat, but I guess Starfleet doesn't go in for snappy head-gear." He subjected Picard's new uniform to a withering appraisal. "Pity. One should never underestimate the effectiveness of a stylish chapeau."

"Enough, Q," Picard barked. "You may be immortal, but I am not. Let's get on with this, unless you're afraid to show me just how big a fool you made of yourself."

Q glared at him murderously, and for one or two long moments Picard feared that perhaps he'd finally pushed Q too far. His body tensed up, half-expecting to be hurled into a supernova or transformed into some particularly slimy bit of protoplasm. *Just so long as he leaves the* Enterprise *alone,* Picard resolved, prepared to meet his fate with whatever dignity he could muster.

Then, to his surprise, the choler faded from Q's face, replaced by what looked amazingly like a moment of sincere reflection. "Perhaps you're right," he admitted after a time, "and I am stalling unnecessarily." He shook his head sadly. "I'm not particularly enjoying this trip down memory lane."

Picard almost sympathized with Q. With atypical gentleness, at least where Q was concerned, he suggested they continue their journey through the past. "It's a truism with humanity that those who do not learn from the past are doomed to repeat it. Perhaps, in your case, reliving your history is the only way we can both learn from it."

"Oh, that's profound, Picard," Q said, regaining some of his usual hauteur. "Very well, let's be on our way, if only to spare me any more of your pedantic clichés."

Why do I even try to treat him like a sane and reasonable being? Picard asked himself silently, but his justifiable irritation could not derail his mixed excitement and alarm at the prospect of actually visiting the Q Continuum for the first time. What could it possibly be like? He couldn't begin to imagine it. Even translated into human analogues, as it would surely have to be, he envisioned a wondrous, tran-

265

scendent realm surpassing the Xanadu of Kublai Khan or fabled Sha Ka Ree of Vulcan myth and legend. As Q swept them away from the decaying ruins with a wave of his hand, Picard closed his eyes and braced himself for the awesome glory to come.

The reality was not what he expected. He opened his eyes and looked upon . . . a customs station? He and Q stood on a stretch of dusty blacktop that led up to a simple gate consisting of a horizontal beam that blocked further passage on the roadway. A rickety wooden booth, apparently staffed by a single guard, had been erected to the right side of the gate. A barbed-wire fence extended to both the east and the west, discouraging any unauthorized attempts to evade the gate. A sign was mounted beneath the open window of the booth, printed in heavy block lettering: YOU ARE NOW ENTERING THE Q CONTINUUM. NO PEDDLERS, VAGRANTS, OR ORGANIANS ALLOWED.

A golden sun was shining brightly overhead, although it seemed to be reserving its warmest beams for the other side of the fence. Picard lifted a hand to shield his eyes from the glare and peered past the barbed wire. As nearly as he could tell, the Q Continuum looked like an enormous multi-lane freeway with more loops, exits, and on-ramps than seemed physically possible. Elevated roadways doubled back on each other, then branched off at dozens of incompatible angles. *Mass transit as designed by M. C. Escher,* Picard thought, astounded by the sight.

"What were you expecting, Shangri-La?" Q asked, enjoying Picard's gawk-eyed befuddlement.

"Something like that," he admitted. *I suppose this imagery makes a certain amount of sense, given the younger Q's description of the Continuum as a shortcut that spanned the known universe.* He could readily believe that this stupendous tangle of thoroughfares connected any conceivable location with everywhere else.

Assuming you got past the gate, of course.

That appeared to be the challenge facing 0 and Q's previous self at this moment. Not far away from where Picard and Q now resided, the young Q and his newfound acquaintance stood before the barricade as the customs official emerged from his booth, clipboard in hand. He was a stern, officious-looking individual wearing a large copper badge upon his khaki-colored uniform. A sturdy truncheon dangled from his belt. Picard was irked but not too surprised to note that this functionary bore a marked resemblance to himself. *Come off it, Q,* Picard thought. *Surely I don't look that humorless?*

The guard scrutinized 0 with a scowl upon his face. "You're not Q," he stated flatly.

"You can say that again," 0 proclaimed, unabashed, "but I'd be grateful if you'd let me trod your fine road. Young Q here tells me it's the swiftest way around these whereabouts."

He clapped Q on the back, sending Q staggering forward toward the guard. Looking on from less than five meters away, Picard noted that the youth had traded his monkish black robe for something closer to what 0 wore, minus the rags and tatters, naturally. He now wore boots, breeches, and a heavy fur coat. *Just what Q needed,* Picard thought sarcastically, *a disreputable role model.*

The guard gave Q a disapproving glance, then inspected his clipboard. "State your name, species identification, planet or plane of origin, and the nature of your business in the Continuum."

0 rolled his eyes, seemingly unimpressed by this display of authority. "Are you sure you don't want my great-great-grandmother's genetic code as well?" he asked dryly. Sighing theatrically, he launched into his recitation. "0's the name, my species is special, my origin is elsewhere, and my business is none of yours. Is that good enough, or would you care to arm-wrestle

for it?" He shook off his shaggy greatcoat and rolled up his sleeve. Right behind him, the young Q placed a hand over his mouth to muffle an attack of giggles.

The guard looked considerably less amused by 0's flippancy. His scowl deepened and he lowered his clipboard to his side. "Where are you from," he asked, and Picard somehow sensed he was speaking for the whole of the Q, "and why should we permit you access to the Continuum?"

0 retrieved his coat from the pavement and threw it over his shoulder. "Well, the where of it is a long story that depends a lot on who's telling it. Let's just say I was once quite a mover and shaker a good ways from here, but I'm afraid that my able accomplishments were not always appreciated by those that should have known better, so it came to pass that the time was right for me to set off for greener pastures." He leaned forward and brushed some of the dust from his boots before straightening his spine, adjusting his hat, and addressing the guard. "As for why you should allow me safe passage through your local stomping grounds, aside from basic hospitality, that is . . . why, this peerless young paragon will vouch for me."

"Is this true?" the guard demanded of Q. He didn't seem to regard the young entity as much of a paragon.

Q gulped nervously, wilting under the guard's censorious stare. He looked to 0 for support and was greeted by a conspiratorial wink. The newcomer's boldness rubbed off on Q, who squared his shoulders and glared back at the guard defiantly. "Certainly!" he announced. "0's word is good enough for me. What's with this siege mentality anyway? We could do a lot worse than open our borders to new ideas and exotic visitors from foreign lands."

0 beamed at him. "That's telling 'em, friend." He poked the guard's badge with his finger. "You should listen to this young fellow if you've got any sense under that shiny, shorn scalp of yours."

That was uncalled for, Picard thought.

"So be it," the guard decreed. "This entity is permitted within the Continuum—on the understanding that you, Q, take responsibility for him."

"They expected *you* to be the responsible one?" Picard remarked, arching an ironic eyebrow. "Why do I get the impression this was a horrendous mistake?"

The older Q averted his eyes from the scene before them. "For a lower life-form, you can annoyingly prophetic sometimes."

Caught up in his newfound bravado, the young Q didn't hesitate a bit. "Agreed," he said grandly. "Raise up the gate, my good man."

"Well done," 0 whispered. He doffed his wide-brimmed hat and plopped it onto Q's head. Grabbing his erstwhile sponsor by the elbow, he dragged his bad leg toward the barricade and the vast interdimensional highway beyond. Picard looked on as the guard retreated to his booth. Moments later, the horizontal beam tilted upward until it was perpendicular to the road, and the newly united fellow travelers strode into the future, embarking on the endless highway for destinations unknown.

"So tell me, Q," 0 asked as his voice receded into the distance, "have you ever considered the fundamental importance of *testing* lesser species . . . ?"

Interlude

WHERE IS Q, the spider hissed. *Q is where?*

His stench was all over the bug over there, but not Q himself. Beneath the smelly smoke, it reeked of Q. Q had been with it, or would be, or should be. What did it matter when? Not at all, not for Q. Never for Q.

Damn you Q, you damn me, damn Q, damn me! He remembered it all now. Q was to blame, Q and all those other Q, parading their pompous, prejudiced, pitiless power throughout perpetuity. There were too many Q to count, far too many to be allowed to exist, but that could be remedied, given the chance. *Hew the Q. Hew Q too. Rue, Q, rue! Your day is through!*

The scent of Q set the spider salivating. Its avaricious arms scraped at the wall, greedy to grab, keen to consume. *Where are you now, Q, my old Q. What have you been doing all this time? What has time done to you and to me and to we. Have you ever thought of me? You should have, yes, you should.*

The time was coming. The voice had promised. Soon.

Q will pay. All the Q will pay. Q and Q

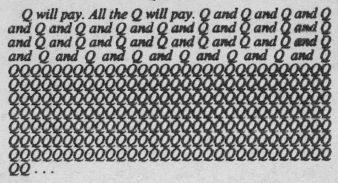

QQ . . .

TO BE CONTINUED

Look for STAR TREK Fiction from Pocket Books

Star Trek®: The Original Series

Star Trek: The Motion Picture • Gene Roddenberry
Star Trek II: The Wrath of Khan • Vonda N. McIntyre
Star Trek III: The Search for Spock • Vonda N. McIntyre
Star Trek IV: The Voyage Home • Vonda N. McIntyre
Star Trek V: The Final Frontier • J. M. Dillard
Star Trek VI: The Undiscovered Country • J. M. Dillard
Star Trek VII: Generations • J. M. Dillard
Enterprise: The First Adventure • Vonda N. McIntyre
Final Frontier • Diane Carey
Strangers from the Sky • Margaret Wander Bonanno
Spock's World • Diane Duane
The Lost Years • J. M. Dillard
Probe • Margaret Wander Bonanno
Prime Directive • Judith and Garfield Reeves-Stevens
Best Destiny • Diane Carey
Shadows on the Sun • Michael Jan Friedman
Sarek • A. C. Crispin
Federation • Judith and Garfield Reeves-Stevens
The Ashes of Eden • William Shatner & Judith and Garfield
    Reeves-Stevens
The Return • William Shatner & Judith and Garfield Reeves-
    Stevens
Star Trek: Starfleet Academy • Diane Carey
Vulcan's Forge • Josepha Sherman and Susan Shwartz
Avenger • William Shatner & Judith and Garfield Reeves-Stevens

#1 *Star Trek: The Motion Picture* • Gene Roddenberry
#2 *The Entropy Effect* • Vonda N. McIntyre
#3 *The Klingon Gambit* • Robert E. Vardeman
#4 *The Covenant of the Crown* • Howard Weinstein
#5 *The Prometheus Design* • Sondra Marshak & Myrna
    Culbreath
#6 *The Abode of Life* • Lee Correy
#7 *Star Trek II: The Wrath of Khan* • Vonda N. McIntyre
#8 *Black Fire* • Sonni Cooper
#9 *Triangle* • Sondra Marshak & Myrna Culbreath
#10 *Web of the Romulans* • M. S. Murdock
#11 *Yesterday's Son* • A. C. Crispin

#12 *Mutiny on the Enterprise* • Robert E. Vardeman
#13 *The Wounded Sky* • Diane Duane
#14 *The Trellisane Confrontation* • David Dvorkin
#15 *Corona* • Greg Bear
#16 *The Final Reflection* • John M. Ford
#17 *Star Trek III: The Search for Spock* • Vonda N. McIntyre
#18 *My Enemy, My Ally* • Diane Duane
#19 *The Tears of the Singers* • Melinda Snodgrass
#20 *The Vulcan Academy Murders* • Jean Lorrah
#21 *Uhura's Song* • Janet Kagan
#22 *Shadow Lord* • Laurence Yep
#23 *Ishmael* • Barbara Hambly
#24 *Killing Time* • Della Van Hise
#25 *Dwellers in the Crucible* • Margaret Wander Bonanno
#26 *Pawns and Symbols* • Majiliss Larson
#27 *Mindshadow* • J. M. Dillard
#28 *Crisis on Centaurus* • Brad Ferguson
#29 *Dreadnought!* • Diane Carey
#30 *Demons* • J. M. Dillard
#31 *Battlestations!* • Diane Carey
#32 *Chain of Attack* • Gene DeWeese
#33 *Deep Domain* • Howard Weinstein
#34 *Dreams of the Raven* • Carmen Carter
#35 *The Romulan Way* • Diane Duane & Peter Morwood
#36 *How Much for Just the Planet?* • John M. Ford
#37 *Bloodthirst* • J. M. Dillard
#38 *The IDIC Epidemic* • Jean Lorrah
#39 *Time for Yesterday* • A. C. Crispin
#40 *Timetrap* • David Dvorkin
#41 *The Three-Minute Universe* • Barbara Paul
#42 *Memory Prime* • Judith and Garfield Reeves-Stevens
#43 *The Final Nexus* • Gene DeWeese
#44 *Vulcan's Glory* • D. C. Fontana
#45 *Double, Double* • Michael Jan Friedman
#46 *The Cry of the Onlies* • Judy Klass
#47 *The Kobayashi Maru* • Julia Ecklar
#48 *Rules of Engagement* • Peter Morwood
#49 *The Pandora Principle* • Carolyn Clowes
#50 *Doctor's Orders* • Diane Duane
#51 *Enemy Unseen* • V. E. Mitchell
#52 *Home Is the Hunter* • Dana Kramer Rolls
#53 *Ghost-Walker* • Barbara Hambly

#54 *A Flag Full of Stars* • Brad Ferguson
#55 *Renegade* • Gene DeWeese
#56 *Legacy* • Michael Jan Friedman
#57 *The Rift* • Peter David
#58 *Face of Fire* • Michael Jan Friedman
#59 *The Disinherited* • Peter David
#60 *Ice Trap* • L. A. Graf
#61 *Sanctuary* • John Vornholt
#62 *Death Count* • L. A. Graf
#63 *Shell Game* • Melissa Crandall
#64 *The Starship Trap* • Mel Gilden
#65 *Windows on a Lost World* • V. E. Mitchell
#66 *From the Depths* • Victor Milan
#67 *The Great Starship Race* • Diane Carey
#68 *Firestorm* • L. A. Graf
#69 *The Patrian Transgression* • Simon Hawke
#70 *Traitor Winds* • L. A. Graf
#71 *Crossroad* • Barbara Hambly
#72 *The Better Man* • Howard Weinstein
#73 *Recovery* • J. M. Dillard
#74 *The Fearful Summons* • Denny Martin Flynn
#75 *First Frontier* • Diane Carey & Dr. James I. Kirkland
#76 *The Captain's Daughter* • Peter David
#77 *Twilight's End* • Jerry Oltion
#78 *The Rings of Tautee* • Dean W. Smith & Kristine K. Rusch
#79 *Invasion #1: First Strike* • Diane Carey
#80 *The Joy Machine* • James Gunn
#81 *Mudd in Your Eye* • Jerry Oltion
#82 *Mind Meld* • John Vornholt
#83 *Heart of the Sun* • Pamela Sargent & George Zebrowski
#84 *Assignment: Eternity* • Greg Cox

Star Trek: The Next Generation®

Encounter at Farpoint • David Gerrold
Unification • Jeri Taylor
Relics • Michael Jan Friedman
Descent • Diane Carey
All Good Things • Michael Jan Friedman
Star Trek: Klingon • Dean W. Smith & Kristine K. Rusch
Star Trek VII: Generations • J. M. Dillard
Metamorphosis • Jean Lorrah
Vendetta • Peter David
Reunion • Michael Jan Friedman
Imzadi • Peter David
The Devil's Heart • Carmen Carter
Dark Mirror • Diane Duane
Q-Squared • Peter David
Crossover • Michael Jan Friedman
Kahless • Michael Jan Friedman
Star Trek: First Contact • J. M. Dillard
The Best and the Brightest • Susan Wright
Planet X • Michael Jan Friedman

#1 *Ghost Ship* • Diane Carey
#2 *The Peacekeepers* • Gene DeWeese
#3 *The Children of Hamlin* • Carmen Carter
#4 *Survivors* • Jean Lorrah
#5 *Strike Zone* • Peter David
#6 *Power Hungry* • Howard Weinstein
#7 *Masks* • John Vornholt
#8 *The Captains' Honor* • David and Daniel Dvorkin
#9 *A Call to Darkness* • Michael Jan Friedman
#10 *A Rock and a Hard Place* • Peter David
#11 *Gulliver's Fugitives* • Keith Sharee
#12 *Doomsday World* • David, Carter, Friedman & Greenberg
#13 *The Eyes of the Beholders* • A. C. Crispin
#14 *Exiles* • Howard Weinstein
#15 *Fortune's Light* • Michael Jan Friedman
#16 *Contamination* • John Vornholt
#17 *Boogeymen* • Mel Gilden
#18 *Q-in-Law* • Peter David
#19 *Perchance to Dream* • Howard Weinstein

#20 *Spartacus* • T. L. Mancour

#21 *Chains of Command* • W. A. McCay & E. L. Flood

#22 *Imbalance* • V. E. Mitchell

#23 *War Drums* • John Vornholt

#24 *Nightshade* • Laurell K. Hamilton

#25 *Grounded* • David Bischoff

#26 *The Romulan Prize* • Simon Hawke

#27 *Guises of the Mind* • Rebecca Neason

#28 *Here There Be Dragons* • John Peel

#29 *Sins of Commission* • Susan Wright

#30 *Debtors' Planet* • W. R. Thompson

#31 *Foreign Foes* • David Galanter & Greg Brodeur

#32 *Requiem* • Michael Jan Friedman & Kevin Ryan

#33 *Balance of Power* • Dafydd ab Hugh

#34 *Blaze of Glory* • Simon Hawke

#35 *The Romulan Stratagem* • Robert Greenberger

#36 *Into the Nebula* • Gene DeWeese

#37 *The Last Stand* • Brad Ferguson

#38 *Dragon's Honor* • Kij Johnson & Greg Cox

#39 *Rogue Saucer* • John Vornholt

#40 *Possession* • J. M. Dillard & Kathleen O'Malley

#41 *Invasion #2: The Soldiers of Fear* • Dean W. Smith & Kristine K. Rusch

#42 *Infiltrator* • W. R. Thompson

#43 *A Fury Scorned* • Pam Sargent & George Zebrowski

#44 *The Death of Princes* • John Peel

#45 *Intellivore* • Diane Duane

#46 *To Storm Heaven* • Esther Friesner

#47 *Q Continuum #1: Q-Space* • Greg Cox

#48 *Q Continuum #2: Q-Zone* • Greg Cox

Star Trek: Deep Space Nine®

The Search • Diane Carey
Warped • K. W. Jeter
The Way of the Warrior • Diane Carey
Star Trek: Klingon • Dean W. Smith & Kristine K. Rusch
Trials and Tribble-ations • Diane Carey
Far Beyond the Stars • Steve Barnes

#1 *Emissary* • J. M. Dillard
#2 *The Siege* • Peter David
#3 *Bloodletter* • K. W. Jeter
#4 *The Big Game* • Sandy Schofield
#5 *Fallen Heroes* • Dafydd ab Hugh
#6 *Betrayal* • Lois Tilton
#7 *Warchild* • Esther Friesner
#8 *Antimatter* • John Vornholt
#9 *Proud Helios* • Melissa Scott
#10 *Valhalla* • Nathan Archer
#11 *Devil in the Sky* • Greg Cox & John Gregory Betancourt
#12 *The Laertian Gamble* • Robert Sheckley
#13 *Station Rage* • Diane Carey
#14 *The Long Night* • Dean W. Smith & Kristine K. Rusch
#15 *Objective: Bajor* • John Peel
#16 *Invasion #3: Time's Enemy* • L. A. Graf
#17 *The Heart of the Warrior* • John Gregory Betancourt
#18 *Saratoga* • Michael Jan Friedman
#19 *The Tempest* • Susan Wright
#20 *Wrath of the Prophets* • P. David, M. J. Friedman,
     R. Greenberger
#21 *Trial by Error* • Mark Garland
#22 *Vengeance* • Dafydd ab Hugh

Star Trek®: Voyager™

Flashback • Diane Carey
Mosaic • Jeri Taylor

#1 *Caretaker* • L. A. Graf
#2 *The Escape* • Dean W. Smith & Kristine K. Rusch
#3 *Ragnarok* • Nathan Archer
#4 *Violations* • Susan Wright
#5 *Incident at Arbuk* • John Gregory Betancourt
#6 *The Murdered Sun* • Christie Golden
#7 *Ghost of a Chance* • Mark A. Garland & Charles G. McGraw
#8 *Cybersong* • S. N. Lewitt
#9 *Invasion #4: The Final Fury* • Dafydd ab Hugh
#10 *Bless the Beasts* • Karen Haber
#11 *The Garden* • Melissa Scott
#12 *Chrysalis* • David Niall Wilson
#13 *The Black Shore* • Greg Cox
#14 *Marooned* • Christie Golden
#15 *Echoes* • Dean W. Smith & Kristine K. Rusch

Star Trek®: New Frontier

#1 *House of Cards* • Peter David
#2 *Into the Void* • Peter David
#3 *The Two-Front War* • Peter David
#4 *End Game* • Peter David
#5 *Martyr* • Peter David
#6 *Fire on High* • Peter David

Star Trek®: Day of Honor

Book One: *Ancient Blood* • Diane Carey
Book Two: *Armageddon Sky* • L. A. Graf
Book Three: *Her Klingon Soul* • Michael Jan Friedman
Book Four: *Treaty's Law* • Dean W. Smith & Kristine K. Rusch

Star Trek®: The Captain's Table

Book One: *War Dragons* • L. A. Graf
Book Two: *Dujonian's Hoard* • Michael Jan Friedman
Book Three: *The Mist* • Dean W. Smith & Kristine K. Rusch
Book Four: *Fire Ship* • Diane Carey